"Hostile armed vehicles detected," ISAC reported.

"Little bit late, but thanks, pal," muttered Colin.

Seconds later the road behind them detonated. The wash of flame dazzled Colin's eyes, and hot air pushed back against the flow of the wind. Unlike them, the Roamers had apparently brought the big guns.

Smaller flashes flickered from the rear, nearly lost in the glare of the headlights. It was time to return the favor. He brought the M60 around and squeezed the trigger. The gun screamed and spat a stream of fire back toward the pursuers.

The tracers were lost against the lights. Colin didn't let it bother him – he wasn't hoping for any precision kills. To that end he hosed back and forth, working the weapon around. A headlight blew out in a spray of sparks, a satisfying result. Return fire thudded against the sandbags and made him duck down, dampening his enthusiasm.

ALSO AVAILABLE FROM ACONYTE

TOM CLANCY'S THE DIVISION®
COMPROMISED

THOMAS PARROTT

ACONYTE

First published by Aconyte Books in 2022

ISBN 978 1 83908 186 6

Ebook ISBN 978 1 83908 187 3

Cover art by René Aigner

Distributed in North America by Simon & Schuster Inc, New York, USA
Printed in the United States of America
9 8 7 6 5 4 3 2

ACONYTE BOOKS

An imprint of Asmodee Entertainment Ltd
Mercury House, Shipstones Business Centre
North Gate, Nottingham NG7 7FN, UK
aconytebooks.com // twitter.com/aconytebooks

For my mews, Kitiara, who cannot read
but keeps me sane so that others may.

CHAPTER 1

There was no power in the abandoned gym. No power was the new normal. The only light came slanting in through the windows on the wall facing the street. One of the windowpanes had been shattered inward. Sunbeams reflected off the scattered fragments, sending dancing rainbows across the ceiling. The exercise area was one large room. The light picked out the dusty shape of treadmills and stationary bikes.

Maira Kanhai sat on a weight bench toward the back. She drank tepid water from her canteen and splashed more onto her face. She had been here for hours already, and her muscles burned with fatigue. She was lightly clad in a sports top and shorts. It was the middle of an April day, but there was no heat to the Kansas sun. She might have caught a chill had she not been driving herself so hard that sweat dripped from her brow.

Maira's gaze wandered over unused equipment and dirty mirrors. She had been coming here for weeks now, but she had never been able to piece together this place's story. She mused about it a lot between sets. The unnamed township nearest to the Kansas Core couldn't have had a population higher than a hundred and fifty people. As small as the town was, ten percent of the people could have worked out here at the same time. It seemed excessive. For all she knew, this place had been abandoned before the Green Poison had come along and kicked over the whole ant hill.

The broken window only made things more confusing. What had someone hoped to find in a gym? There was something darkly funny about imagining someone scavenging all the protein powder they could find as society crumbled. In the end, of course, there were no answers to be had. A million little stories had played out like this across America as the end came. All of them were lost now.

Maira was an archaeologist in her own time. The thought made her shake her head, scattering droplets of sweat to the floor. She stood in a surge. The sudden movement pulled at the scar tissue that covered her back. It ran from the base of her skull to her tailbone, the leftovers of a desperation maneuver with an incendiary grenade. Skin grafts had saved the worst parts, but the damage had been severe. Even now, moving too quickly would set off a cascade of pain sizzling down her spine.

Maira ignored the pain. She wasn't used to it, whatever she told the rest of the Division personnel. She just refused to give in to it. If hurting for the rest of her life was the price she paid, so be it. She would not let herself break over this. Others had been dealt worse hands. If they could keep going, so could she.

She wrapped her hands carefully, flexing her fingers against the stiff fabric. It was stained yellow with old sweat. No amount of washing got it out at this point. The punching bag hung in the shadows. In the back of the gym, it was just a looming shape. Maira liked it that way. It felt more real.

She threw the first punch. It hit hard, a loud smack in the silence. Another, then another. Maira picked up the tempo as she went. Her hands soon throbbed from the pounding rhythm. Leo, one of the more experienced agents she worked with, had given her this training regimen to follow. She pushed harder and faster than he had suggested.

Her heart pounded. Images flooded into her mind's eye.

A body toppled from atop a semi in a spray of blood. Toxic green clouds flooded a town's streets. A machine gun roared, deafening. An Outcast dripped blood onto a sobbing man.

Her jaw ached. She was grinding her teeth.

Her brother, Kazi, fell to his knees, eyes glassy and chest a ravaged mass of bullet holes.

Maira threw her whole body behind the next punch. Her legs buckled and she fell against the bag. She caught herself at the last second, fingers digging into the rough fabric.

"Maira," someone said.

Maira moved, an explosive surge of reflexes. She took two steps to where her gear was and had the shotgun in her hand in the blink of an eye. She came up with the weapon held steady, aimed at the intruder. They were just a silhouette against the light coming in from outside. Maira squinted.

"An agent I trained, that shotgun... Deja vu all over again."

A woman's voice, with a light Georgia accent. Recognition set in. It was Brenda Wells, the cell leader who had recruited Maira into the Division in the first place.

"Brenda." Maira blinked rapidly. She lowered the gun. "You surprised me."

Brenda limped forward. Out of the path of the sunlight, she resolved into the woman Maira admired. She was wearing jeans and a T-shirt, the front emblazoned with some anime-style cartoon character Maira didn't recognize. Her Division watch glowed orange at her wrist. She smiled, a warm expression that lit up her whole face, but there was worry in her eyes.

"Don't fret about it. I would have warned you I was coming, but you unplugged yourself." Brenda motioned to the side.

Maira followed the gesture to her gear. Her own watch sat on top of it, alongside her earpiece and the contact in its case. She mustered a smile and turned her gaze back to her friend.

"I just needed some time to myself."

"I see. I'm sorry for interrupting. Is your hand OK?"

Maira blinked. "What?"

Brenda pointed. "You're bleeding."

Maira looked down at her right hand in surprise. The wrap was soaked red over her knuckles. The skin must have split over her knuckles sometime during the training. She flexed her fingers exploratorily. It hurt, but it wasn't disabling.

"I'm fine." Maira raised her face back to Brenda. "I'm guessing this isn't a social call?"

Brenda frowned but didn't pursue it. "You guess right. Can we take a seat?"

"Of course," Maira said.

They moved over to the weight benches. Maira straddled the bench to face her friend, while Brenda sat sideways. The elder agent rubbed her thigh with a wince.

"Is your leg bothering you?" asked Maira.

"It was just the walk here," Brenda said. "You put a couple miles on it, and it starts to rub you raw."

"How are the phantom pains?"

Brenda shrugged expressively. "A fact of life. The truth is I was lucky to be somewhere they could save my life, much less fit me for a proper prosthetic. The number of places that would be true wouldn't fill a page at this point."

"I've never known you to let anything stop you for long. You'll be up and fighting with us again before you know it."

Brenda started to say something in reply but hesitated. When she spoke, it was clear she was choosing her words carefully. "What about you, Maira? Are you ready to get back out there?"

Maira nodded immediately. "I didn't join the Division to sit around in Nowhere, Kansas watching corn grow."

"Of course," Brenda replied with a wry smile. "I just know that you've been having some troubles. Nightmares, panic attacks. There's no shame in–"

"I'm not ashamed," Maira cut her off. "It's nothing. We needed time to heal, I get that, but I'm good now. I'm ready to get back into the fight."

"Not all wounds are physical, Maira," Brenda said quietly.

The younger woman scratched her cheek and offered a lopsided smile. "Look, I understand what you're worried about, but you don't have to be. It's wasting time, that's the problem."

"I wish we could ..." Brenda trailed off and shook her head.

"If wishes were fishes, we'd all have a fry," Maira said. "Something's up, right? There's too much to do and not enough agents to go around. Well, I'm ready to go. So let's get this show on the road."

Brenda's gaze was steady, measuring. She didn't seem to find whatever she saw completely comforting. She sighed.

"You're not wrong. A situation has come up."

Maira tilted her head. "Something tells me that's quite an understatement. What kind of situation are we talking about?"

Brenda winced. "The kind that threatens to start the dominoes falling and bring the whole thing down. I'm sure you remember the agreement we negotiated with the Freighties?"

Maira gave her a dry look. They had spent weeks traveling by foot from DC all the way down to Tennessee in order to make contact with the I-10 Fleet, informally known as the Freighties. They were one of two major fleets of truckers that had coalesced in the wake of the Green Poison's devastation. The Freighties controlled the southern routes, and largely operated on altruistic lines. Their aid had been a major factor in preventing a famine from wreaking untold havoc on the Eastern Seaboard.

It hadn't been as simple as asking, of course. The Freighties had been locked in a war with their northern counterparts, the Roamers, a vicious armada of raiders and bandits. Freeing up their allies had uncovered the involvement of Rowan O'Shea, a rogue Division agent with a grudge. Stopping Rowan's attack on the Kansas Core was what had brought them out here – and cost Brenda most of her leg. It was a harsh price to pay, but the Cores kept the Division in the fight. It gave them a chance.

"It would be hard for me to forget," Maira replied.

Brenda grinned, but the expression died quickly. "Someone's hitting the food convoys."

Maira's jaw tightened. "The Roamers? I thought they'd fallen back after we took Rowan down."

"They have. It's not them. As best we can tell, it's a new player. At least, new to us."

"What–"

Brenda held up a hand to forestall any questions. "You can ask the rest at the briefing proper. We're assembling the cell down at the Core, and we'll go over the threat profile. Then you'll set out at dawn tomorrow."

Maira frowned. "What do you mean 'you'?"

"Maira…" Brenda sighed. "I'm not going with you."

"What?" Maira didn't bother to hide her shock.

"I'm not fit for field service. I would slow you down and get someone killed." Brenda tapped her replacement leg with a dull thud. "Maybe with time and training, but then again maybe not. Things don't always go how we want them to."

"But we can't… I mean, you're…" Maira could feel her heart racing in her chest as she searched for the words. Brenda's guidance had been what got her through the pain and strife of the last mission. "You are the cell."

Brenda smiled sadly. "Flattery will get you everywhere, but no. I told you, Maira – we need agents who can think on their own, not ones that will do whatever I tell them. This only makes that truer."

"You can't just turn me and Leo loose on the countryside," Maira said weakly. "I'll go crazy from having no one to talk to."

That got a genuine laugh from Brenda. "Oh, come on, he's not so bad once you get to know him. But no, you won't be sent off into the world just the two of you. We've been able to make contact with others. Reinforcements for you."

Maira frowned. "Reinforcements?"

As thin as the Division was spread these days, that could only mean a desperate crisis, indeed.

"Well, I figure this is your stop," the truck driver said.

Colin Harrison leaned forward and peered through the windshield. There was nothing to be seen except endless fields of corn, waving gently in the breeze. He tilted his head curiously.

"How certain are you?" he asked.

The Freighty driver grinned and resettled the baseball cap on his head. "Pretty damn sure. Last time I was here it was a battlefield. It's the kind of thing that tends to burn a place into your memory."

Colin nodded. "Fair enough." He held out a hand. "I appreciate you volunteering to bring me all this way."

The driver gripped his hand firmly. "My pleasure. The Core had requested some supplies anyway, so it let us kill two birds with one stone."

"They needed food?" Colin was surprised. "I figured a Core would be stocked up for years."

The driver smirked. "Oh, they are. But you got a military look about you… the kind of food that lasts for years, would you want to live off nothing but that if you had a choice?"

Colin chuckled. "I suppose not. Do you need help unloading?"

"Nah, you go on ahead. They'll send some folks out to get the goods when they're ready. I'm sure you'd like to stretch your legs."

Colin nodded and opened the door. Gear rattled as his boots hit the dirt. The breeze ran along his scalp through his buzzed hair, a relief after the stuffiness of the truck cab. He turned his face into it and smiled.

"Proximity to Core," ISAC announced in his ear.

It highlighted the entrance to the Core on his visual display. Colin nodded and set off through the corn. Stalks slapped lightly at him as he walked. He rested a hand on the butt of his M4 to keep it steady.

He didn't bother to walk quickly. Maybe it was funny, but he was nervous to meet his new cell. He'd run through gunfire and stopped arterial spray in battlefield conditions, but meeting strangers could still make him anxious. It didn't help that this particular group was the subject of spreading rumors. They said the Kansas Core would have been destroyed without them, and if they needed reinforcements, that meant he was replacing someone.

How did you step into the shoes of the dead without it feeling awkward?

Colin shook his head. It was a stupid thing to worry about. They were Division agents, the same as him. Their first concern would be the mission, and he could help them see that through. That was all that mattered. Everything else was a distraction.

Of course, thinking about the mission carried its own freight of concerns. The details had been scarce when the all-call had gone out requesting volunteers to make the trek to Kansas. He could have stayed. There was plenty of work left to do in New York; there was always a demand for trained medics these days. His days had been full with organizing relief efforts and seeing to a variety of injuries and illnesses.

One key piece of information caught his attention though.

The cell would deploy into the area of the Texas-Louisiana border. News from that region, like most of the country, had been spotty. Yet it had come with a name that grabbed him by the throat.

Marcus Georgio.

Colin sighed. Even if Marcus was there, as people were saying, he didn't know what speaking to the man would accomplish. Some things couldn't be healed by words alone. Who knew that better than a medic? But Colin felt like he had to make the attempt, and this mission might give him a chance to do so.

He had reached the entrance to the Core. It wasn't much to look at from the outside. It looked like nothing so much as a tiny shed in the middle of a huge amount of nothing. Colin had been in this life long enough to know that appearances could be deceiving.

"Security system interface detected. Present identification," ISAC said.

Colin held up the wrist which bore his Division watch. The glow pulsed a comforting orange. There was a pause, during which Colin entertained a variety of worst-case scenarios. None of this equipment was new anymore. Was it possible for the recognition telemetry to fail? Would he be warned off if that did happen, or would he just be turned into Swiss cheese by half a dozen automated machine guns?

"Identification confirmed: Agent Colin Harrison. Status: Active. Core access granted," ISAC said.

The door on the shed unlocked with an audible *ka-thunk*. It swung open and revealed a stairway down into the earth. Colin stepped inside and shut it behind him. He turned and gave his eyes a moment to adjust to the transition from sunlight to dim interior. The stairway terminated in a tunnel at the bottom.

"Colin Harrison," someone said.

Colin blinked. He had the butt of his rifle tucked into his shoulder in an instant. His alarm faded as quickly as it had come. Obviously, they'd sent someone to greet him. He flushed. He was too in his own thoughts about all of this. He needed to get his head in the game. He cleared his throat, irritated with himself.

"That's me."

The man who had startled him watched impassively. He was geared out similarly to Colin, and if that hadn't been enough to confirm his identity, he also wore the telltale watch. Another agent. He made no move for his own weapon despite Colin's motion. He had dark skin tones that shone warm even in the pallid installation lighting. His expression might have been carved from granite, but Colin got the impression there was a lot going on behind those dark eyes.

"Last one to get here. Come on," was all the man said, and he turned away to walk down the stairs.

Colin followed him. The tunnel he'd seen wound downward, deeper and deeper. He would make sure to stay alert from this point on. That was how he spotted the gouges in the walls. He ran his finger across one as he passed. Bullet impacts was his educated guess. It seemed like stories of the Core being invaded weren't complete fabrications. The idea of an enemy actually making their way inside a Core was a grim one. It must have been a hairsbreadth from disaster.

"Were you here when all this happened?" Colin asked.

The other agent nodded. He didn't say anything. The silence stretched long enough that Colin started to get uncomfortable. As they moved deeper into the Core, the sounds of activity began to pick up. The hum of electronics mixed with conversations in low voices. No apparatus could be completely automated, and this place housed those who kept the Division running.

"I didn't catch your name," Colin said finally.

"Didn't give it." The other man sighed quietly after a moment and relented. "Leo Fourte. Agent."

Colin nodded. "I'm… well, you already know, right? Heh." He cleared his throat again. "Are you going on the mission headed south?"

Leo nodded. Colin took a few seconds to look the man over with a medic's eye. A slight limp spoke of a severe leg wound some time in his recent past. Besides that, the other agent was in fighting trim. He wasn't a big man; the top of his head only came up to Colin's chin. Nevertheless, there was a steady confidence to him that spoke volumes.

"Guess we'll be traveling together, then. You ready to get back out into the field?" Colin asked.

"Yes," Leo said. There was a pause. "You'll meet Maira soon. She's a talker."

"Like you" felt like it belonged at the end of the sentence, but Leo left it unsaid.

They made their way into the depths of the complex. Rooms branched off the main corridor regularly. Some were dark and abandoned, others active with people going about their work in neat cubicles. Colin wondered if this site had been a missile silo during the Cold War. It had that weird mixture of "very expensive" and "barebones" that he expected from facilities from that time period.

"Maira – she's another agent in the cell?"

Leo nodded. "New recruit."

Colin tilted his head. "Is that some kind of joke?"

Leo shook his head. "Newest agent in the Division. Picked her up out in the world." He hesitated, then added with great care, "Proved herself. She's good."

"Feels like there's a long story behind all of that. Guess we'll have time for it on the road." Colin scratched at his jaw. "You, me, Maira... that's three. Is that all?"

Leo shook his head again. He didn't get a chance to elaborate on that, assuming he would have. They had arrived at their destination. A doorway branched off the tunnelway. It led into a small conference room. There was a table surrounded by chairs, and an immense screen took up one end of the room. There was room in here for twenty people, but only three others waited for them.

All were women. Two of them Colin didn't know. The youngest looked to be of Indian descent with short-cropped hair. It had the appearance of a buzz cut that had spent a few months growing out. She alone out of those gathered wore a long-sleeved shirt. There were smile lines on her face that spoke of a good nature, though her face was currently very serious.

The next had East Asian features and sat across from the first. Her dark hair was pulled back into a small ponytail. There was a remarkable stillness to her. Most people Colin knew fidgeted at least a little. Not this woman. Every small movement she made stood out and seemed carefully chosen.

She radiated self-assurance in a way that would doubtless be a relief in the chaos of a firefight.

The last person in the room stood by the screen, and Colin smiled upon seeing her. She was a middle-aged Black woman with strong features. She returned his smile with a bright grin and stepped to meet him halfway across the room. They clasped hands warmly.

"Brenda Wells! I hadn't imagined I'd encounter you here." Colin frowned immediately as he noticed the pain with which she walked. "What happened?"

"Colin, you clever dog! It's good to see you again. I've been worried about you since I heard you were part of the first wave into New York." Brenda glanced down at her leg with a wince. "Did you know shotguns can hurt people? Really badly, in fact."

"I'd heard someone mention the possibility before," he replied drily.

"Is there anyone in the Division you don't know, Brenda?" asked the first woman.

"Well, I told you I was a recruiter and trainer before the Poison. Tends to put you on a first name basis with just about everybody," Brenda acknowledged. She turned her face back to Colin. "Grab a seat. Let's go around the table and get the introductions out of the way."

"Oh man, is this gonna be like the first day in class type thing?" asked the first woman.

"Whine too much, and I'll make you give a whole presentation on what you did during your summer break," Brenda replied.

"Anything but that! I'm Maira Kanhai," the first woman

said as Leo and Colin settled into seats. "Formerly a Navy cybersecurity specialist, now in the professional world-saving business like all of you."

Brenda turned her gaze on Leo expectantly.

"Leo," he said.

"And?" Brenda asked.

"Last name Fourte," Leo offered after a few seconds of contemplation.

Brenda sighed. "Leo used to be an officer in the Army, and commanded tanks. He's a valuable asset to the team for his tactical acumen." She shifted her gaze to Colin and raised an eyebrow. "Are you gonna make me speak for you, too?"

Colin chuckled. "I think I can spare you that. I'm Colin Harrison, and I'm Navy, too."

"At last, a fellow salt here to save me from these mudsloggers!" intoned Maira soulfully.

Colin grinned. "Alas, I was a Corpsman and spent my time among Marines, so I'm afraid I may have been irrevocably contaminated."

"Well, at least we have a medic now," Maira replied. "Somehow working for the Division keeps getting people shot."

They all turned to look at the last person. She inclined her head politely, apparently unbothered by being the focus of the room.

"Cha Yeong-Ja. My prior experience was with the FBI Hostage Rescue Team as a sharpshooter. A pleasure to meet all of you."

Maira's eyebrows went up. "You're the first agent I've encountered with no military background."

"It's actually far from unusual," Brenda said. "The Division recruited from all walks of life in the old days. Military and first responders tend to have useful skillsets, but the primary criterion was psychological profile."

Colin nodded. "I met a man who was a heart surgeon before activation. There's some folks in NYC that owe their lives to that fact."

"A medic, a sniper, a hacker, and a Leo," Maira said thoughtfully. "Quite a crew. So, what's the mission?"

"I thought you'd never ask." Brenda picked a remote up off the table. "First, some background."

She clicked and the lights in the room dimmed. An image of the southern reaches of the United States came up on the screen. It had major highways stretching the width of the nation highlighted.

"These are the trade routes we've established with the assistance of our friends in the I-10 Fleet. They reconnect settlements from the Southwest all the way to the Eastern Seaboard, with much needed goods flowing in both directions."

Colin nodded. "It's definitely saved some of the survivor enclaves up around New York City. The largest might have gotten through on their own, but some of the smaller ones were at risk of completely depleting their supplies."

"I think it's safe to say the arrival of food and fuel saved millions of lives over the winter," agreed Brenda. "Unfortunately, we've hit a snag. Hostile forces have ambushed several supply convoys as they passed through Texas and Louisiana. They've shown sufficient organization and armament to be able to overwhelm the Freighties' defenses."

"Keep taking losses, the Roamers will get bold. Push south again," mused Leo.

"That is a concern, but it's not our biggest danger," said Brenda. A tap showed the reported attacks in blinking red dots on the map. "If you notice, there are signs of a greater strategy at play here. These bandits aren't just taking goods. They're choking off supply lines to a specific area."

She clicked again, and the display zoomed in on a region along the Texas Gulf Coast.

"The whole I-10 Fleet is kept running thanks to oil production centered on this area. As you can see, the platforms and refineries that we depend on are close to the area our new bunch of hostiles are operating in. Division Intel thinks that's no coincidence, and that the fuel production is their actual target."

"What are they after?" asked Yeong-Ja.

"We're not completely certain," admitted Brenda. "We know they call themselves the Reborn. We know they're heavily armed – not just small arms like you'd expect from any local militia, either. There's reports of high explosives and other military grade weaponry among their arsenal."

"Well, that's fun," Maira said quietly.

Brenda nodded. "I wish I could give you a full layout of their capabilities and organization, but we don't have much in the way of an active presence in that area. You'll be our advance team."

Colin nodded and popped his knuckles thoughtfully. "So, what's our first objective?"

"You'll deploy into the region and make immediate contact with the enclaves working on oil production. We can't let a hostile force cut us off from our fuel supply and endanger everything we've fought for. Whatever you can do to strengthen the defenses of those communities will be priority one."

"So we're not looking for a fight?" asked Yeong-Ja.

"Only if they force your hand. Use whatever tactics you deem necessary, but realistically speaking we don't have the assets to fight a war. More importantly, we don't want one. The Division's reputation has suffered as it is. Better to keep a low profile," Brenda said.

"Are there any people of interest we should be concerned about in the area?" Maira asked.

"A couple," Brenda said.

She clicked through to the next image. It showed a heavyset, mustachioed man in an ill-fitting business suit. The picture was candid, the man in the middle of a discussion with several workers in hard hats.

"Douglas Rychart," Brenda said. "He's the one who is requesting our help."

"Doesn't look like some slick executive," commented Colin.

"He's not. When the Green Poison hit, all the big money types fled the area. Rychart was a middle manager, and the highest man left on the totem pole. He's the kind who worked his way up from nothing, and he's apparently popular enough with the people that he's still in charge to this day."

"Small favors that we're not propping up some oil tycoon," Maira offered.

Brenda smirked. "I think if I put you and a CEO in the same room, Maira, you'd mutually annihilate like matter and antimatter."

"God, you are such a nerd sometimes." Maira grinned.

Brenda restrained a guffaw into a snort and clicked on to the next person. This time it was a man in the dress uniform of the United States Marine Corps. He had a powerful build and a weathered face, clean shaven. His hair was dark black to match his eyes, and even in image form his gaze was piercing. He wore a colonel's eagles on his shoulders.

"Marcus Georgio," Colin blurted. He winced as everyone turned to look at him.

"That's correct," Brenda said. "Are you familiar?"

Colin swallowed and shook his head. "Never met him. Just heard of him while I was with the Corps. He was considered one of the sharpest field commanders of his generation."

He felt a surge of regret at the lie of omission. It was unlikely to matter, after all. Colonel Georgio would not come looking for him. Colin would have to seek the man out on his own time. Brenda's eyes were measuring. Colin wondered if she knew more about the connection, but if so, she didn't say anything.

"That's correct," Brenda said instead. "He had retired by the time the pandemic started. No information for a while after that, then he reappears in the Dallas-Ft. Worth area. He'd assembled a private army, called the Molossi, and cracked down on the chaos. Most JTF elements in the area ended up rallying to his banner rather than fight him."

"Friendly?" asked Leo.

Brenda frowned. "Let's put a big question mark on that for right now. We haven't had enough direct contact to evaluate his stance."

"OK, question," Maira said.

Brenda raised an eyebrow. "What now?"

"What on earth is a Molossi?"

Brenda sighed and touched the bridge of her nose. "The fabled warhounds of ancient Greece, thought to be extinct now. It's a callback to the colonel's Greek heritage, we assume."

"Huh," Maira said. "I like it better than the True Sons, at least."

"Damned with faint praise," Brenda said. "There is one more complication."

"Of course," muttered Maira.

"The projection ability of the Division network has been increasingly compromised as time has gone on. Communication infrastructure is decaying from a lack of maintenance, and that's essentially unavoidable at this point."

Colin paused as that sank in. "Wait, so we'll be cut off while we're there?"

Brenda hesitated. "Not completely. Long range communication may be difficult. We do have a stop gap, however. We'll be sending you with a Mobile SHD Server. It will keep your SHD tech operational while you're in the theater."

"Well, that's something at least," Maira said. "What sort of supplies will we have in that regard?"

"We'll send you with everything we can spare. I'm not going to sugarcoat this for y'all. You're going to be outnumbered and possibly outgunned in this fight. You're going to need every advantage you can get. Don't hesitate to use the tech to get an edge."

"That all?" asked Leo.

Brenda nodded. "That's all I can tell you for now. If we get any major breakthroughs on this end, I'll do my best to push them through to you somehow. Be prepared for departure in the morning."

The meeting broke up with no further ado. Yeong-Ja slipped out the door with little fanfare. Leo and Maira left together, talking quietly. Colin stood and walked to the end of the room to look at the map more closely. There were too many unknowns for him to feel comfortable. It reminded him of that first push into New York, and the carnage that had followed.

And now he had confirmation. Marcus Georgio was in the region. Was trying to find him and talk to him a fool's quest?

Brenda stepped up beside him. "Sorry you volunteered now?"

"Which time?" Colin asked with a humorless smile. "But no. This is the job, right? Truthfully, I haven't really been in the field since the debacle in New York. Maybe it will be good for me."

"I heard about that," Brenda said softly. "I'm sorry about what happened to your team."

"Thanks," Colin said. He took a deep breath. "This is a chance to do it better. To do it right."

Brenda didn't reply to that, but her eyes were sympathetic.

"Come on," she said finally. "I'll set you up with a room where you can get some sleep before you leave."

"'Once more unto the breach, dear friends. Once more,'" Maira quoted as they walked down the corridor.

Leo nodded. "Ready?"

"Yes. No. Maybe?" Maira shook her head. "It will be better than sitting around here counting corn stalks."

"Stay sharp. Stay smart. We'll be fine," Leo said.

"I'm starting to suspect you're a closet optimist," Maira observed.

Leo snorted. They had reached the juncture where they'd separate to head to their own quarters.

"It won't be the same without Brenda there," she added softly.

Leo paused. "No. It won't."

He walked off down the hallway. Maira watched him for a moment before turning away. She flexed her hands. Her knuckles still stung from the training earlier, but it was a good pain. It made her feel stronger. More prepared.

"Maira," Leo called.

She looked up in surprise to find him standing at the end of the hallway. "What is it?"

"Don't forget your gas mask," he said.

Maira grinned. "Don't worry. I never leave home without it."

She headed down the hallway toward her room, and her smile faded. It was easy enough to put up a front around others. If she kept that up long enough, it might even become real, she told herself. She didn't know what else to do.

CHAPTER 2

"Dixie Dog!" Maira called delightedly.

The truck driver looked up with a grin. He leaned against his engine with an air of practiced nonchalance.

"That's what they call me! Whether I want them to or not," he added.

Maira stepped forward and pulled the man into a hug. He laughed and slapped her on the back in return. She flinched at the impact on her burn scars, even covered, but did her best not to let him notice.

"It's so good to see you again," she said.

"Likewise," Dixie said. "You look good. I'm glad they gave you some R&R after all that wildness six months ago. You all looked about like bugs freshly scraped off a zapper after that."

Maira winced at the memory. Her back burned to char, and the blood besides, from friend and foe alike… She shook her head.

"We didn't feel much better than we looked."

Dixie squeezed her arm sympathetically and looked past her to the other three agents approaching. He spread his hands welcomingly.

"Please, please, come forward and make yourselves comfortable aboard the finest engine that has ever graced these highways and byways."

Leo gave him a quick nod. "Dixie." He climbed aboard with no more than that.

"He's still like to talk your ear off, I see," Dixie noted cheerfully.

"Leo never changes," Maira said. "That's the best and the worst thing about him. Here, let me introduce you to the other two."

"We've met," Colin said brightly.

Dixie nodded. "This will not be the first time this gangly fellow has had to fold himself up inside my cab for a bit of transportation."

"Well, that saves time! Last piece of the puzzle, then, is Cha Yeong-Ja here." Maira nodded to the sharpshooter.

"It's a pleasure, Mr Dog. There seems to be quite a history here," Yeong-Ja said pleasantly.

He chuckled. "Please, call me Dixie. And yeah, I seem to have made a foolish habit of hauling Division agents around. Not a healthy hobby to have, I can tell you that much."

Yeong-Ja smiled. "You must be a brave man. We're very grateful for your help. It would be quite a walk."

Dixie blushed, to Maira's delight. "Well, I mean, I never figured it was bravery as such. But thank you. Please, make yourself as comfortable as you can."

Yeong-Ja reseated her rifle strap on her shoulder and

climbed up past him into the vehicle. He turned his attention back to Maira after she passed.

"Did you just develop a crush before my very eyes, Mr Dog?" asked Maira.

"Hey!" hissed Dixie. "Shh. No! Don't go… saying stuff. All right? Just hush."

Maira grinned. "Of course, of course, mum's the word. How have things been with the fleet?"

Dixie motioned for her to go ahead and climb inside as he spoke. "They were going well until these latest attacks started. We had the damn PWR on the run, and then this all kicked off. It's like we can't get a moment of real peace these days."

Maira clambered up into the cab. It was an expanded sleeper setup, which would make things as comfortable as possible at least. There were two beds structured like bunks, along with various facilities like a sink and some seating. Colin had already settled into the passenger seat, while Leo and Yeong-Ja sat at the small lunch table. It was similar to the arrangement the first time she'd ridden with him, but thankfully it wasn't exactly the same.

"I see you were able to trade up," Maira said.

"Oh, trust me, I didn't drive that radioactive hunk of junk any longer than I had to," Dixie replied.

He got behind the wheel and started the vehicle up. The engine woke with a growl, and they pulled away from the Core to head toward the nearest road. The drive until then was a bumpy rattling mess of dirt roads.

"Radioactive?" Yeong-Ja called over the engine's sound, her eyebrow arched.

"An unfortunate incident with a dirty bomb," Maira answered.

For a moment, she was back there that night in St Louis. The dust rained down all around them as they careened through the city streets. Bullets sparked off the truck. She clung to the machine gun with frozen fingers, teeth locked in a grimace behind her mask.

"Anomalous elevated heart rate detected," ISAC noted in her ear. "Signal for aid?"

Maira swallowed and shook her head.

"–off?"

Colin had said something. She'd missed it. "What?"

He tilted his head. Maira didn't like the way his eyes were gauging her. She realized her hands had tightened into fists and forced them to relax.

"I said I thought the fighting in New York was ugly. Who set that off?" Colin repeated.

"A band of Outcasts in DC, working for a rogue agent." Maira chuckled drily at his expression. "It's a long story."

"Full of dashing heroics from your cell, and a lot of screaming on my part," noted Dixie.

"You kept driving while buildings exploded and people shot at you," said Maira. "A little screaming can be forgiven."

"Well, how long is this trip going to take us?" asked Colin.

Dixie glanced at the clock on his dash. "Call it twelve hours, give or take. That's if everything goes smooth and nothing blows up, mind you."

"Sounds like enough time for a story to me," Colin said.

"I'd like to hear it, too," Yeong-Ja said.

"Well, all right," Maira said. She looked at Leo. "Do you want to tell it?"

The other agent pointedly got up and went to lie down on one of the cots.

Maira grinned. "OK, so, for starters I met Brenda and Leo in the outskirts of DC…"

Colin frowned. He didn't like the situation. Unfortunately, that didn't change anything. There was no way around it.

"Do you have any eights?"

Yeong-Ja shook her head. "Go fish."

Colin sighed. "I thought so."

He reached forward and plucked the top card from the deck. A three of clubs. Useless. He did his best to keep disappointment from his face.

It had been a couple of hours. They were driving through a rainstorm. It was coming down hard, an endless drumbeat against the roof that dissolved the distance into gray obscurity. There was nothing but abandoned suburbia and rushing dark clouds outside. Maira and Leo were both sleeping on the bunks. The other two agents had decided to pass the time as pleasantly as they could. Yeong-Ja had produced a well-worn deck of cards from her kit. Colin wasn't sure how one managed to be a card shark when it came to Go Fish, but he felt certain he was being swindled somehow.

"Do you always keep that deck with you?" he asked.

"Everywhere I go," she confirmed. "It is my lucky deck."

Colin could have sworn the corner of her mouth quirked slightly when she said it. He narrowed his eyes. Before he could probe that subject any further, however, he realized she was looking past him with a small frown. He glanced over his shoulder, but all he saw was Dixie driving.

"What's wrong?"

"He keeps looking in the mirrors. Something has him anxious," Yeong-Ja said.

Colin set his cards down. "Dixie, something we need to know about?"

The trucker jumped a little. Definitely on edge, Colin noted. He looked back over his shoulder, and Colin could see the worry in the man's eyes.

"I didn't want to spook anybody because I wasn't sure what I was seeing at first. The rain, you know? Coulda been anything."

"Better safe than sorry. What's up?" Colin said.

"I think we're being pursued."

That got the attention of both agents. They stood from the table. Colin grabbed his carbine, noting that Yeong-Ja had likewise gone for her rifle. Maira came awake at the rush of movement. She sat bolt upright immediately.

"What? What's going on?"

There was an edge to her voice that Colin didn't like. He'd heard it earlier as well. Maira was personable, sharp, and by all reports a skilled agent. He didn't challenge any of that. His instincts just told him she was hurting, too.

There was no time to deal with that now, even if he'd known how.

"Dixie spotted someone on our heels," Colin said.

Leo's eyes were open, he realized. Whether he'd been awake all along or woken up, too, was moot. He sat up smoothly now and began to collect his own weaponry. Maira hopped down from the top bunk.

"Do we have any idea who it is, Dixie?" she called forward.

"I'm not even sure they're really there," the trucker said anxiously. "This storm makes it hard to see."

Yeong-Ja had gone to the front with the driver and was peering into one of the mirrors. She opened the door and without hesitation leaned out into the whipping wind and rain. When she came back, she was dripping water and her expression was grim.

"They're out there," she confirmed. "Three semis. Upgunned, and they're gaining."

"Roamers," said Leo darkly.

"Maybe," Maira said. "Could they be friendlies?"

Dixie shook his head. "We haven't even crossed I-40 yet. We're still too far north for it to be anyone but the PWR."

"Don't suppose there's any chance they think we're just one of them?" Maira asked.

"This isn't that captured engine anymore. They might not realize who we are yet, but all it would take is a radio check," Dixie said. "And if they get close to us, they'll definitely know."

"Outrun them?" asked Leo.

"I can try, but if they aren't suspicious yet, they will be when I bolt."

"Sounds like they're going to catch on sooner or later regardless," Colin put in. "Better if they never catch up at all, right?"

"You got it," Dixie said firmly.

He put the pedal to the metal, and the truck's engine roared. Colin staggered a bit and caught himself by grabbing one of the nearby cabinets. Dixie glanced into the mirror, and his jaw tightened.

"They just turned all their lights on. Yeah, they're onto us now."

"All right," Maira said. "The Roamers are with Black Tusk now. They're no friends of the Division. If they catch us, we're as good as dead. So, let's do what we can to discourage them. Do you have any onboard weapons?"

"Got a gun nest and a mortar launcher up top. Might be enough to make them think twice, at least, but we aren't hauling anything big enough to take them out of action easily," Dixie answered.

"It's a start," Maira said.

Colin nodded. "I'll go up top and get on the gun."

"Call for help," Leo said to Dixie. Then he motioned for Colin to lead the way. "On the mortar."

"Breaker breaker, one-nine, this is Dixie Dog putting a call out to any friendly faces on the way south through Oklahoma." He paused from the radio to call to them, "There's a door in the back, takes you to a ladder up."

"Where was that last time?"

Colin heard Maira asking that as he pushed open the rear door and stepped out into the storm. Anything else anyone might have said was lost to the wind. It was pouring down. The drops seemed huge, splashing home against Colin with chilly force. He pulled himself up the ladder and clambered onto the top of the semi's trailer. The wind whipped against his back, snatching at his shirt and pack. He steadied himself against the force and staggered onward, moving past where the mortar was set up.

"Hostile armed vehicles detected," ISAC informed him. The AI interfaced with the advanced contacts each agent wore. It highlighted the vehicles behind them, already picked out by their headlights. They had gained on the agents and their Freighty ally in the meantime.

"Little bit late, but thanks, pal," muttered Colin.

There was a brilliant flash from that direction. Seconds later the road behind them detonated. The wash of flame dazzled Colin's eyes, and for a moment hot air pushed back against the flow of the wind. Unlike them, the Roamers had apparently brought the big guns.

"Fuck!" Colin opined.

The nest was just up ahead. It was a circle of sandbags secured to the top of the trailer. In the center was an M60 on a tripod, along with several cases of ammunition for the weapon. Colin scrambled over the bags and behind the gun. With fumbling, rain-soaked fingers he pulled a belt of ammunition from the can and fed it into the machine gun.

Smaller flashes flickered from the rear, nearly lost in the glare of the headlights. Small arms, Colin thought. A hot hiss of a near miss confirmed his guess. It was time to return the favor. He brought the M60 around and squeezed the trigger. The gun screamed and spat a stream of fire back toward the pursuers.

The tracers were lost against the lights. Colin didn't let it bother him. The goal was simply to discourage the enemy – he wasn't hoping for any precision kills. To that end he hosed back and forth, working the weapon around. A headlight blew out in a spray of sparks, a satisfying result. Return fire thudded against the sandbags and made him duck down, dampening his enthusiasm.

The distinctive thump of a mortar behind Colin announced

that Leo was joining the fight. The first shot went wild, landing off to the side of the road and kicking up a cloud of smoke and debris. All Colin could do was hope these dark suburban houses were as abandoned as they appeared, because one had just gotten its roof staved in.

The Roamer cannon answered. The blast thundered right to the side of their engine, close enough that smoke washed over the roof of the trailer. Colin coughed and spat, wiping his wet sleeve against his eyes. One direct hit with that and all the sandbags in the world weren't going to save him.

Another mortar shell set off with a howl. It managed a glancing hit against the cab of the nearest Roamer truck. The vehicle came roaring through the blast, but it was weaving. That one slowed down, letting one of the other PWR engines pass it. They might still be in the fight, but that had been close enough to put some fear into them. They were going to let one of their friends take some of the heat for a while.

The M60 pinged empty, the belt spent. Colin's arms ached from the gun's vibration. He turned to grab another and reload. Yeong-Ja was there. She hadn't entered the nest with him, she was just standing with surprising steadiness alongside. She was laid out directly against the roof of the trailer on her belly, her M700 braced against her shoulder.

"Which one has the cannon?" she yelled.

"Hell, uh… ISAC! Spotlight the cannon for her!" Colin called.

The AI made the leftmost truck flash on their enhanced vision. The only sign that Yeong-Ja actually noticed was a slight nod. She was consumed entirely in what she was doing. She squeezed the trigger and her rifle thundered. There was no effect. The only concession she made, to Colin's eye, was a twitch of her cheek. She fiddled with the rifle's sights briefly and then put her cheek back to the weapon.

Colin focused on pulling more ammo from the box and getting the M60 working. A bullet striped a bag to the left of him. Wet sand spilled out onto the metal. He put it out of his mind. It didn't change what needed to be done. He locked in and unleashed a new barrage against their pursuers.

Yeong-Ja's rifle spoke again. The left truck went out of control. It veered sideways, tore across a driveway at cross angles, and smashed into a house. The impact tore the whole structure apart. The shells for the cannon cooked off a heartbeat later, sending a massive fireball skyward and lighting up the area for miles.

"That's one," Yeong-Ja commented with calm satisfaction.

The loss stripped the Roamers of their biggest weapon. The other two engines killed their lights and were soon lost in the rain and gloom behind them. Colin took a deep breath. He let go of the M60 and shook his hands out wearily. The entire interlude couldn't have taken more than a matter of minutes, but he felt exhausted. His clothes were rain-plastered to him, and he was cold.

He stood from the nest and offered Yeong-Ja a hand up. She accepted gratefully and they stood a minute more looking back to make sure the enemy really had given up. Leo came forward to stand beside them. He was bleeding from where a bullet had skimmed his shoulder. The moving truck jolted over a bump in the road. All three agents grabbed ahold of each other to avoid falling.

"Area secure. No hostile vehicles detected," announced ISAC.

"Not bad," Leo allowed. He slowly released the others.

Colin gave a shaky laugh and clapped Yeong-Ja on the shoulder. "Yeah, not bad at all." He turned his attention to Leo. "Come on, let's get back into the cab and I can get that sewn up for you."

Maira yawned, her boots up on the dash. They had left the Roamers behind hours ago. Having remained with Dixie during the battle, she had let the others get some rest while she stayed up to keep watch. The only problem was staying awake as the monotonous miles flowed past. They had eaten a few minutes before, packaged food that Maira heated up for both of them so that he could keep driving. Now they were listening to Johnny Cash, and Dixie was noisily chewing gum.

"Where did you even get that from?" Maira asked him.

"Oh, we found like a whole crate of the stuff in one of the bases the Roamers abandoned when they went back north. Guess they didn't figure it was worth packing."

"Isn't it stale by this point?" she asked.

"For sure. But I can tell you this, it's not the worst thing I've ever put in my mouth even so." Dixie gave her a big grin.

Maira snorted and threw an empty food container at him.

"Hey, hey, no harassing the driver! That's basic road etiquette. Also basic I-don't-want-to-die etiquette," Dixie said.

Maira was about to reply when she spotted the smoke column up ahead. It was the afternoon, and the black haze stood out sharply against the blue sky. She dropped her feet to the deck with a thud and sat forward. Her hand came to rest uneasily on the butt of her sidearm.

"Do you see that?"

Dixie craned forward then nodded grimly. "More trouble?"

"Could well be. Looks like it's in our path, so I think we're going to find out one way or another." Maira turned her head to call to the others. "On your feet, agents. We might have another problem on our hands."

The others had gathered within a matter of minutes. By that point the column had resolved into a dozen smaller blazes. Leo rested a hand on Maira's chair to lean forward and get a better look.

"Roamers again?" he asked.

Dixie shook his head. "Hell, we're south of Dallas now. If this isn't fleet territory, then I don't know what is."

"Perhaps radio in, see what your comrades may know?" suggested Yeong-Ja.

Dixie nodded and picked up the radio mic. "Breaker breaker, this is Dixie Dog. South of Dallas, headed on Houston way. Spotted a smoke column. Any word? Over."

The silence stretched for a few seconds.

The radio crackled. "Dixie, this is Jukebox. Only thing out that way other than you is a convoy that was headed south to try to get through to the roughnecks. Over."

They came around a curve and into sight of a scene of devastation. The ruins of several semis littered the road ahead of them. Each one showed signs of catastrophic battle. Most of them were completely cored and actively burning, the source of the smoke they'd spotted in the distance. The road itself was pocked with a number of craters.

Dixie hit the brakes hard. They squealed in complaint, but the truck obligingly slowed to a crawl then came to a complete stop. Maira braced herself against the deceleration but couldn't look away from the carnage in front of them. The driver beside her appeared shaken by the sight.

He licked his lips uneasily and then queued the radio again. "Jukebox, this is Dixie. Just found the convoy. Someone hit them hard. Do you know how many trucks were involved? Over."

"Should be six, Dixie. Over."

Yeong-Ja's eyes swept the battlefield. She shook her head sadly. "That's all of them."

"God above," muttered Dixie. He hit the radio again. "Jukebox, they're gone. They got all of them. Clean sweep. Over and out." He hung the mic up and shook his head. "They were carrying enough food to keep an enclave going for months. Damn."

"The Reborn?" asked Colin softly.

"It's got to be," Maira said. "Who else would have the nerve to jump an entire Freighty caravan?"

"Looks fresh," Leo noted grimly.

Maira nodded. "Hold up here for a minute, Dixie. Stay in the cabin and keep the engine warm. We're going to do a sweep, see if there's any survivors." *And make sure there aren't more hostiles waiting to kill us, too,* she added silently.

The four Division agents geared up. Maira took point this time, hopping down to the asphalt with her Winchester in hand. She could have traded the weapon out at the Core, but she hadn't. It hadn't let her down, and she didn't want to forget the people who had given it to her. She walked forward toward the shattered convoy with the weapon held ready.

The heat of the fires soon had her sweating. The whole battlefield stank of burning rubber and hot metal. There were hints of other smells, too. The kind that reminded Maira of unpleasant things. The scents of burned flesh and scorched blood. She wiped sweat off her face onto her sleeve, wincing as the motion pulled at the scar tissue on her back.

It wasn't long before her eyes confirmed what her nose had already guessed. The crews of the trucks hadn't somehow been miraculously spared. A corpse was sprawled out in the first cabin she checked, already burned into unrecognizability. The passenger side door hung open. A more intact body lay in the grass beside the road, bullet holes punched into its back.

"Not the merciful types," Colin remarked behind her. "That's an execution. That person was running."

Maira could only shake her head in response. Her eyes were on one of the nearby trailers. The rear hatch had been blasted open. Whatever cargo had been inside was long gone. Others they had ripped asunder but not plundered, simply leaving them to burn. She glanced inside one of the more intact ones. It was smoke-filled and charred. She thought she could make out consumer goods, electronics, and clothes. Most of the convoy's tonnage would have been given over to food, but people needed more than calories to survive. Apparently the Reborn disagreed.

"Maira," called Yeong-Ja.

Maira walked over to stand beside the sniper. Yeong-Ja pointed at the road in the middle of all the destroyed trucks. There was a symbol spray-painted onto the asphalt in dark green. Maira tilted her head and walked around it in a circle, trying to make sense of it. She was a quarter of the way before understanding dawned.

It was a stylized deer skull, mounted by antlers. Creepers

covered in thorns wove through the eye sockets and wreathed the whole. Morbid imagery to be sure. Maira felt certain it must be the symbol of the Reborn. This attack must indeed have been their work.

"ISAC, take a snapshot," Maira said.

They were beyond the reach of the Network now. The version of ISAC they were operating with thus had severely restricted capabilities. The AI could capture the image for later use, but they would have to wait until they got their node set up at their destination before they could access any of the intel databases or comm networks.

"A calling card," said Yeong-Ja quietly.

Maira nodded. "Not only did they do it, but they want people to know they did it. They're proud of it." She couldn't keep the disquiet out of her voice.

Leo stood off toward the far end of the battlefield. He was staring at the ground as well. She walked over toward him and found him gazing not at another tag but at a deep crater near a semi toppled on its side.

"Anything interesting?" Maira asked.

Leo raised his head and chewed his lip thoughtfully for a moment. "IEDs on the road. Knocked out the first trucks, smashed them over, forced the others to crash." He stepped over to the side and pointed at the wreckage of one further back. "Then RPGs on the rear vehicles. Busted them methodically. All of them would have been burning in seconds. Shot anyone who got out and tried to run."

Maira had encountered more than her fair share of dangerous gangs in the post-Poison world. Outcasts, Hyenas, True Sons… all of them had been more than capable of gratuitous violence and cruelty. Something about this disturbed her in a new way. It felt like a combination of the worst things she'd seen previously. The firepower and organization of the True Sons. The brutality of the Hyenas. The curious sense of righteous anger of the Outcasts.

"I don't think we're going to find any survivors," she said quietly.

The four agents were quiet as they walked back to their own waiting engine. Even after they'd left the scene of the battle behind, Maira could still smell the burning on her own clothes. It made her nauseous. She resolved to change as soon as she got a chance.

Dixie saw it in their faces as they climbed back aboard. He didn't bother to ask them if they'd found anyone alive. He just lowered his head and got the truck moving again.

Their destination was only a few hours away now.

CHAPTER 3

The quiet stayed with them the rest of the way. No one felt like sleeping or playing games anymore. They didn't even turn the music back on. Colin saw each of his fellow agents lost in their own thoughts and wondered what form that took for them. He sat at the table and mindlessly picked at his hands. He couldn't stop thinking about that body lying in the grass where they'd tried to run.

Yeong-Ja seemed to have focused her attention completely on her rifle. She had disassembled it and meticulously cleaned every part, then reassembled it. Was that just a distraction? Colin wondered. Or a dream of getting revenge for those murdered in the convoy's ambush?

The other two agents were even more opaque, if that was possible. Leo sat at the dining table. His gaze was in the middle distance, and his fingers twitched. It was as if he was imagining conducting some invisible symphony. Maira lay on her back on the top cot, but she wasn't sleeping. The restless swinging of her leg, hanging over the side, made that clear.

Dixie, of course, just stayed focused on the road. The good cheer he'd shown for most of the drive had evaporated completely. Colin felt for him. There was no telling how close to home the ambush had hit. At the very least, it must be easy for the man to imagine himself in their place. At the worst, he might well have known some of those people. If he did, he didn't say anything about it.

"We're close now," Dixie said.

Colin unfolded himself to his full height and headed to the front of the cab to peer out. It was now progressing fast into the evening. The colors of the sunset were fading into gray twilight. There was smoke on the horizon. Colin's heart fell. Then he realized what he was looking at: the smokestacks on an oil refinery. Artificial light was burning there as well, coming on as night closed in. It was strange to see signs of life after so much empty country.

"Is that our destination?" he asked.

Dixie nodded. "Someone told me it used to be the biggest oil refinery in North America." He scratched his head. "I suppose it still is. Just now it's one of the only ones still working at all."

Colin clapped him on the shoulder. "Thank you for getting us here safely. I'm guessing you'll be grateful to be back to your normal routes soon."

Dixie gave him a wry smile. "I have to admit, it'll be nice to go back to just hauling food or something. I'm glad to help you Division types, but it feels like every time I do a few years get shaved off my lifespan."

Maira stepped up next to them to take a look. "So, this is Roughneck HQ, huh?"

"Yep. Think you'll be able to help keep them safe?" Dixie asked.

"We'll do our very best," Maira said firmly. "After what happened to those people back there? I'll be damned if I let it happen to anyone else on my watch."

"You've got that right," agreed Colin. "I wondered at first if I was doing the right thing, leaving New York to volunteer for this mission. But after seeing that... we can't let that keep happening, much less let it spread."

"What are those?" Yeong-Ja asked.

They might have only spent a day together, but Colin had already learned not to doubt her keen eyesight. He followed her pointing finger to see if he could puzzle out what she was talking about. There were dark shapes gathered in the lots in front of the refinery. That was odd in the modern world, but not inconceivable. After all, if anyone had the gas to keep cars running it would be these people.

"Those are military trucks," Maira said suddenly.

Colin blinked and looked again. To his surprise, he realized she was correct. It was a gathering of military vehicles. They were painted black instead of army green, but there was no mistaking the silhouettes now. Humvees and LMTVs. These weren't demilitarized either. He could make out the gun cupolas on the Humvees.

"It's not JTF, is it?"

Leo shook his head. "We'd know."

It made the skin between Colin's shoulder blades itch. He had been there for the Division's first encounters with the Last Man Battalion in the early days in New York. This reminded him of that. Military hardware in the wrong hands had almost always meant bad things for everyone in the area. Then again, even elements of the JTF had gone down a dark road in DC, some of them falling in line with Black Tusk and the new regime. Maybe no one was trustworthy.

"Are we walking into another firefight already?" Colin asked grimly.

"There's no shooting yet, and we're not going to be the ones to start it," Maira said. She smiled bleakly. "For one thing, we'd be seriously outgunned."

"Information first," Yeong-Ja agreed. "We'll gain nothing by being belligerent off the bat. Our job is to get the lay of the land, not go in guns blazing."

Maira nodded and stepped up beside Dixie. She rested a hand on the back of his chair to brace herself. "Just pull in to the edge of the lot, and we'll walk the rest of the way across. Can you keep it warm this time, too? We might need to get out of here quick."

Dixie nodded. "I was planning to pass the night here anyway. Even I have to sleep at some point, you know."

Yeong-Ja rested a hand on his shoulder briefly. "Thank you for watching out for us."

Dixie blushed crimson. Colin shared an amused look with Maira. Each of the agents went over their gear quickly. Colin made sure both his M4 and his X45 sidearm were loaded and ready to go. He blew out a shaky breath. There were always nerves before a possible fight. The memories of the Last Man Battalion had him on edge. *This doesn't have to go the way that did*, he told himself. *It won't.*

Leo held something out to him. A pair of incendiary grenades.

"Better to be ready," was all Leo said.

Colin frowned but took them and clipped them to his vest. In truth, he had never loved fighting. He knew plenty of people who did, or at least claimed to. He couldn't walk ten feet during his time with the Marines without stumbling over someone longing for some proper violence. Colin was a healer at heart. He would much rather close a wound than inflict a new one. Sometimes reality didn't cooperate with his qualms, so he reluctantly carried a weapon anyway.

The semi slid to a halt and Leo led the way out into the evening gloom. Colin followed just behind. The group of agents spread out as they walked to present a less easy target. There was something very strange about the simple act of walking across a parking lot toward a working facility. It felt like they'd stepped through a time warp and arrived in an alternate timeline. One where everything hadn't gone wrong, where life had gone on never knowing what a Green Poison was.

Spotlights came on. They picked out the Division agents. Colin held up a hand against the actinic light, wincing. It didn't seem necessary; they hadn't been trying to sneak up on the refinery. He could just make out the silhouettes of armed people among the vehicles ahead of them. Two of the mounted guns had swiveled to aim at them. His pulse accelerated, and he swallowed against a dry throat. If one of those .50 cals opened up…

"Stop where you are," someone demanded through a megaphone.

"Unknown hostiles detected," noted ISAC. "Twenty-seven targets and weaponized vehicles detected. Threat level: severe."

"Great," muttered Colin.

Leo pulled up short immediately. Colin and the others followed suit. He decided not to wait for the laconic man to try to take point on talking to these people, whoever they were. Instead, he eased forward and held his hands up, well away from his weapons.

He raised his voice to be heard. "We're not looking for a fight."

"Identify yourselves," came the reply.

"We're agents of the Strategic Homeland Division," Colin said.

He turned his arm so that the telltale orange glow of the watch would be more visible. Before mass media had shut down, people had come to associate the symbol with the Division. That wasn't always a pleasant association, to be fair, but he figured it was best to be honest and straightforward as much as possible. He didn't know anyone who appreciated being lied to.

"The Division," the person said. It was a high voice underlying the bark of the loudspeaker. "I thought your operation had been shuttered."

The megaphone and the blinding lights made it hard to gauge what kind of reaction that had gotten. Colin felt certain it hadn't been a warm one, though. It definitely had not had the desired effect of getting all those weapons aimed somewhere other than his vital organs. Colin was very knowledgeable about the effects of gunshot wounds on the human body. He had no urge to make the experience personal.

"We'd be happy to talk with whoever is in charge," Colin offered. "What can we do to convince you we're not a threat?"

"What is going on out here?" a new voice yelled.

"Get back inside, Mr Rychart. We have this situation in hand," boomed the loudspeaker.

Rychart. That was the name of their contact. Only he didn't sound like he was in control of this site. Colin glanced back at the other agents in confusion. Maira looked as lost as he was. Leo was as unreadable as always. Yeong-Ja gestured with her head toward where the new arrival's voice had come from. She mouthed something. Colin wasn't certain but it looked like, "It's him."

"Be damned if I will. You heard these folks, they're Division agents! We invited them here to help us! Stop hassling them like they're common criminals," demanded Rychart.

So this was indeed the person the cell had been sent here to meet. By implication, the militants were a different group entirely. Colin had suspected as much. The locals doubtless had small arms to protect themselves, but they'd just be a militia. These people had brought significant hardware with them, and seemed to know how to use it.

"We are here to provide security now. There's no need for–" began the loudspeaker.

"Kill the lights," a new voice said firmly.

"But… yes, sir." The megaphone crackled, and the spotlights went out.

Being plunged instantly back into semi-darkness did nothing to help Colin make sense of the situation. He was left with blobs of color floating in his vision. He took a breath and tried to stay calm as his eyes adapted. It left his mind wondering. There had been something about that new voice. It was familiar.

"So, the mighty Division has finally come to Texas, armed to the teeth and ready to save us all."

It was the newest arrival, and he wasn't bothering to hide his contempt. He had a faint Greek accent. It was barely noticeable. The only reason Colin picked up on it was he was familiar with the sound. It made the hair on the back of his neck stand on end. Surely there was no way...

Colin's eyes were adapting now. The speaker was walking toward them. He was dressed in an outfit with the cut of military fatigues, but all black. It reminded Colin of the way some of the most heavily militarized police forces in the country had dressed, but this one lacked any insignia whatsoever save one: a snarling hound's head on the shoulder and breast pocket. His features were tan and tough, like weathered oak, and his head was topped with a recon flattop of salt and pepper hair. He was older than the picture, but it was him. He was here.

"Allow me to introduce myself. I am Colonel Marcus Georgio, commander of the Molossi. We are here to protect the civilians of this region, and your presence is a waste of everyone's time."

Maira frowned. The silence was beginning to stretch. The colonel's approach had obviously hit Colin on some level. He'd gone taut like someone had jabbed him with a live wire. She didn't want to step on his toes, but this situation was already unfriendly. They didn't need to let it get any worse by losing what grip they had on it.

"Colonel," she offered calmly. "I am Agent Maira Kanhai, and this is my team."

That was a stretching of the truth, of course. No one was in command of a cell, as Maira had learned to her surprise. Right now, though, it helped to focus attention on her and away from whatever was going on with Colin.

"If you'll excuse me for saying so," she continued quickly, "your declaration isn't really up to you. As Mr Rychart indicated, we're here at the invitation of the locals."

Rychart was visible now, too, thanks to the dazzling spotlights being out of the picture. He was revealed to be a large-framed man, balding, with hunched shoulders and a bristling mustache. He carried most of his weight on his gut. His face was sweat-sheened and red. Maira had the feeling he looked that way most of the time.

Rychart nodded rapidly and mopped his face with a handkerchief. He hurried to involve himself in their conversation now that she'd provided an opening. "Yes, exactly. These folks are here because we asked them to come. They've traveled a long way. I won't have you send them packing like vagabonds."

Colonel Georgio looked less than pleased. In fact, Maira thought he looked like someone was forcing him to take a swig of fish oil. He forced a thin smile, however, and spread his hands.

"Of course. This is your home, and you can invite anyone you like to it. The Molossi are guardians, not warlords. Forgive me for being somewhat overzealous – these are fraught times."

He turned and waved a hand at his band of soldiers. They lowered their weapons. The machine guns turned away from the group. Maira felt some of her tightly wound muscles ease in relief.

She offered a sparse smile of her own. "These days you can't be too careful."

Rychart nodded again. "Good, good. Glad we could get that resolved. Now, Agent... Kanhai, was it?"

"That's me," she said. She allowed her smile to become more genuine.

"Please, come on inside. We can discuss the security situation where it's more comfortable. It's as muggy as a swamp out here, which ain't much of a coincidence seeing as it used to be one." He turned to walk toward the building.

Colonel Georgio's voice caught him mid-step. "With your permission, I'd like to be present at this discussion, Mr Rychart. The security of the region is a shared concern, after all."

Rychart shot her a nervous look. To be honest, Maira wouldn't have minded if this black-garbed man and his air of understated violence left entirely. That was a personal feeling, however. What would Brenda have done? she asked herself. She would have...

The Molossi were well outside their usual stomping ground. From a Division point of view, these people and their place in this jigsaw puzzle needed to be figured out. So Maira just smiled again and nodded.

Rychart looked relieved. "The more the merrier, I suppose! Come on."

The group walked toward the building. A couple of Georgio's people moved to fall in with him. Rychart glanced over but didn't say anything about it. Their interactions intrigued Maira. All these armed people obviously did make the roughneck leader nervous. That was normal.

What was more interesting was that he was neither deferring to Georgio nor eager to challenge him. It had the air of people who were still figuring each other out as well. If they'd been here for an extended period, the relationship would feel more set. Unless Maira missed her guess, that meant the Molossi were new arrivals, too.

Maira set those thoughts aside for now. They headed through the doors into the refinery proper. It was odd to step from the heat into climate control and fluorescent lights. This was a working space, and people were actively at their jobs even now. The dress might have been a little more casual, and everyone might have looked a little thinner. Even so, this was a scene that might have come from the times before the smallpox chimera devastated the world.

The workers were shooting nervous looks at them. That was understandable. Two groups, both heavily armed, showing up in your home might put a wrinkle in anyone's day. Even more so when both were claiming to be here because a third, even more dangerous, group might soon invade. Maira made sure to smile warmly at them. *We are not the enemy.* She tried to emote the thought as clearly as possible.

Maira let her steps slow until she was walking beside Colin. Even now he seemed lost in his thoughts. He didn't even react to her presence. She gave him a subtle poke with her elbow, and he jumped a little bit.

"Where's your head at?" she asked quietly.

"A couple thousand miles away." Colin grimaced and shook his head. "Sorry."

"No need to apologize. We've all got our buttons. How did the good colonel push yours so quickly, though?"

"He didn't. Not on purpose, anyway." Colin took a deep breath. "There's history here."

"Old boyfriend?" she asked.

He shot her a dry look. "No. I served with his son."

Maira frowned. "In the military?"

Colin shook his head. "In the Division. We were activated at the same time, put into the same cell. We were both part of the first wave into New York."

Maira winced. "That didn't go well, as I recall. Where's his son now?"

Colin just lowered his gaze and shook his head.

"Fuck," Maira said. That was an unexpected complication. "Does he know who you are?"

"No. I don't think so. How could he?"

What would Brenda have said? she pondered. It didn't take much to figure it out. She would have told Colin to keep it that way. To do otherwise was an obvious risk to the mission. Yet Maira had seen the fruits of Brenda's methods, and they weren't always good. A lie might keep the peace now, but it planted the seeds of future conflict.

Colin was watching her mull this over with anxiety in his eyes. She patted him on the shoulder.

"Just… be careful, all right?"

"Yeah," he muttered.

Maira disengaged with an internal sigh. *Wonderful job, Kanhai. Way to make a really excellent non-decision there.* Then again, was it even her decision to make? Maybe no decision was the right decision. Maybe trying to control the cell – trying to be Brenda – was just going to lead to disaster.

Maybe she was overthinking all of it.

She fell back further until she was walking in between Yeong-Ja and Leo. She glanced between them and immediately resolved to never play poker with either one. Leo had all the emotion of a slab of marble, and Yeong-Ja radiated nothing but pleasant attentiveness. Maira was somewhere between impressed and jealous.

"Analysis?" she asked softly.

"Molossi weren't civilians," Leo said immediately.

Maira frowned. "Obviously not. They've armed themselves."

"No, weren't. Ex-military, almost to a person. In the walk, the talk. In their blood."

"That helps explain the access to the hardware. Are we thinking this is a True Sons situation?" Maira asked uneasily.

The True Sons were elements of the Joint Task Force in DC that had gone bad in a big way. They'd decided soft methods just didn't cut it anymore, and they'd turned to butchery and slavery. They'd maintained a facade of patriotism, but anyone who had lived in the area knew better. What the True Sons craved was power, and they'd been willing to take it at the barrel of a gun.

"No, I don't think so," Yeong-Ja said. "Or not yet. If that were the case, they would have killed us when they had the chance. Georgio hates us, but he does think he's protecting these people."

"I might have a lead on that hatred," Maira said.

Yeong-Ja raised an eloquent eyebrow.

"His son was a Division agent. He was in the same cell as Colin, apparently, those early days in New York," Maira said. "He didn't make it."

"Would a soldier take that so personally?" asked Yeong-Ja.

"The death of his son?" Maira was surprised she'd asked.

"Oh yeah. I mean, maybe some wouldn't, but plenty would. I'm more surprised Marcus knew his son was a Division agent in the first place."

"Family ties don't break easily," Leo said quietly. "Also, too old." He added it as an afterthought.

"Too old?" asked Maira, confused.

"True Sons were younger. Angry. Brash. Look at them."

Maira followed his gaze and measured the Molossi who walked nearby. The colonel was in excellent shape, but was in his fifties or sixties. His aides, though, were either the same age or not much younger. A blonde woman among them locked eyes with Maira. Her gaze was cold and challenging. Maira looked away quickly.

"So, what? Retirees?"

"Separated. Retirees. Veterans. Experienced and dedicated, that's what's important," Leo said.

"The old salt brigade, taking up arms once again," mused Maira. "Interesting."

"All right," Rychart said. He came to a halt next to a door.

Both armed groups turned their attention to him. He visibly wilted a bit. To his credit, though, he didn't lose his train of thought. He wasn't a soft man, Maira thought. Just not a killer, and not comfortable around those who were. In other words, a normal and sane person. A precious rarity nowadays.

"We have plans and a scheduling room just through here where we can talk things out. Figure a path forward," Rychart continued.

He took a key ring out of his pocket and opened the door.

It was a small auditorium beyond. Maira could imagine the old presentations. Numbers and dollar signs. Barrels of oil and production costs. A world with its own heavy problems, but at least that had had fewer murderous hordes running amok.

The two groups both chose seating with a gap between them. Maira couldn't help but find that a little bit funny. They were like high school cliques with a grudge. Well, assuming high school cliques had carried enough firepower to bring down a city block.

A few more of the locals joined Rychart. They were having a hurried discussion in low tones. Maira wasn't able to make out any of it.

"Is there a problem?" Colonel Georgio asked.

Rychart mopped his brow with his handkerchief again. "Oh, no, no, of course not. Just a few logistical details on the next oil shipment that needed ironing out. The work never stops, you know."

Maira suspected he was lying. Her alarm bells weren't ringing, though, so she let it slide.

"Please, Mr Rychart. Tell us your situation," she said instead.

"Well, what would you like to know?" Rychart seemed eager to help. Relieved, perhaps, to not be facing down the Molossi alone.

Maira smiled. "I know what I was told when we set out, but I'd like to hear your version of what's going on. What can we do to help you? Why did you ask for our presence here?"

Rychart blew out a tremendous sigh. "Well, if I'm going to be completely honest, it's because folks are scared. I have about twenty thousand people living here or at our other facilities, Agent Kanhai, and they're more afraid than I've seen them since the early days of the Green Poison."

"Understandable," put in Georgio. "But it is no longer necessary. I assure you, my people will see to it that you and yours are safe and sound. You have my word on that."

"A comforting thought, I'm sure," Maira said. She tried to make it sound sincere. "But I'd like to hear more. What are they afraid of specifically?"

Rychart nodded. "Well, there's the obvious. The Reborn are moving into our area, and they're wreaking havoc as they come. We're obviously on good terms with the I-10 Fleet, a relationship that predates even the Division's arrangement with them. Seeing them take such losses trying to keep us supplied isn't making anybody happy."

"Could you elaborate on your connection with the I-10 Fleet?" asked Yeong-Ja.

"Of course. They saved us, not to put too fine a point on it. In the wake of the Poison, we were a scattered group of oil workers and their dependents. We were doing our best to keep the lights on and the machines running. We knew that someone would need what we were producing. After all, like it or not, the modern world is built on fossil fuels."

The surly man said that with a certain wounded pride. Maira noted it with dark amusement. There had been a time when Big Oil and the climate catastrophe it had helped create had seemed the worst apocalypse looming over human civilization. Maira herself had lost sleep on the topic. Then, the Green Poison had lunged onto the scene and caught everyone off guard instead. Now they had bigger fish to fry.

But old habits die hard, and he was used to being on the defensive.

"But you can't eat oil," was all Maira said, sympathetically.

"Exactly," he said and nodded vigorously. "My people don't know anything about growing wheat or whatever, we just knew how to do our jobs. But the way things were going, we would have to abandon the facilities anyway. Sooner or later you gotta figure out where your next meal is coming from."

"Enter the I-10 Fleet," Maira said.

"Yes, ma'am, that is it. Good folks, them. They showed up on our doorstep with trailers full of stuff we needed. You'd think they had us in a choke hold, but they just wanted to make sure we were OK. They gave us food, clothes, parts. We gave them oil, and they made sure that got to other people as needed it. And we kept their trucks running, too, of course."

"And now these attackers, the Reborn, they kill your benefactors. You are afraid you will be reduced to the same situation you were in before the Fleet came on the scene," Yeong-Ja said.

Rychart nodded. "Feels like they're out for us, and the Freighties are just a side way to get at us, if I'm honest. Sooner or later, they'll go for the throat." He didn't bother trying to hide how worried he was.

"And in the face of your very real fears, the Division sends you four agents." Georgio's voice was cold and dismissive. "I am here with real soldiers, enough to secure your facility. Your other facilities? I am happy to do the same for them as well."

Let's try the diplomatic approach, Maira thought.

"You seem to be approaching this as a competition, colonel. I'm not clear on why that has to be the case. The Division has liaised with local militias and JTF forces at every opportunity. I'm glad you want to see the oil facilities secured. There's no reason we can't work together toward that end."

"I'm not here to 'liaise' with your organization," he replied sharply. There was some fire in Georgio's dark eyes. "It is rotten to the core. Listen to how you talk! I am not concerned with 'oil facilities'. I am here to save the lives of American citizens."

Maira's jaw clenched. "We're not concerned investors here protecting our percentage. The fuel is important because it's needed to save lives, too. Or were you not paying attention when he talked about how they'll be starved out without shipments of food? Now apply that to every survivor enclave across the nation, for one thing or another. No one is an island. We were invited here to preserve a web of trade that is keeping people alive."

"Ladies and gentlemen, please–" Rychart began.

"Then do not worry yourself," Georgio cut him off, his attention still locked on Maira and her cell. "We can protect both. The Molossi are capable of securing production and saving these people. Based on your track record, I am not sure the Division could manage either task."

"Track record?" Leo growled. He was bristling under the assault on the SHD's competence.

"Are you in denial? Then let me open your eyes. The Division has mangled every attempt they've made to 'save what remains'. From the moment your people went boots down in New York, you have done little other than commit mass murder and shred infrastructure in petty wars."

"Rogue agents–" Leo started.

Georgio rose to his feet, fists clenched, and cut him off with a barked laugh. "Ah yes, I remember those claims from the early days. The Division can do no wrong, anything that has gone poorly has only happened because of a few bad apples. Well, agents, I regret to inform you that a few bad apples spoil the whole bunch, and I am not here for your shield of fallacies."

Silence hung over the chamber. Maira glanced at the rest of the cell. Leo was seething. Colin looked downright anxious. Yeong-Ja had a small smile on her face for reasons Maira couldn't begin to fathom.

For her own part, Maira didn't know how she felt. She had been there personally when Division agents had saved lives, including her own. She also knew the damage they had done along the way. Some of their villains had been self-made. She knew that all too intimately after her own clash with the rogue agent Rowan O'Shea.

"The Division has made missteps," Maira admitted slowly. "We've also done a lot of good. We've restored the flow of supplies across a significant portion of the nation. We've secured both DC and New York against major threats."

"At what cost? Face it, you were reckless cowboys from the start. Now with the president gone, you wreak havoc unchecked, driven only by your whims. In any saner time, you would have stood down when ordered." Georgio punctuated the last word with a dismissive wave of his hand.

"That's not what your son thought, sir," Colin burst out.

Oh no, Maira thought. Oh, Colin, no. But there was no taking it back. The words hung in the air. The colonel stared at Colin with apparent astonishment. His jaw worked momentarily, but no sound came out.

"Your son David believed in the Division and its mission, sir," Colin hurried on in the silence. "I know that for a fact. I was there with him when we went into New York. David was proud to be there, proud to wear the watch. He was everything good about the Division."

The fire had gone out of Georgio. Now his eyes glittered colder than ice. His hands clenched so tight that his knuckles stood out white, but otherwise he was stock still.

"You were there," the colonel repeated distantly.

"Yes," Colin said.

"You fought at his side?"

"I did," Colin said. "That city was trying to tear itself apart, sir, and we did everything we could to save it."

Colin might as well not have wasted the breath. Georgio only heard the first two words. Maira could see it in his face.

"So, you saw him die, then," the colonel said. "And yet here you are."

Colin hesitated. He looked away. There didn't seem to be anything to say. Maira closed her eyes for a moment in sympathy. Oh, what a mess we have on our hands, she thought. Brenda, where's your silver tongue when we need it most?

"Well, I will give you this credit," the colonel continued. "You were right about one thing. David was the good in the Division, and it is gone now, just as he is. And I will be damned if I let you add the bodies of these people to the Division's sacrificial pyre."

The words hung in the air. Rychart was literally wringing his hands. Maira could just imagine it from his point of view. This whole tableau must have looked about ten seconds from turning into a shooting war.

"Well," the local headman offered weakly. "I don't think these are issues we're going to reach a resolution on tonight. May I suggest we adjourn for the evening, perhaps reattack these matters in the sober light of day?"

"That sounds like a good idea," Maira said softly.

The colonel snorted and turned away. Rychart nodded and seemed to consider that agreement enough. He hastily exited through the side door and motioned for the Division agents to follow. Maira got to her feet and went with him out into the hallway. He ushered them on quickly to get some distance before he started speaking.

"The Molossi showed up a week ago. It's not the first time we've heard about them, but most of their operations were up toward Dallas." Rychart sounded weary. "At first, I assumed it was the Reborn that were drawing them east, spoiling for a fight. Now I'm starting to wonder if they learned we'd called the Division and were looking for you."

"I'm sorry if we brought this down on you," Maira said.

"I'm sure neither one of us is pleased with how this is going," Rychart said. He shook his head slowly. "Well, c'mon. I'll set you folks up with a place to hang your hats."

"Do you trust them?" she asked as they walked.

"Hell no," he said emphatically.

"Will you ask them to leave?"

Rychart gave her a steady look. "I'm not a dictator, Agent Kanhai. I represent these folks, that's all. And I'll tell you true, they brought more guns than you did. And with murderers closing in, that's looking real good to my people right now."

Maira nodded slowly. "That's fair. What do you suggest we do?"

"Right now? I suggest you get some rest. Tomorrow? Either figure out a way to convince my people you can protect us or figure out how you're getting home."

CHAPTER 4

"So, I royally fucked that up, huh?" Colin said into the silence of the room.

The four of them had been placed in what looked like a storage chamber from the old days. It wasn't as bad as that made it sound, Colin thought. They'd been provided with a quartet of cots, complete with blankets and pillows. They'd moved the rest of their gear from Dixie's trailer to here. The driver had stayed but elected to sleep in his cab. As an added small bonus, the roughnecks kept the room nice and clean for them. Colin could even still smell the lemon tang of the cleaner in the air. Perhaps most importantly, it had air conditioning.

Each of them was at the cot they'd chosen. Leo was sitting down, busy removing his boots. Maira was laid out on her stomach, feet kicking above her rump. Yeong-Ja was carefully arranging the blankets on her cot, making sure they were laid out with crisply aligned edges. As Colin spoke, they all turned to look at him.

He shrugged. "I figured it was what all of us were thinking, so I might as well say it out loud. Better out than in, right?"

"We might have to confront the fact that the urge to blurt things out isn't your best feature," Maira said.

"Familiar," Leo said and gave her a sardonic look.

Maira offered a lopsided grin. "Touché. There may be an element of the pot calling the kettle black here." She focused her gaze back on Colin. "Look, it wasn't great, yeah? But I don't think it actually changed the outcome."

"There was not a great deal of flexibility in that man," Yeong-Ja offered.

Maira nodded. "Marcus had made up his mind to not work with us long before he walked into that room. All you did was strip away the veneer of civility a little faster."

"What do we do now?" asked Colin. He slumped onto his own cot and scrubbed a hand over his face. His head was starting to hurt. "Wait for the shooting to start?"

"Even if we wanted a fight – which we don't – they've got us outnumbered and outgunned," Maira said.

"SNAFU," said Leo.

"Yeah, no kidding," Maira said. "I know we're always fighting uphill, but it doesn't change the fact that a fight won't get us what we want here. We have to keep these people and the facilities they run safe somehow. We fought too hard for this to just let it fall apart now."

Yeong-Ja had finished fiddling with the blankets. She sat cross-legged on her cot now and grabbed a pillow into her lap to rest her chin on. "Are we best served by staying here? Our goal was the security of this region, like you said. Is it possible that the Molossi are capable of doing our jobs for us? Should we just leave them to it?" she asked.

Maira tilted her head and raised her eyebrows. "It's not the worst idea I've ever heard, but I do have concerns. Namely, Georgio himself. He says this is all about keeping people safe, but you heard him in there. There's a grudge here. He wants the Division taken apart."

"And if he ends up in tacit control of the oil supply for half the country, he'll have the chokehold he needs to see it done," Colin agreed morosely.

The silence stretched as all of them imagined that playing out.

Maira sighed and shook her head. "Let's set up the SHD Node and get some rest. If we're lucky, maybe tomorrow we can get some advice on where to take this. And even if we're unlucky, at least we'll be coming at it with fresh eyes."

They opened the crate they'd brought with them to reveal the equipment needed to establish the Node. Once deployed it would interface with their ISAC bricks and bring their SHD tech to full functionality by restoring connection to the Network. The actual creation and programming of such a device was undoubtedly a feat of remarkable engineering. Luckily for the cell, save perhaps Maira with her tech expertise, in the field it was mostly as easy as "plug and play".

"So, I don't want to hit you on a sore subject, but what happened with you and his son?" Maira asked as they finished assembling the Node.

Colin sighed. It wasn't a pleasant set of memories to delve into. "You have to remember how quickly things went wrong in the early days. People were dying in droves, both from sickness and increasingly from violence. We were activated and we moved fast. We were constantly bouncing from objective to objective, struggling to keep a lid on the boiling pot."

"That's a lot for anyone to have to handle," offered Yeong-Ja sympathetically.

Colin gave her a small smile. "It was, but we thought we were handling it. After all, we were the last line of defense. If we didn't keep things locked down, who would? And David – Marcus's son – he fought harder than anybody. It was like he had something to prove."

"So where did it go wrong?" asked Maira.

Colin looked down at his hands. It was easy to remember how they had been that night. He'd worn gloves in an effort to keep his fingers warm and flexible. It hadn't helped much. By the end of the night the fabric had been stiff with blood, freezing in the winter air.

"We got a distress call. An agent in need of assistance. I never found out for sure, but now I think it must have been a trap. We found out later that some of us were already going rogue. Some had cut a deal with the worst factions in the city."

"Ambushed," Leo said quietly.

Colin nodded without looking up. "We walked right into the arms of the Last Man Battalion. One of us got killed right off the bat, picked off by a sniper. The rest of us holed up in an abandoned store. We put out our own distress call, but they had us right where they wanted us. They kept us pinned down and just hammered us with explosives."

"Damn," Maira whispered.

"Wasn't far off from hell," Colin agreed. "Last thing I remember, David took shrapnel. I was staunching the blood loss with one hand and trying to get a bandage out with the other. Then the whole roof came down on us."

"You're lucky you're alive," Yeong-Ja said.

"I guess so," Colin said. "Didn't really seem that way at the time. Turns out eventually reinforcements did come. They dug my body out of the rubble, but David must still be under there. I didn't wake up for three days. By then it was too late to go back to look for him, and the whole area had been pronounced under quarantine anyway."

"That's not your fault," Maira said.

Colin swallowed hard. He shrugged and forced a smile. "I doubt his father sees it that way. Some days, I don't know if I do either. I was their medic. It was my job to keep my cell alive. And instead, I was the only one to come back in one piece."

The silence stretched in the wake of the story's end. They weren't judging him, Colin knew. They just didn't know what to say. It didn't stop him from judging himself. He should have done more. There was no going back in time to change David's fate. He had hoped he could make amends to the man's father somehow. But now that, too, seemed increasingly impossible.

Colin stretched out on his bed and put his arm over his eyes. His mind began to wander to back then. What was the point of being a medic when so many things could never be healed?

"You can't fix everything, doc," drawled David.

That Texas manner of speech was an affectation, Colin knew. David was a military brat. He'd lived everywhere during his childhood. Texas was the last place before he'd reached adulthood, but he used the accent on purpose. Colin guessed it had been an effort to fit in at one point. Maybe now it was just a habit.

"It's my job to fix everything that I can," Colin replied lightly.

Colin turned his attention back to the kid sitting on the bed in front of him. He shone a light into the boy's eyes and checked his ears. He got a tongue depressor out of his kit.

"Say *ahhh* for me," Colin said.

"Ahhhhh," the child said.

"Yep, that is an unhappy throat right there," Colin said. He stood and faced the parents. "Strep throat. I can't run a culture, obviously, but I'd bet money. I'll give you some antibiotics. Make sure he takes them all."

A round of vociferous thanks later, and the two agents were back out on the street. It was bitterly cold. The December chill had a way of working through your clothes and climbing into your bones. Colin blew on his hands to try and keep them warm as they walked. David hardly seemed to notice.

"I guess I just don't get the point," David said.

"Of what?" Colin asked.

"You turn every patrol into a hundred house calls, and for what? Most of these people aren't going to make it no matter what you do," David said.

He said it so casually. Colin frowned.

"You don't know that," Colin said.

"You've seen the same numbers as me. No matter how you slice it, this city is full of dead men walking."

"So what?" Colin asked. "We do nothing?"

"Hell no. Are you kidding? This is our chance to shine. Just stop sweating the small stuff. You'll drive yourself crazy," David said.

"These people aren't 'the small stuff.'"

There was a huge crash up the street. Someone screamed. Glass shattered. Colin startled and pulled his gun from the clip on his pack. David was already sprinting up the road in that direction.

"C'mon, doc!" he yelled back. "This is the real shit!"

With a sigh, Colin took off after him.

Maira woke with a jolt. She had been in the midst of a nightmare, judging by the fact that she was soaked in sweat. The pieces of it were already falling away, however. She couldn't remember what it had been about exactly. Only that there had been fire. Her back itched.

Another chime sounded in her ear. That must have been what woke her. She frowned and did a quick check for the time. It wasn't even dawn yet. To her surprise, the other agents were beginning to wake up, too. Leo immediately put a hand to his ear. He must have been getting the same alert.

"Hostile broadcast detected," ISAC said.

"What?" Maira said, surprised.

"Hostile broadcast detected," the AI repeated.

Maira met Leo's eyes across the room. He shrugged, evidently as confused as she was.

"Access the broadcast and play it for us," Maira instructed.

There was a burst of static in Maira's ear. She winced. It quickly resolved into a woman's voice. Maira didn't recognize it. Whoever she was, she spoke with the clear diction of someone used to public address. She had the cultured, unplaceable accent of the well-traveled and highly educated. She also spoke with absolute certainty.

"This is Cassandra Raines, and I speak on behalf of the

Reborn. I am the voice of the future. I will tell you nothing but the truth. If you find my words to be unwelcome, it is because you are clinging to lies. Hear me well. It is better for you to learn from my words than wait until you know us by our deeds.

"We take action because we must. We are decisive because we cannot afford to be anything else. We are bold because we have no other choice. It is you that has made us all of these things. If you find us extreme, it is because you have driven us to the very edge."

The other agents were all sitting up now, obviously listening. Maira found she was sweating again. Something about Raines's voice put her on edge. She sounded cool and in control, but there was something underneath it. Something broken, in the way of shattered glass: made more dangerous in its destruction.

"This world is not yours. It never was. That was an illusion, one of the lies you have told yourself. The world cannot belong to anyone. The world must belong to everyone. It is the birthright of every living thing ever born, or that ever will be. For that reason, if no other, your acts have been criminal. You are a thief and a despoiler, and if you cannot change your ways, you will be treated as such.

"The Reborn are the vessel of our wounded world's wrath, but we are not without mercy. We will begin your reeducation simply and clearly. There is an oil refinery located in what was once the town of Groves. It should have died with the old world. Instead, you have kept it running. We will now correct that error."

"ISAC, you're recording all this, right?" asked Maira.

"Hostile broadcast recording confirmed," the AI replied.

Raines was still talking. "You have until noon tomorrow to remove all personnel from the site. We will then wipe it from the face of the earth. This is the only warning you will receive. Do not discard our mercy lightly. Anyone who does not heed our warning – anyone who chooses to remain – will be destroyed along with the facility.

"I am Cassandra Raines, and I speak for the Reborn."

The broadcast dissolved into static and left the agents staring at each other with alarm.

"Broadcast recorded. Incoming hostile broadcast," ISAC said.

"This is Cassandra Raines, and I…"

"Thanks, but I think once through that was enough. Cut the feed." Maira got to her feet unsteadily. "Continue to monitor it, ISAC, and let us know if any new information is detected."

There was a knock at the door. Maira tensed. Her sidearm was next to her boots. She drew the weapon and held it down by her side. A glance to the others confirmed they had likewise armed themselves. Whoever it was knocked again, impatiently. She eased her way over to the door and opened it a crack.

Rychart stood there, as red-faced as ever. "We have a problem."

"Did your people get the broadcast, too?"

He raised his eyebrows, apparently surprised she already knew. "Yes. It's been playing over and over for a few minutes now. The Reborn must have brought a radio station online for the purpose."

"I'm less concerned with how they did it than what they're

going to do." Maira ran a hand across her short hair. "Do you know the refinery she's talking about?"

Rychart nodded. "There's some of my people there."

"That's it, then. They're making their move on you, and far sooner than we had hoped."

"What do we do, agent?" he asked desperately.

Maira shook her head. "We'll figure it out. Give me a few minutes to get my people ready, and we'll meet you at that presentation room, all right?"

Rychart nodded and stepped away. Maira shut the door and leaned against it. Her head felt like it was going about a hundred miles an hour. This was supposed to be an information gathering mission. They didn't even know the scope of the threat. It was all moving too quickly.

The others were already getting dressed when she looked up. She hurried to join them, throwing her clothes on. She buckled her body armor and gear into place. Her pistol went back into the holster at her thigh, while the shotgun locked into place on her backpack. The Winchester she kept to hand for now, ready to go. It never hurt to be prepared.

"Target identification complete," ISAC said.

Maira raised an eyebrow. "Show me what you've got, ISAC."

The information piped directly into her vision overlay. The translucent figure of a woman, drawn in glowing orange. She was fairly tall, to judge by this, maybe around five foot eight. A mugshot came with it. Sharp features and a grim expression. She had dark hair that fell to her shoulders in the picture.

"Cassandra Raines," ISAC identified her. "Born August 2, 1975. Awarded Doctorate of Atmospheric Science from

Princeton University in 2003. Married to Alexander Raines in 2005. Widowed in 2010. Convicted of the following crimes: criminal trespass, criminal damage to property, public disturbance, breaking and entering, terroristic threats, aggravated assault."

Yeong-Ja swiped quickly through various information files attached to the upload. "She was an environmental activist. She became increasingly extreme in the face of public apathy, ultimately resulting in the criminal record that ISAC just ran through. It spiraled out of control when her husband died in a car crash while driving her car. She believed it was a murder attempt, arranged by the oil companies and meant for her."

Colin listened with a serious mien. "So where was she when the Green Poison hit?"

Yeong-Ja frowned. "She went to prison for that aggravated assault charge. Got out in 2011 on good behavior. After that she pretty much disappeared from the public eye. She's connected to significant land purchases in Texas and Louisiana. There's some talk of compounds being built on the grounds. And that's it."

"That broadcast made it sound like she hasn't forgotten the old grudge," Colin said. "The world has changed, but she's still out here fighting the same fight."

"Not exactly the same," Maira said wryly. "So what, she goes to ground and founds a cult? Builds an army? Then the Green Poison happens, so she feels like it's time to cut loose and really make her dreams come true?"

"It's not impossible," Yeong-Ja said.

"Dangerous," Leo commented.

Maira looked at him questioningly.

"Thinks she's doing the right thing," Leo clarified. "The necessary thing."

Maira nodded. There was an unfortunate ring of truth to that. They'd seen a similar mindset with Rowan. If someone convinced themselves their goal was important enough, they would do anything to see it done. Including atrocities that the merely selfish and cruel might even blanch at.

"This is important information, but it is not everything we need to know," noted Yeong-Ja. "Reconnaissance may be the wisest next step. We don't even know what game we're playing, much less what our next move should be."

Leo nodded agreement. "Need to know the forces involved. Platoon? Company? Regiment? Could change the entire strategy."

"All right," Maira said. "Let's bring all this information to the roughnecks and see what they think."

"Marcus will be interested, too, I'm sure," Colin said gloomily.

"I'm sure he will," Maira agreed. "We'll just have to be ready for him, too."

Maira could hear raised voices before they ever reached the door. Several of the local workers were gathered in the presentation room, along with Rychart and a group from the Molossi. Several of the locals were locked in an argument of some kind. Rychart stood nearby with an anxious expression. The soldiers kept themselves completely apart but seemed to be listening with keen interest.

"We have no choice but to pull our people out of there," a

man was saying. He had the drawn look of too little food and too little sleep.

"And what?" an older woman replied. She had her arms crossed on her chest challengingly. "We run away, and these bastards just go, 'Thanks, that's all we wanted'?"

"Perhaps it is, perhaps it isn't. The point is they're going to slaughter anyone who doesn't leave."

She snorted. "And if we leave, they'll just blow it up, and then it will be the next site and the same demand. Sooner or later, we don't have anywhere to run."

Rychart had noticed their arrival. He raised a hand in greeting.

"Agents, thank you for coming. I hope you got some good rest."

Maira offered a smile. "Thank you, we did." She swept her eyes across the gathering. "I take it there is some debate about the best response to that broadcast."

"Only from cowards," the woman said sharply with a glance at her opponent.

The man stiffened. "I am not a coward. I just don't want to throw anyone's lives away."

Maira glanced toward Colonel Georgio, expecting him to intrude on the conversation at this point. Instead, he seemed content to sit by with a small smile on his face. It did nothing to make her more comfortable.

"You're the ones who were sent to protect us, right?" the woman demanded of Maira.

Maira tried to meet the woman's gaze but found herself looking at the floor instead. She hesitated at the way that question had been phrased. To say there was an agenda at play here felt painfully obvious.

"Protecting the people of this region is absolutely one of our top priorities," Maira said.

"Then you're going to do something, right?" the woman asked sharply. "You can't just let them destroy one of the plants we still have up and running. Our people are there. Our purpose is there."

Maira glanced at the other members of her cell. She was getting more familiar with the mannerisms of the whole group. None of them seemed any happier about the situation than she did. She had a host of concerns. The question was whether she could make these people understand her fears.

"We're gathering information, currently," she said carefully. "We've already learned a great deal about the person we all heard on that broadcast. The 'voice of the future.'"

"Cassandra Raines," Rychart said with a twist of his mouth.

"You're familiar with her?" Maira asked.

Rychart sighed. "To some extent. I'd say she was fairly notorious in our business a decade ago. She led all kinds of protests and marches, then she started actively sabotaging equipment. By the end, her actions had led to several workers being hospitalized. I knew some of those folks. We were all relieved when she went to prison."

"Did you know she was involved before now?"

Rychart shook his head. "Truth be told, I hadn't thought about her for years."

"We think it clarifies the motives of the Reborn. They may be seizing cargoes, but they're not just raiders. We're dealing with an ideological crusade," Maira said.

"What does that mean for us?" asked the cautious local man.

Maira winced. "Unfortunately, it does mean she is unlikely to be satisfied with just a withdrawal from Groves. She's not trying to acquire territory."

"Hell," Rychart said frustratedly. "She's still out to destroy all fossil fuels, isn't she?"

"See?" the woman said. "I told you. She's not going to be satisfied until she's brought us all down. Running won't do us any good."

"That's not exactly what I'm saying," Maira hedged.

"If a prison stint and the Green Poison didn't stop Raines, why would you think anything else would?" asked Rychart with a frown.

Maira took a deep breath. The knowledge that Raines was involved had Rychart full of bluster. Just the same old fight, and he was ready to toe the line for Big Oil again. Maira was less in love with black gold. Right now, though, it was a necessary evil. Lives were on the line.

"Like I said, we need to be focused on gathering information at this point. Yes, we have some idea of who's leading the Reborn and what they want now. But we still have a lot to learn about their methods, their numbers, their organization…"

The blonde Molossi woman leaned over and whispered something to the colonel. He laughed in response, to all appearances in genuine good humor. Maira fought the urge to scowl at them. She had a hard time feeling like all of this wasn't playing directly into their hands somehow. At the same time, she wasn't sure what else to do.

"We don't have time for a fact-finding expedition," the local woman said in disbelief. "They've demanded we have our people out by tomorrow. We only have a little more than a day."

Maira nodded. "I understand that. I'm not saying it will be an easy decision. We need to assess the factors at play. How many people are located there? How much of your production does it represent?"

Rychart scratched his jaw thoughtfully. "I'd need to check records to give you an exact number, but I reckon it's under a thousand people. Maybe five percent of the total refinement capacity."

Reminding Rychart of the people involved seemed to have calmed his burst of bullishness. He was back in manager mode now, trying to think of how to handle a crisis.

"Could you absorb the logistics of having to relocate all of those people?" Maira asked.

She could see the more aggressive local was slowly turning red at these questions. She didn't even want to hear the possibility discussed. It reminded Maira of some of the people back in the community of Athena, near DC. She had been in charge of security there. They had struggled to face hard truths as well.

Rychart took a few seconds to think it over. He slowly started to nod. "I think we could. We'd have to move fast to get them all out of there by tomorrow, but there's plenty of room to set them up somewhere else. It wouldn't even be a complete production loss, because there's always more work than people at this point."

"That is their home!" the local woman finally burst out, arms spreading wide in exasperation. "You're going to demand they just pick up and abandon it?"

"I'm trying to be realistic," Maira said with careful calm. "We have no idea what kind of forces the Reborn can commit to destroying that refinery. If we try to stand our ground, how many of them will show up? Ten? A hundred? A thousand? What kind of weapons will they be carrying?"

The woman stared at her with a disapproving sneer. "So you're scared."

"Ella," Rychart said reprovingly. "That's not helpful. I'm sure that's not what's happening here."

He shot Maira a sideways look that as well as said, "you need to change this topic quickly." Maira felt sick to her stomach. This was exactly like Athena. She'd never been able to get the recalcitrant elements on side there either. She'd ended up the scapegoat for everything that went wrong. Sometimes that had been fair, sometimes it hadn't. She looked to the other agents desperately. Yeong-Ja stepped forward quickly.

"It's not a matter of fear," she said smoothly. "It is a matter of practicality. They picked the time and the place. If you play by the house's rules, the house always wins."

Colin frowned behind her.

"'Therefore, the clever combatant imposes his will on the enemy, but does not allow the enemy's will to be imposed on him,'" Leo added abruptly.

Maira stared at him. "Sun Tzu?" she guessed.

He gave a satisfied nod.

"I am telling you," the woman now identified as Ella said angrily, "these people are fighting for their homes. If you help them, they will stand their ground. We can stop this here and now."

"We're not questioning their willingness," Maira said.

"But will alone doesn't make someone a soldier. I've seen the handiwork of our enemy. The Freighties are fighters, but they've lost to the Reborn repeatedly. They're sharp. Battle-proven. If we pit untrained civilians against them, it could be a slaughter."

"So, if I understand you correctly–"

Maira flinched at Colonel Georgio's voice. He'd finally decided to speak up, apparently.

"–you're suggesting you don't have the combat-capable forces necessary to hold Groves," he continued.

Maira turned a cold glare on him. "I'm saying we don't know what forces would be necessary, because we don't know what our enemy is bringing to the table."

"You are coming at this from a very cautious angle, agent. Your concern for the lives of the people of Groves is commendable. I understand your fears."

"How kind of you," Maira gritted out.

Georgio smiled benignly. "I understand them, but I do not share them." He stood and swept his gaze across the room. "We have all heard the Division's stance. They wish to fall back and fight another day. I mean, I assume at some point they would make a stand? Stalling tactics can only work for so long, after all."

"Obviously we won't–" Maira tried to answer.

Georgio talked over her as if she wasn't there. "I can offer you a different way. Here is my truth: I do not care what the Reborn are bringing to this fight. The Molossi will meet them at Groves, and we will break them there."

"You can't promise that," Maira said with a surge of anger.

Colonel Georgio raised an eyebrow. "Perhaps you cannot.

These people went against their better judgment and asked for your help. The Division saw fit to send a mere four agents. Your resources are understandably very limited. As for me? I can have two mechanized companies at Groves by tomorrow.

"Let me be clear, I am not speaking of an untested citizen's militia. These are Marines, Army, National Guard, with armored vehicles for support. We secured the Dallas and Fort Worth area and will secure your homes for you as well."

Maira's back itched. She flexed her fingers uneasily, sore knuckles aching. She had played her part beautifully, she knew. She could see it in Georgio's satisfaction, and in the expressions of the locals. Even the ones who didn't think the Division were running scared were accepting they simply weren't ready for this fight.

Were they? The vast majority of the Division's forces were underground. Maira trusted her cell, even the new members. Pushovers didn't make the cut. Everyone could pull their weight. But they weren't invincible. They could be overwhelmed. The fight at the farm in West Virginia would have taught her that if nothing else had. Innocents had died there, too.

"–for your help?"

Maira broke from her reverie to the realization the world had not held still. Rychart was asking Georgio something. The other agents were tense around her. This was all going wrong.

"We don't expect payment. We are not bandits or overlords. But if I secure a territory, I want it truly safe. The Division, for all that it may mean well, has a penchant for going rogue. They will not be welcome in any area that we are protecting."

There it was. The stinger on this scorpion. If the locals asked them to withdraw, and the Molossi were prepared to enforce that, they would have to pull back. As Colin had predicted last night, the fuel supply would be all the leverage Georgio needed to take things further than that. He'd have them on the run without ever firing a shot.

"Maira," Leo said.

She couldn't stand to look at him. The expectation was clear. She had to say something. Do something. Brenda would have been able to figure this out. Why couldn't she? Maira's hands were clenched so tight now that her nails were digging into her palms.

"We'll fight," Maira said.

"Now hold on just a minute," Rychart said.

He seemed genuinely surprised. Georgio had raised an eyebrow, too, though his face was unreadable aside from that.

"I said we'll fight," Maira repeated. "You invited us here to see this region secured. We will do exactly that. At least give us a chance before you turn to the Molossi. I will take my cell to Grove and prevent the refinery from falling into the hands of the Reborn."

"Maira," Leo said again, urgently.

Maira held up a hand for him to wait, keeping her eyes on Rychart. "Give us a chance. The Division can stop the Reborn. If the Molossi are concerned about saving this region, we welcome their assistance. But we don't need it. We can save your people. I know we can."

Rychart looked utterly miserable. He glanced between Maira and Georgio, then looked to the other locals. Ella appeared nonplussed. The more cautious man was shaking his head with a frown.

"All right," Rychart said. "You'll get your chance."

Maira nodded. Her heart was pounding in her chest. "Evacuate your people all the same."

"Then what's the damn point?" demanded Ella.

Maira locked eyes with the woman. "They'll be able to come back after the fight. But I don't want them in the way. I don't want anyone getting hurt that doesn't have to."

Ella looked away, breaking eye contact first.

Rychart nodded rapidly. "Good. Yes. We'll get them out of there, and you'll have plenty of room to deal with these Reborn bastards."

Maira nodded agreement. She turned her fierce stare on the Molossi. The various aides and underlings looked satisfyingly frustrated. To her surprise, however, Georgio's face had gone completely stoic. He met her gaze evenly, before turning and leading his contingent from the room.

The agents had reassembled in their room to pack what they needed for the trip to Groves. The silence between them was uncomfortable. Colin resisted the urge to say anything multiple times. The tension in the air was unpleasant. He wanted to smooth it over somehow. This whole mission had started off choppy and was turning into a worse mess by the hour.

"Maira," Leo finally said flatly.

"We should be able to just leave the Node here," Maira said.

She didn't look at Leo as she said it. Colin winced. He hadn't been with the cell for very long, but this already felt like having mom and dad mad at each other. He locked eyes with Yeong-Ja, and she gave a tiny helpless shrug.

Leo turned to face Maira and crossed his arms over his chest. "This is a bad idea," he said.

"What, leaving the Node here? No, Groves is only an hour aw—"

"You know that's not what I mean," Leo said.

Maira paused. She kept flexing her hands. Colin had seen the scars she bore last night. She was lucky to be alive. If his own near-death brush in New York weighed on him, he couldn't imagine what was going on inside her head.

"We don't have a choice," she said.

"We do," Leo disagreed empathically.

"What? Cut and run? Let those Molossi assholes take control of the whole region? We can't let them."

"You have a crystal ball now?" Leo asked.

She turned to face him in a surge. Her eyes were wide. "Fine. You tell me what we should do then, Leo."

"Anything but walking into a fight with a complete unknown."

There was no cruelty in his voice, Colin noted. He just sounded worried. About the mission, to be sure, but also about her.

"If we have to fall back, we fall back," Leo continued.

"No," she said flatly. "If we let Georgio swoop into the rescue, we're done here in Texas. Do you get that? He will control the oil supply, and he'll use it to destroy us."

"He might," Leo allowed. "We don't know what he'd do. I do know this: we can't do anything if we're dead."

"I guess you're the one who can see the future then. Who says we have to die? We have our advantages. They're coming to us. We can prepare the field, use the tech."

Maira's shoulders were visibly tight. It was like she was expecting someone to hit her, even though Leo hadn't made any aggressive moves.

"Prepare how?" Leo asked patiently. "We don't know what we're up against. That's the whole point. If Georgio wants to lead his people in blind–"

"No," Maira repeated sharply, cutting him off. "I will not let him get his hand around our throat like that."

"Maira…"

"I will not let him destroy what's left of the Division!" she shouted.

Everyone froze at the sudden outburst. Colin looked at Maira, and swiftly looked away again. She stood there shaking. Fear or anger, he wasn't sure. It wasn't clear if she knew herself.

"I've already given up too much for it," Maira said quietly.

Leo hesitated. He nodded slowly. "All right. OK, Maira. We're in it now, one way or another."

Maira nodded shakily and took the radio off her shoulder. "Dixie. We're ready to go."

CHAPTER 5

"I should stay, help you fight," Dixie said.

The semi was idling near the refinery they had agreed to defend. It was early morning, before the heat of the day started to build. The town was more forested than Colin had expected. Directly in front of the building was what had once doubtless been a pleasant little park, in fact. All of it was overgrown nowadays, of course. Meanwhile the facility itself was all concrete and metal, exactly as he'd imagined. Huge concrete reservoirs were visible from where they sat. He wondered if they were full of petroleum even now.

"How would you do that, exactly?" Maira asked.

Dixie looked hurt. "Park the truck and man a weapon."

"And get yourself killed?" she asked sharply.

They hadn't been able to park in the actual parking lots. Those were full of the local workers preparing for evacuation. They were packing everything they could take with them. Colin had seen their faces. They didn't have a lot of faith that the Division agents were going to save their home. He would do everything in his power to surprise them. He had to hope it would be enough.

The agents were unloading some useful supplies from the trailer. Dixie stood nearby, radiating worry. Colin fancied himself an empathic person, but it didn't take any special insight to see he felt guilty just leaving them here. He touched Maira on the arm and gave her a look.

Maira glanced at Colin and winced. She clearly made an effort to soften her tone. "Look, I have no idea what's headed for us on this one, OK? But I saw that ambush site. We all did. They've got the weapons to blow your truck to kingdom come, and I can't have that."

"So, I get down and carry a rifle. Not like my arms don't work. My people are the ones they've been killing, you know."

Yeong-Ja set a crate down and wiped her forehead with her sleeve. She stepped over toward the driver with a smile. "You already helped us. You got us here swiftly. We'll at least have time to explore our surroundings and prepare. That could make all the difference."

Leo nodded. "Time is everything now."

Colin decided to pile on. "Besides, they'll need your help getting the workers out of here before everything goes down. They have some of their own trucks, but nothing like your girl here. That's something no one else can do."

Dixie sighed and swatted at a mosquito hovering around him. "Can't say it feels right all the same. But OK. I'll help with the evacuation and leave the big hero stuff to y'all, same as usual."

Maira hopped down from inside the trailer with a box full

of ammunition. "Trust me, I wish this wasn't necessary."

Colin and Yeong-Ja traded looks. She was still holding on to the idea that they had no choice but to make a stand here. There was a level of wildness in her eyes that hadn't left since the argument with Leo. No one wanted to push her on it now. Everyone was walking on eggshells.

"I have family near here," Leo noted.

Colin looked at him in surprise. It wasn't like him to initiate a conversation topic. Even he must be trying to change the subject for Maira's sake.

"Where do they hail from?" he asked.

"Haiti originally. Settled in Louisiana here in the States." Leo gave a small smile. "Big family. All over the place. Baton Rouge. Lafayette. New Orleans."

"You never told me that," Maira said with some surprise.

"Never asked," Leo replied with a shrug.

Maira laughed exasperatedly and shook her head. "I did ask about you once! I think you tried to tell your life story in ten words or less."

"Can't get words back after you let them loose. Better to not speak in the first place," he said.

"Huh," Colin said, thinking that over. "Makes sense. So, uh… Your family…"

He wasn't sure how to ask. When a virus kills ninety percent of the population, there's no easy way to broach the subject of family. Everyone had lost someone. Most people had lost far more than that.

"Don't know," Leo said. "Got activated, been in the fight ever since."

"Maybe it is better that you don't," Yeong-Ja said softly.

Colin turned to her with some surprise. "Why do you say that?"

"Because I know what happened to my parents. I was there to see it," she replied.

Colin closed his eyes. "Jesus. I'm sorry. That's rough."

Yeong-Ja started to say something, then shrugged. After a moment she tried again. "They were the only family I had. The only people I had really. I have never had an easy time bonding with people, and I traveled a great deal for my work."

"Family is important," Leo said. "Left the Army for my family."

"Maybe when we've got this whole thing handled, you can stop in and try to find some of them. I'm sure they must be thinking about you, too," Colin said.

Leo gave a slight smile and a single nod.

"All right," Maira said. "Let's get a drone in the air while we split up and look the area over. We'll meet back here in thirty minutes and see what we're dealing with terrain-wise."

Yeong-Ja released the drone, and it rose into the air, propellers humming, then zipped away to begin its survey.

Maira walked alone down the road a short way. The sounds of the evacuation had faded behind her. The air had the brackish tang of nearby bodies of saltwater. It was oppressively humid, and there were vastly more mosquitoes around than she would have preferred. It would be a hell of a thing to survive battle after battle, only to be ushered out of the world by malaria. She snorted and shook her head at the thought.

"Bold of me to imagine I'm going to be alive next week to have to deal with that."

Her voice seemed loud against the silence. It sounded unsteady to her. She frowned and kicked a rock that was in the road. It skittered off into the grass. The asphalt here, as with most of the country, was suffering without maintenance. It was graying and cracking, grass springing up through the gaps.

"Nothing lasts forever. That's something we have in common," Maira told it.

Maira wasn't an idiot. She had seen how the other agents were looking at her. Like she was made out of porcelain, ready to crack under pressure. They were wrong, of course. She was the strongest she'd ever been. What choice did she have? She'd been through the crucible and come out harder on the other side.

Who cared if she saw Rowan's face every night in her dreams? The way her expression had lingered for a second, then slowly gone dull. Those empty eyes right beneath the neat hole in her forehead. Maira had done what she had to do. She knew that for a fact.

"Except she had agreed, hadn't she?"

Maira flinched and looked around. It was her voice. There was no one else here. No one to hear. She was the only one saying these things anyway. All the hostages had seen what happened. So had Brenda. None of them had chastised her. None of them had pointed out that Rowan had agreed to let them all go right before Maira shot her.

"I had to. She was going to destroy the Division."

Maira didn't sound convinced, even to her. It was true, though. Rowan had made her intentions clear. She was going to tell everyone the truth and do everything in her power to bring the Division crashing down. What was one life against that? It wasn't like she was the first person Maira had killed. Why was this one any different?

She could remember so many faces. Hyenas, Outcasts, True Sons, Roamers. Lots of labels. No names, though. Maybe that was the difference. The faces stayed with her, but she hadn't known who they were. She hadn't known their grievances, their struggles, the way she had with Rowan.

The Division was more important than any one life. Including hers. More important than the lives of the whole cell? Yes. Maira had to believe that, or else how could she do what they did? Violence never strayed far from her side now. It was a part of her, or maybe she was a part of it. It was a meaningless distinction. It didn't matter.

The only thing that mattered was what had to be done. Someone else was out to destroy the Division now, and she would stop them. It was as simple as that.

A mosquito was on her arm, busily drinking her blood.

Maira stared at it. She slapped it with a lightning-fast hand. It splattered under her palm. A red smear across her skin both on her arm and on her hand. She blinked a few times and looked around. She had reached the end of the road at some point. There was nothing further on except for more concrete, metal, and short grass.

Time to head back. The clock was ticking.

Colin looked around as he returned from his perimeter check. He was grateful to see that the civilian evacuation was already making progress. Dixie had departed to assist them. That was good, too. It would get the man out of harm's way, and besides, Colin hadn't been lying. The semi would make a huge difference in moving supplies or people to a safe new location.

The others hadn't gotten back yet. He thought he might as well do a quick gear check while he had the time. Colin headed over to a picnic table in the park. He gave his rifle a once over. The barrel was clear and clean. He set it aside and did the same for his handgun. Both were in good condition. It was no surprise, he'd always been meticulous about his equipment.

Colin pulled the bottom of his shirt up to wipe some sweat off his face. He was no great fan of southern latitudes. They were always too hot for comfort. Then again, that winter in New York hadn't been any fun either, even after the pandemic and riots. Give him a nice brisk fall day, thank you. Maybe somewhere in the middle. Was Virginia nice this time of year?

Colin waved mosquitoes away and pulled his medic kit from his side. There was no reason for it to have magically become unstocked since the last time he'd looked. Still, it paid to err on the side of caution. Better to replace anything missing before the shooting started. He knew too many medics who had scrambled for a pair of scissors in the heat of battle.

The kit only weighed four pounds but opened out to reveal surprisingly voluminous contents. Everything had been carefully selected for maximum effectiveness. The odds might be stacked against them tomorrow, who knew, but he refused to make it any worse. Colin had failed his last cell. He'd be damned if he let that happen again with this one.

He had an itemized list in his mind, clear as day. Colin

went down it, double-checking each item. Bandages, sutures, tourniquets, and more. The lip balm and sunscreen were there, too. Those hadn't been on any required lists he'd ever seen, but he'd learned to bring it all the same. Taking care of Marines hadn't been a hundred percent different from taking care of kids, to be honest.

Everything was there, even the special-issue SHD tech items. Hopefully he wouldn't have to administer any combat cocktails today. They kept people on their feet when nothing else would, but they were incredibly addictive, and the withdrawals were a nightmare. Personally, Colin considered them a tool of last resort.

He began to pack the kit away again, neatly returning each item exactly to its assigned spot. Approaching footsteps made him raise his head. It was Yeong-Ja, carrying her rifle across her shoulders. She gave him a smile as she approached.

"Anything interesting in your direction?" she asked.

"Do you count 'lots of mosquitoes and an unpleasant odor' as interesting?" Colin asked.

"Mosquitoes? I hadn't noticed any."

Colin peered at her. It was hard to tell if she was joking or not. Her smile remained as serenely pleasant as before. He was coming to believe that if Yeong-Ja had a sense of humor, it was as dry as the Sahara. Before he could ask her, he saw Leo approaching as well. Maira was visible, too, off in the distance still but on her way.

The four of them gathered around the picnic table. A small breeze had started to blow through, a blessed relief from the increasingly hot sun overhead. Colin supposed it must be getting past noon now. If the Reborn were as good as their word about timing, this was going to be the kind of heat they had to fight in.

"All right," Maira said. "Let's take a look at the footage from the drone."

The vision overlay contacts each of them wore made reviewing the information easy. It was simply projected into the air right in front of them. Everyone spent a few silent seconds studying it. The refinery complex essentially marked the end of dry land. Wetlands surrounded it on three sides, leading out into the ocean to the east. The only solid direction was south, through the park and into the town itself.

"Looks like the Reborn have two choices," Colin said. "Wade through a swamp or come at us from the south."

"Marsh," said Yeong-Ja.

"Beg your pardon?" Colin asked.

"These are marshes. It's different from a swamp. Less trees, lower water levels," she explained.

"Even better," Maira said. "So, if they did decide to try and come at us from the wetlands, we could see them coming a long way out."

Yeong-Ja nodded. "I am confident that I can make them regret that choice."

"Let's hope they do it, then. We could do with a few boneheaded moves on their part," Maira said.

"Highway," Leo said. He motioned, and the road was pinged in their vision, cutting through the swamp from the north.

"Ah, yeah, I see it," Colin said. He grimaced. "OK, so they could ride the road in and come out to the east of us. So that's two feasible approaches."

"They have to cross this bridge if they go that route. That's a pretty defensible choke point," Maira said.

"Could just blow it," Leo said.

"I don't think the locals would appreciate us collapsing their already decaying infrastructure," Maira said wryly.

"Better than losing everything." Leo shrugged.

"If we don't destroy the bridge, we have to make some effort to guard both approaches," Yeong-Ja said.

Maira nodded slowly. Colin noticed she was slowly flexing her hands as she thought. In and out, open hand to closed fist, over and over. Her knuckles were healing, but whatever she'd done to them was recent. It had to be hurting every time she did that.

"OK, so, we compromise. We mine the bridge for demolition and keep an eye out that way. If we see them using it, we blow it. Otherwise, we focus our attention on protecting the south," she said.

"Sounds smart enough to me," Colin agreed.

"Guarding the south, easier said than done," Leo noted.

"Lay it out for me, Captain Fourte," Maira said.

Leo snorted but gestured. "It's a mile across. Hard to watch it all at the same time. Lots of cover, too. Trees, buildings. Too much to have any hope of clearing beforehand."

"We have four drones at our disposal," Yeong-Ja said. "If we dedicate one to watching the bridge approach, that leaves three and all four of us keeping eyes on the south."

"I wish we had a JTF company to back us up," Colin said. "Hell, I'd take a squad. I can't believe Marcus is really going to just sit this out and let us hang."

"If wishes were fishes..." Maira said distantly. She drummed her fingers restlessly against the wood of the table. "We do have a quartet of turrets, but only one has active sensors to help with spotting."

"The additional firepower will be our ace in the hole," said Yeong-Ja.

"We have some deployable barricades, too," Colin said. "Which I think we'll be very grateful for, given we know the enemy has used RPGs in the past."

"Spread thin no matter what," Leo said quietly.

No one replied. Colin wasn't sure what they could have said. Everyone knew this was a bad situation. It all depended what kind of forces the Reborn could bring to bear. All they could do was try to prepare for anything.

"All right," Maira said. "Let's start setting up the defenses."

"Any word on comms with the Kansas Core, ISAC?" asked Maira.

"Processing request," the AI replied.

She had just finished setting up one of the turrets they'd brought with them. All the SHD's devices were miraculous by the standards of widely available technology. This was one of the standard assault turret models. It was equipped with a machine gun capable of three hundred and sixty degree rotation. As long as it had access to the Network, it could independently target threats under battlefield conditions.

Maira had only seen them used once before. That had been during the battle at Cumberland Gap. The Roamers and Freighties had clashed in one of the largest conflicts of their road war. Brenda had decided to throw their weight behind the Freighties to try to tip the balance and earn their trust.

SHD tech had been the key and proven a decisive resource, until the rogue agent Rowan O'Shea had seized control of them.

The odds had been against them then, too. The only Division agents had been Brenda, Leo, and nominally Maira. She had not yet earned her watch at that point.

"We came through then. We won the day," she said.

Never mind that they hadn't fought alone. That really, the Freighties had done most of the fighting and all of the dying. How important could that little factoid really be?

"Fucking hell," Maira whispered. "What am I doing?"

"Processing complete," ISAC said. "No accessible line of communication."

Of course. It was to be expected. Brenda had warned them it would be difficult to maintain contact down here. Besides, what could the senior agent really have done? Wish Maira good luck? Promise them all plaques on some future memorial?

Maira was surprised to feel tears start in her eyes. She wiped them away with her sleeve. There was no time for all of that. There was no room for weakness. Her weakness had gotten Kazi killed. It had gotten Johnny and Andrea killed. That wasn't going to happen this time. She wasn't going to let it.

One of the drones buzzed past overhead. They'd set them about thirty feet up on slow loops, constantly scanning in all directions. The Reborn had set a time, but Maira saw no reason to trust them on that. They would be prepared for anything, at any time. Anything else just wasn't an option.

"Maira," Leo said.

Maira's hand dropped to her sidearm before recognition set in. She hadn't heard him approaching. He was always so quiet, and not just verbally either. He must choose his steps just as carefully as his words.

"Hey, Leo," she said. "How are the barricades?"

"Did what we could," he said. "There's too few for the need. Will be like trying to catch gnats with a net."

Maira nodded. She needed to say something. She knew it. She just wasn't certain what. Smart remarks and clever quips always came easily to her, but this didn't seem like the time. What was there to joke about? Even she couldn't tell any more.

Instead, the silence between them stretched. Maira gave a jerky nod and turned on her heel to walk away. The sharp movement pulled at her scars with a sizzle of pain. She hated the way he was looking at her. Leo had never thought she was fit to be a Division agent. Maybe he had been right all along. Maybe—

"Brenda wouldn't want this," Leo said.

Maira froze.

Leo spoke like it was tearing out of him. Like he didn't know what else to do.

"Brenda made a lot of mistakes," he said. "A lot of them you didn't even get to see."

And what? Maira thought. Recruiting me was the biggest one?

"She put the mission ahead of the people a lot. Too much. It caused problems. You saw that with Rowan. And with you—"

Maira turned her head but didn't quite look at him. She couldn't bear it. She cut him off sharply. "It doesn't matter.

What's done is done. We're here now, and we have to deal with it."

Leo frowned. "I'm not… I'm trying to… You're not in this alone."

Maira laughed bitterly. "You think I don't know that? You think every minute I don't think about the fact that I've dragged you and the others into this with me? Trust me, I know, Brenda would never have. She would have avoided this whole mess somehow."

Leo shook his head and seemed frustrated. "No, I just… That's not… Things could have been done better with–"

"I get it, OK? I wish she was here, too. I didn't want to leave without her in the first place. But she's not here, and I am. And that's all there is to it." Maira drew herself up. The tears were threatening to return. It was time to make her exit. "Focus on the job, Leo. If you have something to say, say it tomorrow. If we live."

Leo hung his head. Maira turned and walked away as fast as she could. She wiped a sleeve across her eyes again furiously. There were still so many things left to check before night set in. She had to focus. Everything else was a distraction they couldn't afford.

Night had fallen. Blessedly, it had brought some relief from the afternoon heat. The air was full of the croak and creak of animals and insects in the surrounding marshes, trees, and grasses. It was like the whole area came to life when the sun set. Colin strolled through it with a massive yawn.

"You'll catch flies that way if you aren't careful," Yeong-Ja said.

At least, Colin heard her voice. He looked around in confusion, but she was nowhere to be seen.

"Yeong-Ja?" he asked cautiously.

A low whistle came from above him. "Up here."

Colin looked up. Yeong-Ja's legs were dangling overhead. She was sitting at the edge of one of the corrugated steel roofs, her rifle laid across her knees. She gave him a cheerful little wave as their eyes met.

"How did you…"

"There's a ladder around back," she answered. "Seemed like a good spot to me. Good visibility. Want to see?"

Colin chuckled. "Sure."

He went around to the rear of the building. The ladder was exactly where she said it was. It went up around twenty feet. He climbed up swiftly and walked over to her. There was a nice breeze blowing through at this height. His boots rattled against the roofing; no one was going to make a stealthy escape from up here, that much was certain.

Colin stepped up beside her. Their height difference made it almost comical. Sitting down, her head came to just above his knee. The stars were out overhead. He turned his gaze to the horizon. She hadn't been wrong about the vantage point. Up here you could see the dark shapes of the town beyond the trees of the park. Everything was still.

"It's so peaceful," he said.

Yeong-Ja nodded. "It is one of those moments when you could convince yourself all is right with the world."

"I guess if it was, we'd be out of a job," Colin mused.

"I would be OK with that retirement," she replied.

"Heh. Yeah, me too," he said.

The silence hung comfortably between them. Colin had taken a liking to Yeong-Ja. She wasn't personable, exactly, but she was steady. Solid. In a world that had descended into chaos, that seemed important. It was good to have things he could rely on.

"You said that you don't really have any people left in the world," he said after a while.

Yeong-Ja simply nodded.

"So why volunteer for this mission? Or... did you? I suppose they would have assigned someone if no one did," Colin said.

The quiet returned. He wasn't sure if she was thinking it over, or if she just didn't want to answer. He felt a moment's regret thinking it was the latter. He hadn't meant to make her uncomfortable.

"I volunteered," Yeong-Ja said at last.

"Oh," Colin said. "Cool. Better than being forced to be here, I guess."

"A sniper is extremely useful, but only if applied carefully. Tight confines, poor sightlines, and more can waste my talents."

Colin nodded. He wasn't sure how this applied to his question, but there was no need to rush her. She was going somewhere at her own pace.

"So, because of this, I never actually attached to a cell long term. I served in an auxiliary capacity. I would appear for a single mission, help out, and then be on my way to the next."

"If I'm going to be a hundred percent honest, that sounds very lonely," Colin said.

Until then, Yeong-Ja had kept her eyes on the horizon. She looked up at him and smiled. "Yes, very much so."

"This one was a more long-term assignment. Is that why you...?" Colin trailed off.

Yeong-Ja nodded once. "I am very tired of being alone. They wanted volunteers, I wanted a chance to get to know people. It seemed like a lucky draw."

"Wow," Colin said. "And now here you are. Was it fun, at least? I mean, for as long as it lasted."

Yeong-Ja looked back out to the trees and the darkness beyond. Her smile did not go away. "Yes. I wish we'd had more time."

The radio crackled. Maira's voice came through. "It looks like we're as ready as we're ever going to be. I know it's easier said than done, but we should all try to get some sleep. Shall we take watch shifts? Just in case?"

Colin picked up his own radio. "That sounds good to me. I'll take the first watch."

"Copy that," Leo said.

"Got it," Maira said.

Colin looked down to Yeong-Ja. "You better go get some rest while you can."

"Yes, that would be wise. I only hope I'll actually be able to sleep. It is a cliché, but it's always the waiting that is the worst part."

Colin offered her a hand up. She accepted and then stretched and yawned.

"Catch flies that way," he noted.

Yeong-Ja chuckled and walked away. Colin stood watching the horizon and listening to the rattle of her boots as she departed. She paused over by the ladder, and he looked back.

"I'm glad we met, Colin."

"Me too, Yeong-Ja," he said. "Me too."

CHAPTER 6

The next day was oppressively hot. There was no breeze at all at ground level. The stink of the marshes hung over everything. The last of the civilians had long since departed. Now it was just the four Division agents, restlessly waiting for the Reborn to arrive.

Maira drank from her canteen. She was pretty sure she was more sweat than skin at this point. The container shook as she put it to her lips. She frowned at it. Her grip was white-knuckle tight, causing the tremor. She took a few deep breaths and forced her hand to relax.

It was the waiting. They had done everything they could to be ready. Now there was nothing but the passage of time. The waiting was always the part that got inside her head. The heat of battle was no fun, she thought, don't get her wrong. But she was too busy to think about it once the shooting started. The waiting was like an itch she couldn't scratch.

Her Winchester rifle was unpleasantly warm in her hands. The heat of the sun had soaked into it. She checked it over for the fifteenth time. Everything seemed to be in place. The weapon was old, but it had never let her down. Johnny had been as good as his word.

Thinking of him threatened to bring memories boiling to the surface. It had only been a short interlude on their journey southwest from Maryland, but it had been a precious moment of peace. Some of the memories were good. Fixing things around the farm with Johnny. Cooking with his wife, Andrea. That was only the tip of the iceberg, though. Underneath was all the horror. Their brutal murder at the hands of the Outcasts, brought down on their heads by the presence of the Division agents.

Maira took a deep breath and shoved the thoughts away. This was different. The civilians were out of the way this time. She had made sure of that. No matter what happened today, those people were going to be OK. At least for now.

"Radio check," Maira said.

"Here, over," Leo said.

"This is Colin, I'm here, over," the medic said.

"Yeong-Ja, read you loud and clear, over," the sniper finished.

It was far from the first radio check she'd done. To their credit, none of them sounded like they wanted to strangle her for it. Maira turned her gaze to the park. She had taken a central position on their line. The once-pleasant grounds were directly across the road. Even overgrown as they were, it was strange to have the situation turn them so ominous. Every rustling squirrel plucked at her nerves like guitar strings.

Gnats buzzed in her ear. Maira scattered them with a sweep of her hand, but they were back an instant later. She started to pace to try to get away from them. In all truth, if she kept pacing this same track back and forth, eventually they would have a trench they could take shelter in. A worry rut for the ages.

She needed to think about something else, she told herself. Anything. Maira had hobbies once, didn't she? Video games, right? She hadn't picked one of those up since she'd left Athena back in Maryland. To be fair, that was the kind of luxury that was harder to come by nowadays. Video games required a way to play them, and the power to run it. Not to mention she would need the game itself. There was no internet – and no servers being maintained – to jump on for a quick download.

OK, Maira said to herself. Books, then. She loved to read. So, what was the last book she had read? She had to admit she had no idea. It was like whole parts of her had fallen away.

"Incoming hostiles detected," ISAC said.

The words hit Maira like an electric shock. She snapped around, rifle to her shoulder. Her eyes frantically searched the trees. ISAC was interfaced with everything that they had set up. It was monitoring the turret, the drones, even their own vision, thanks to the enhancement contacts. The question was what it had picked up. One of the SHD mobile barriers was nearby. She ducked behind it swiftly to be safe.

"Oh my god," Colin said, his voice scratchy over the radio.

One of them stepped into Maira's view. They were a white shape in the park, walking forward slowly but openly. Light clothes, with a white bandanna wrapped around their face. She could see they were holding a sickle in their left hand, the sunlight glinting off the blade. Another one stepped into view nearby. Similar clothes, only this one was carrying a hay hook.

Another then, and another behind them. They were flooding into the park. Maira lost count within seconds. She looked through her scope, disbelieving her own eyes. They wore a curious mishmash of clothing. Some had elements of modern dress: jeans, baseball caps, sneakers. All, however, wore some amount of handmade garb. Homespun shirts and pants, left undyed white.

Every single one carried a crude weapon. Many had repurposed farming tools, like the first two she had spotted. Others carried the detritus of the world before, pipe wrenches and baseball bats and more. Not all of them were fresh, either. Many were spattered with old crimson stains.

"ISAC, what are we dealing with?" Maira asked softly.

"Data incomplete. More than five hundred hostiles detected."

Maira's stomach twisted. She was shaking. This was a nightmare beyond anything she'd conceived of. Athena had never numbered much more than a hundred people, including children. The Outcasts had overrun their defenses with numbers, but even they hadn't brought half this many. Underneath that awe, she was bewildered. These weren't the hardened professional soldiers she had imagined from the ambush of the Freighties. The Division agents stood no chance, yet simultaneously were about to be the perpetrators of a slaughter.

"Gunmen spotted," Yeong-Ja called.

The sniper's indicators highlighted what she was talking about on Maira's vision. There were more of the Reborn toward the back of those gathered. They were little more than dark blobs at this distance. A check through her scope confirmed what Yeong-Ja had said, however. Unlike the rest, these carried modern firearms and wore body armor.

"Cannon fodder," Leo said darkly.

Maira was forced to agree. This arrangement painted a horrifying picture of the enemy's plan. The Reborn would funnel barely armed people forward in a human wave to absorb the brunt of their defensive fire. In the wake would come their actual hardened killers, to break whatever resistance remained. Maira carried twenty-four rounds for her rifle, and a similar amount for her shotgun and pistol.

They literally couldn't kill enough of these people to stop them.

They weren't attacking yet, though. Maira could see how restless they were. They shifted from foot to foot, swung their crude weapons back and forth. There was a stink of sweat on the air, perceptible even beyond the smell of the marsh. It had a bitter tang. Maira knew it all too well. Fear. It occurred to her that the gunmen at the back might be there as much to force the rest forward as anything else.

"What are they waiting for?" Maira asked.

"No idea," Colin replied uneasily.

"Someone is headed your way, Maira," Yeong-Ja said.

Maira swept her gaze across the crowd of hostiles facing her. They blurred together into an inchoate mass. They weren't silent, but there was no talking. Only that uneasy shuffling, the rustle of hundreds of breaths on the wind. Sweat ran down Maira's forehead and dripped from the tip of her nose.

The crowd parted to allow someone through. A much

larger figure was headed in her direction. This must have been what Yeong-Ja was warning her about. Maira had difficulty processing what she was seeing. It had the air of a fever dream, it was so out of place with the world she knew. They were just a gray blur at first, and then it finally clicked.

It was a person on horseback. They approached at an unhurried pace. As the figure grew closer, she could hear the snort of the horse and the rattle of its tack. The man on its back was a slender figure dressed in simple, undyed homespun. This included a bandana used as a mask, the same as the crowded figures.

Even so, there was no mistaking this one for part of the mob. For one thing he had a rifle in a long holster alongside the horse's saddle, plus a sidearm at his hip. For another he lacked the air of unease that hung over the rest of them. He might as well have been out for a pleasure stroll for all the concern he showed.

"I have a shot," Yeong-Ja said calmly.

"Hold your fire," Maira said. "We're not going to be the ones to kick this party off."

Maybe they could still talk their way out of this, she thought. There was no hope behind the thought. These people hadn't marshaled by the hundreds to turn around and go home. They had come here to see their task through.

Brenda would have...

Maira dashed the thought. It didn't matter. Brenda wasn't here. Maira was. She had to see this through.

Maira emerged from cover to meet the rider. The horseman pulled up across the street from her. The strip of asphalt was all that separated them. The horse stamped impatiently, and the rider locked gazes with her. She could make out the dark skin of his brow and his eyes above the bandana.

"You're Division," he said. "You're not supposed to be here."

He seemed genuinely surprised. Maira furrowed her brow. There was something familiar about him, too. She couldn't put her finger on it.

"Yes, we heard your broadcast," Maira said. "I'm hoping we can still discuss this like reasonable people."

"The broadcast? What does that have to do with it? I thought you were supposed to stay out of the way and let us handle this." The man tilted his head. "This place is an offense. It can't be allowed to stand."

"We're the Division. We protect people. People live here," Maira said. She was bewildered at this assumption that the Division would stay out of the Reborn's way. Why would he think that? "What's more, there are lives depending on what they produce here. Surely you can understand that?"

"That's the old world in you talking. This is the new. We have a chance at paradise, a world without the weight of a thousand old mistakes. I shouldn't have to explain this to you again."

He said it with a disquieting mixture of flatness and reverence. It had the air of rote memorization, of something repeated a thousand times until it had lost meaning. Even so, she didn't feel like that represented any give in him. The words had been drilled into him, and so had obedience. Still, through it all, she couldn't shake the sense of familiarity. Something about his face? Or his voice?

"Look, I don't know who you've talked to before, but this is my first chance to speak with one of your group. I'm not without sympathy," Maira said. "If we're not going to rebuild the world better than it was, what's the point, right? But we're playing a game of necessity at the moment."

"That was always the excuse. Things can't change because it would be too much trouble. Too many consequences. We were told to be patient, to do as we were told until the time was right. It was a lie then, and it's a lie now. The world's addiction to oil has been killing our world for centuries. It stops now."

"It's not, though," Maira said, desperately earnest. "We can reach an agreement. I'm sure of it. We'll arrange the talks. Get everyone at one table. We can figure this out without any more bloodshed."

The rider stared at her. "The time for talk is past."

Maira's heart sank. "It's not, if you don't want it to be. You don't have to do this."

He scarcely seemed to have heard her words. Instead, he pointed to the watch she wore, the orange glow almost lost in the bright sunlight. "I don't know why you've decided to get involved. Cassandra will hear of this."

Maira glanced down at the device in confusion. "I don't–"

"I'll give you one chance. Leave. Take your people and go." He hesitated. "I shouldn't do that much. But …"

Maira frowned. Something clicked. A sudden surety of where that strange familiarity was coming from. "Let me see your face."

The rider glowered. "What?"

"I want to see your face. Is that so much to ask? What, you'll kill us, but you won't show me your face?"

The whole thing sounded absurd said out loud. It *was* absurd. If you had told Maira three years ago that this was where she would be in a few years, she'd have laughed. Hundreds of millions of dead later, and here she was frantically trying to prevent more bloodshed. And failing.

The rider hesitated, then reached up to the bandana he wore. He pulled it down with a sudden tug. Maira blinked. Her jaw dropped open. She was at an uncharacteristic complete loss for words, her brain scrambling to catch up.

"Leo?" she finally managed.

It wasn't, of course. The resemblance was uncanny, though. The same eyes, the same nose, the same mouth. Younger, though, and less careworn. Perhaps, she thought dizzily, this is what Leo had looked like before he joined the Army.

"What did you say?" the rider asked in surprise.

"What, Maira?" Leo responded. There was a pause. He might have been accessing ISAC. When he spoke again, he sounded more shaken than Maira had ever heard him. "Raffiel?"

"Raffiel?" Maira said.

The rider's eyes narrowed instantly. "How do you know that name?"

"Maira, that's my brother," Leo said. He was somewhere between astonishment and horror.

"What?" Colin said, bewildered.

Maira felt just as confused. "What is your brother doing here?"

She had meant the question for Leo. Words didn't restrict who could hear them, though.

"What do you know about my brother?" Raffiel demanded. "What do you know about Leo?"

"Listen," Maira said hastily. "Your brother, he's here. I don't know what's going on here, but–"

"You have to leave," Raffiel said. There was a new urgency to his voice. "You have to take all of your agents and go."

He turned his head and froze. Leo was sprinting up the road toward them. Maira looked between them with genuine dismay.

"Let's just slow down," she begged. "Obviously this is an unexpected element for all of us."

"You don't understand. There's no stopping this. If I don't give the word, someone else will." Raffiel wheeled the horse away and set it to moving with a sharp, "Hyah!"

"Maira, don't let him leave!" shouted Leo.

Maira took a step forward. She could feel the heat radiating up off the asphalt of the road. She reached out a hand, not sure what she hoped to do. Raffiel was already out of reach and headed back toward the waiting crowd of Reborn fighters.

A gunshot rang out. Maira heard the hot snap-hiss of a near miss. Panic surged from deep inside her. She fell back instantly. It was a smart move. That first shot set off a fusillade of more. Maira dove behind the SHD barricade again. She could hear bullets impacting the far side with rattling crunches.

Leo closed in fast. Maira sat behind the cover, staring in horror. Leo was always the tactically minded one, the most cautious. He had abandoned all of that now in a headlong rush.

"Leo, get down!" Maira screamed.

With Maira out of sight, the Reborn gunmen switched their sights to the other visible agent. Stray shots kicked up clouds of dust on all sides of him. Maira could see the precarious nature of his situation sink in as his eyes went wide. Before he could do anything, something snatched at him. He spun to the ground in a heap.

"Agent down," ISAC announced.

"Fuck!" snarled Maira. "Give me covering fire!"

"Maira, most of these people don't have guns!" Yeong-Ja said urgently.

"Shoot over their heads! Just cover me!" Maira barked.

The chatter of Colin's M4 carbine started up. The thunderclap of Yeong-Ja's rifle was half a heartbeat behind. Maira rolled to a sprinter's starting stance right at the end of the barricade. The other agents were doing their best, but there were simply too many Reborn to suppress. Maira could still hear the pop and twang of nearby impacts.

It doesn't matter, she screamed inside her own head. *Leo is out there.* Maira bared her teeth in a mixture of rage and terror and broke from cover to rush toward him. A bullet punched through a corrugated steel wall near her head with a sharp twang. She bit back a scream. Leo was only a few feet away.

Maira executed a textbook baseball slide down next to him. Leo was breathing. She knew that immediately because he coughed and clutched at his chest. Any further examination had to wait. She hooked her fingers into his body armor and dragged him toward cover. A shot impacted so close that it kicked dirt into her face. She spat to the side, the world lost in a blur of tears.

"ISAC!" Maira sputtered. "Start the turrets!"

"Belay that!" snapped Yeong-Ja. "These are unarmed civilians!"

"Conflicting commands," ISAC said. "Clarify."

"Don't hurt him!" rasped Leo. "Don't hurt my brother!"

They were around the corner of a building now. Maira slumped against the wall and scrubbed her face with a sleeve.

Sweat, tears, and mucus came away slick. She coughed and spat and turned to look at Leo. He had sat against the wall and winced, touching his chest. There was a crater in his body armor, but no sign of blood. Maira took in a gasp of relief.

"Is he OK?" Leo demanded shakily.

"Your brother made it back to their lines," Yeong-Ja said. "Maira, we have to shut the turrets down—"

The sniper was cut off by a resounding roar. Maira blinked rapidly. It took her a second to place it: hundreds of people shouting together. Maira struggled to reconstruct what was happening in her head. She'd reached out for their leader. They must have thought she was trying to hurt him. The gunmen had opened fire in response. And now...

The sound of an onrushing horde confirmed it. They were charging. Terror and fear alike sank their claws into Maira. Images flashed into her head in rapid succession. Athena swarmed by Outcasts. The farmstead burning. Bodies strewn across the cold floors of a concrete tunnel.

"We don't have a choice!" Maira yelled.

"We always have a choice!" Yeong-Ja said.

"Fire! ISAC, fire for effect!"

The AI was incapable of hesitation. The turrets spun up instantly. Machine guns roared before Maira had taken her next breath. Bullets spewed toward the ranks of the gathered Reborn. Screams resounded from across the park.

Bringing her rifle up she looked around the side of the building. The light-garbed foot soldiers were already halfway across the park. They were charging directly into the merciless machine gun fire of the quartet of SHD turrets. Too late, what she had ordered truly sank in. Maira's eyes snapped wide.

"Don't!" she screamed. "Stop!"

The sound was lost completely. The slaughter had already begun. The turrets did their work methodically. They were not made for moral ambiguity. They swept the onrushing human wave like a harvester cuts wheat. Blood sprayed grass and trees. People toppled, cut down midstride. One man's head was shattered upon impact. A woman took several bullets through her legs and fell, screaming. Her efforts at dragging herself away ended as the Reborn behind her trampled her on their way forward.

Maira stood frozen. Everything in her head was screaming at her simultaneously. She needed to turn the turrets off. They needed to run. They had to stand their ground. They had to–

An RPG howled in on a smoky tail. It hit one of the turrets dead on, an ace shot. The SHD tech vanished in an eruption of smoke and flame. When it cleared the automated weapon was gone, leaving nothing but a smoldering crater in its place. Another shared its fate a second later, reduced to so much shrapnel in the blink of an eye.

The rate of fire thus halved, the surviving Reborn surged forward. They poured across the road in a torrent. Five hundred must have been an underestimation. There seemed to be no end to them. Maira's thousand concerns fell apart under a wave of very real fear. They were screaming and blood soaked, eager to come to grips with the people who had killed their fellows.

Maira shot the closest in the torso as the woman came around the corner. Her target fell back screaming and clutching at the red ruin in the middle of her abdomen. Maira couldn't spare her another thought. A dozen more were on her heels. She backpedaled rapidly and shot two more as fast as she could work the lever. One went down with a geyser of blood where his throat had been. The other toppled with a hole clear through their chest and out the back.

The nearest was now within reach of her. They came on swinging a hatchet wildly. Maira ducked the first sweep and smashed them in the stomach with the butt of her rifle. The attacker's howling battle cry died off into a choking gurgle. Maira kicked them in the side to knock them into the dirt.

Another crashed into her at full speed. The momentum picked her up off the ground and brought her down onto her back with a resounding thud. Air was ripped from her lungs with a stifled cry. The world exploded into stars. Her rifle tumbled away across the dusty ground.

Her foe was on top of her. Maira lashed upward with her fists. A series of rapid punches broke something under their bandana. It turned from gray-white to crimson red within seconds. Maira followed up with an elbow to the throat that left them choking. She shoved the person off her and staggered to her feet.

Maira had barely stood when a baseball bat smashed her in the shoulder. White hot pain surged. She staggered with a yelp of pain. Her assailant pressed her, not wanting her to recover. Maira shielded her head as best she could as blows smashed into her arms, each one a new flame of agony.

A series of gunshots rang out. The bat wielder fell to their knees and toppled. Blood stained their clothes and the dirt in swiftly widening pools. Colin was there. He grabbed her by the unhurt shoulder and pulled her back. With his other arm he fired his carbine from the hip. There was no need for precision aim. A new wave of attackers fell back under the barrage, if only for the moment. Colin and Maira seized the chance to retreat around another corner, deeper into the complex.

Maira gasped desperately, unable to catch her breath. She reached back and unlimbered her shotgun from her pack. Preloaded and ready to fire. Colin had emptied his magazine covering them. He threw the empty one aside and slapped a new one home. Another Reborn was already coming around the building after them. Maira unloaded the shotgun into the attacker's chest. Their legs folded under them, and they flopped back with a choking screech.

"Leo?" Maira finally managed to cough out desperately.

"I don't know!" called Colin.

She couldn't remember what had happened to Leo. He had been sitting against that building. The Reborn had charged. Maira had been fighting – had he still been there? She thought so. He had been fighting, too. They'd been separated instantly in the flood of assailants.

"We have to go back–"

More of the Reborn rushed around the corner in a knot. Maira shot one instantly, pitching them into the wall. They hit and slid down, leaving a smear of blood in their wake. Colin gunned down another in a spray of fire. One with a pipe wrench held wide lunged at Maira. She swung her shotgun like a baseball bat. The reinforced frame struck the Reborn's jaw with bone-breaking force. Shattered teeth scattered, and the man stayed down, screaming.

Another foe came to grips with Colin. They had a hay hook snagged on his carbine. Agent and Reborn fell back into a nearby metal wall with a crash, struggling with each other for control of their weapons. Maira pulled her sidearm from her thigh and fired a trio of shots into the attacker's side. It was sloppy. It also worked. The Reborn fell with a disbelieving wheeze, folding around their wounds.

"They're among the storage tanks!" Yeong-Ja said.

"What?" barked Maira. She returned her M9 to its holster with half a thought.

"A team of them came from behind on a fanboat!" the sniper replied.

Maira and Colin traded looks. They set off at a sprint together. Weaving through the buildings, Maira discovered there was no escape from the Reborn. She couldn't hear any turrets still firing. They were flooding through the complex. Unrelenting panic turned her heartbeat into a strident tattoo. They had to save this place, or else the people... the Division...

Howling, one of the Reborn charged them with a pitchfork held out before them. Maira cut him down with a blast from her SPAS-12. She worked the slide, sending the spent 12-gauge shell tumbling away into the dirt. One leapt at them from the side, sledgehammer raised high for a crushing blow.

"Watch out!" Maira yelped.

She and Colin both leapt to the side as the heavy tool arced down. It hit the ground with a thunderous crunch. At a distance of only a few feet Colin shot the wielder dead with a burst from his M4. The next walked right into his line of fire, and Colin emptied the rest of his magazine into them. They tumbled into the dirt, improvised weapon falling from a nerveless hand.

"I'm out!" Colin called.

He slung his M4 around his back and pulled the X45 he carried as a sidearm. The lightly armed Reborn cannon fodder were serving their role perfectly. For one reason or another, Maira and Colin were both already down a weapon. Soon they would run out of ammunition completely and be helpless.

This place was going to be overrun.

"They're planting C4," Yeong-Ja said.

Even now she seemed preternaturally calm. She might as well have been discussing the weather. Maira, for her part, could feel her heart jangling in her chest. She felt like an exposed nerve, with every sound and sensation becoming too much too quickly.

We're going to fail, and the Division is going to be destroyed, Maira thought.

"Yeong-Ja, you have to stop them!"

Colin caught Maira by the shoulder. "There are too many of them! Maira, we have to go!"

Maira shook his hand off with a flare of unthinking rage. "We are not cutting and running! Leo did not die so that—"

"Leo might not be dead!" Colin stared at her as if she had grown a second head. "If we stick around, we will be!"

"Yeong-Ja, stop them!" barked Maira.

The thunderclap of Yeong-Ja's M700 rang out. Once. Twice. A third time.

"That's one. That's two. That's three… Oh." Yeong-Ja sounded nonplussed. "That's got their attention."

"Yeong-Ja, get out of there!" roared Colin.

An RPG leapt from among the containers in the distance.

Maira could see it on its tail of smoke. The world slowed. It screamed to the roof of a nearby building and detonated. The entire building caved in under the impact, collapsing and releasing a pillar of dust and smoke that clawed skyward.

"Agent out of action," ISAC said. "Serious trauma detected. Immediate medical assistance required."

"Shit," Colin said.

The medic was off at a headlong sprint. Maira watched him go, mouth working silently.

"I didn't mean…" she managed.

The words were tiny, helpless. No one seemed to hear them over the cacophony of battle. Maira took an unsteady step. The world was spinning. She caught herself on a nearby wall, hot metal under her hand. Vomit rose in her throat, burning.

"Maira, I need your help!" Colin yelled on the radio.

Maira swallowed hard. No weakness. There was no time for it. She staggered off after Colin.

Colin ran through the compound, teeth bared in a desperate snarl. He didn't know if he could save Yeong-Ja. He didn't know if it was too late for all of them. Maybe all of it was going to happen again, and there was nothing he could do to stop it. But he'd be damned if he didn't try.

He skidded around the corner to see the collapsed building. It was burning in a half dozen places, pumping black smoke into the sky. One of the dark-garbed Reborn gunmen stood amidst the rubble, with a submachine gun in his hands. He looked up. Colin hit an isosceles stance and fired his X45.

The shots were pinpoint accurate. The first two hit the Reborn directly in his armored chest. He staggered backward, losing his balance on the loose rubble and scree. The third hit him in the forehead and dashed the contents of his skull across the rocks. As that foe fell, the return fire tore through the smoke. Colin sidestepped behind what remained of a wall with a curse.

"Maira, I need your help!" he called into the radio.

Colin peeked out with a grimace. There was a flash of movement amidst the obscurity. He fired off a pair of shots just to discourage an advance. Yeong-Ja had not specified how many of the hitters there were. She had claimed to kill three, though, and Colin had now eliminated another. If they had come on a fanboat as she said, he guessed from experience with the craft that there would be two more of them at the most.

That, of course, didn't account for the hundreds of friends they had in the area.

"ISAC, do we have any eyes in the sky left?" he asked.

"Two drones operational," the AI replied.

"All right, I want them on tight patrol on my loc signature. Suppress any hostiles attempting to close with my position."

"Confirmed," the AI said.

Within seconds he heard the chatter of the drones' turrets in the background. Hopefully that would buy them a little time. Colin coughed and wiped streaming eyes with his sleeve. The fire was spreading and the smoke with it. For a lot of reasons, he had to find Yeong-Ja fast and get them all out of here.

A footstep crunched right next to his hiding place.

Colin came around prepared to shoot. The Reborn was there with an assault rifle held ready. They shot each other in the chest at the same time. It was like being punched in the sternum by a heavyweight boxer. Colin stumbled backward, his cough turned to a choking wheeze. His vision was badly blurred. He fired blindly, desperate to kill his attacker before they did the same to him.

A gun spoke nearby, and he flinched. A second shot followed right on its heels. Colin held up his hands in a desperate defense, well aware that this would not save him. He waited for the white-hot pain.

"ISAC, where is Yeong-Ja?" Maira said.

Relief flooded Colin. He scrubbed his face on his arm and shoulder until his vision cleared somewhat. The Reborn gunman was sprawled out several feet before him, chest savaged by a pair of close-range shotgun blasts. Maira was only a few feet away from Colin. He let out a breath. His chest still ached like fire, but maybe he wasn't going to die this instant.

A ping on his vision showed ISAC's answer to Maira's question. Yeong-Ja was nearby, apparently under a fallen section of wall. Her vitals showed next to her. She was hurt badly, but she was still alive, too.

"Here, help me," Colin wheezed and stepped up to the broken wall.

Maira moved beside him, and between the two of them they managed to lever the slab of metal off their fellow agent. Yeong-Ja was laid out on the ground, battered and unconscious. Her left leg was twisted at an impossible angle. Nevertheless, Colin was surprised she was intact. He glanced up.

"She must have jumped when she saw the RPG," he said.

Maira nodded. "Come on, let's pick her up."

They levered her up between them, with the sniper on Colin's left shoulder and Maira's right. He kept his handgun in his grip and looked around anxiously. An explosion overhead punctuated his worries. That was one of their drones gone, and with it the only screen that remained to them against the enemy's overwhelming numbers.

"Maira, we have to go," he said urgently.

Maira hesitated. Colin felt his heart sink. Surely, at this point, she had to see how pointless this fight was. What was he going to do? he asked himself. This place was already lost. Staying here and dying wouldn't change that. He couldn't let her throw their lives away for nothing.

"ISAC, where is Leo?" she asked instead.

There was a pause. "Agent location and status unknown," the AI said.

"What does that mean?" Maira asked despairingly.

Colin shook his head. "I don't know. Maira, I'm sorry."

She didn't look at him, but she nodded. "Let's go."

They set off, carrying Yeong-Ja as carefully as they could. She moaned without waking, a low sob of pain that pulled at Colin's heartstrings.

"We've got you," he said soothingly, hoping she could hear him on some level.

"The fanboat she mentioned," Maira said.

Colin nodded rapidly, following her thought process. Maira looked badly shaken by the events of the day. He didn't have much comfort to offer, but he was glad she was at least still trying, still thinking.

"Since we killed the crew, that's our best way out of here," he agreed. "ISAC, can you get us to the fanboat?"

"Processing request. Projecting optimal route to destination," the AI replied.

It showed up as a glowing orange guideline through the complex. The pair of agents hurried along as fast as they could with their burden and their own injuries. A distance counter showed in the corner of his vision. Three hundred feet away and counting. Soon it was less than a hundred. He could see the drop off into the wetland, across another road.

"I'm surprised we're being left alone," Colin said uneasily. "Where are the—"

The world turned to fire behind them.

The blast caught them like the hand of God. It snatched all three of them right off their feet and sent them tumbling. The world spun around Colin, a dizzying cavalcade of images that he couldn't sort into sense. He hit the edge of the marsh with enough force to send sludge splattering. It flooded his nose and mouth. He came up choking and spitting.

"Maira," he rasped, trying to get to his feet. "Yeong-Ja!"

Colin staggered upright. He found Yeong-Ja first. She was still unconscious, but blessedly she had not ended up with her face in the marsh. He scooped her up in a bridal carry for lack of a better option and stumbled on toward the next marker in his vision. Maira was curled into a ball, her arms clutching tightly at her legs.

She was saying something to herself, over and over. Colin struggled to make it out over the ringing in his ears. He crouched down on one knee, balancing Yeong-Ja's small frame as best he could.

"I'm on fire," she was saying. "Oh god, I'm burning."

"Maira!" he called.

Colin reached out and shook her shoulder. Her head came up in a snap, eyes wide with terror and bloodshot through and through.

"Maira, you're not on fire. You're OK. Do you hear me? You're gonna be OK!"

She clutched at his arm, but her eyes didn't show any comprehension. Either she was deafened, too, or she was going into shock. Either way, they had to get out of here now. If their enemy realized they hadn't been wiped out by the blast, they would doubtless hunt the Division agents down. None of them were in a condition to put up a fight at this point.

"Fanboat, ISAC," he wheezed.

Colin pulled Maira up with one arm. She got to her feet, at least, supporting her own weight. He kept Yeong-Ja's battered body clutched close to him with the other. As a tattered trio they staggered to where the fanboat waited. In the way of silver linings, the explosion had not capsized it, only pushed it out into the wetlands several feet.

Colin waded out into the muck and set Yeong-Ja in the boat. He turned and helped Maira climb onboard, too. Then he levered himself over the side, hitting the deck with a thud and a grunt. Slowly and painfully, he pulled himself to his feet yet again. He started the engine, the propeller kicking on with a roar.

They pulled away from the destroyed complex. Colin glanced back. The blaze consuming the complex was massive, a glowing ember of hell that filled the horizon with reddened smoke. Maira had slumped at the front of the boat, her gaze hollow. Yeong-Ja lay nearby, still unaware of her surroundings.

They're alive, Colin told himself. At least they're alive. One thing at a time.

CHAPTER 7

The island appeared abandoned from a distance. There was a cabin visible from the shore, but there was no sign of life. Colin killed the fan and watched it for several minutes as the boat drifted. It was a strange thing to have to worry about. Whole swaths of the nation had been depopulated by the horror of the Green Poison. Here he was floating along through a marsh and worried about hermits.

In all fairness, though, they were in no condition for a confrontation of any kind. Maira had not spoken a word since they left the destruction in Groves behind them. Yeong-Ja had stirred briefly, only to lapse back into stillness. Colin hoped she had at least switched over to a more healing sleep. Colin himself ached throughout his entire body. He longed for a shower, sleep, and a big meal, and he wasn't particular about the order.

With a sigh, Colin heaved himself over the side of the boat. He hit the muck and immediately sank up to his thighs. He grabbed at the boat to avoid falling over and getting immersed completely. Once he had his balance back, he slogged his way toward the shore, pulling the boat with him. He dragged it up onto the beach as far as he could.

Beach was probably being overly generous. For that matter, dry land might have been flattery. The water table was high here. The ground squelched with each step Colin took, and that wasn't just because he was now soaked in marsh crud. He had to hope they could actually get inside the cabin he'd seen. This wasn't a good place to bivouac.

"Maira," Colin called. "Can you get out of the boat on your own?"

The other agent slowly turned her head and blinked at him. There was no understanding in that gaze. Colin felt a surge of worry. It was no secret that Maira had been in a vulnerable state from the moment they'd left Kansas. Whatever demons she was carrying around in her head, they had driven her to seek that fight in Groves. The disaster she'd found there had clearly torn those wounds wide open.

"Maira," Colin repeated gently. "Can you hear me? I need your help."

It didn't seem to do any good. Then, Maira blinked again, and gave something between a hiccup and a sob. She reached up and wiped at her face, only managing to smear around the ash and grime that coated all of them at this point.

"What's up? What are we doing?" she croaked out.

Colin favored her with a broad smile. "Hopefully finding a place where we can get some rest and plan our next moves. I'm worried about Yeong-Ja, though, and I need your help getting her over there."

Maira nodded and got to her feet unsteadily. Colin wasn't

sure how much help she would be in her current state, but Division agents all shared certain traits. In this particular case, the one that mattered was an unstoppable drive to fix things. Maira's recruitment might have been unusual, but he was willing to bet she had that same fundamental urge.

Under his direction, Maira scooped up the sniper and eased her over the side of the boat into Colin's waiting arms. Yeong-Ja stirred uneasily and coughed. Her eyes opened a crack, full of nothing but confusion and pain.

"Easy does it," Colin said softly. "We're safe."

He hoped that was true. He kept an eye on the cabin the entire time. There was still no sign of activity. That didn't prove anything, of course. Someone could be lying low. They could be drawing a bead on the Division agents at this very moment. They might have the entire shore mined, their finger poised over a detonator.

Colin snorted at himself. Dithering in the swamp was going to kill them a lot faster than imaginary minefields.

"What's your weapon situation, Maira?" he asked.

Maira hopped over the side of the boat onto the shore. He could see that she'd lost her rifle during the battle. It was a pity. Judging from the way she'd clutched to that weapon, there had been an emotional connection there. It was gone now. Even if they were able to go back, he doubted it would have survived the raging firestorm that consumed Groves.

Maira raised her shotgun and looked it over. She frowned and patted at the pouches on her vest.

"Four shells left," she said. "I must have lost ammo at some point."

"God knows there were enough chances to," Colin said

wearily. "That blast back there must have carved a decade off my life. Just stay ready while we check this cabin, all right?"

"Yeah, I'm ready." Maira straightened her shoulders.

They set off toward the little building. Yeong-Ja couldn't have weighed more than a hundred pounds, but she might as well have been a concrete slab at that moment. It was all he could do not to stagger back and forth along the way. He gritted his teeth and did his best to stay steady. Her leg would be agonizing already, no need to make it worse.

"She said they were setting C4," Maira said.

Colin nodded. "Clever of them. A huge spectacle up front that holds our attention completely, and a strike team at the back to hit us where it hurts."

"Seems a little hypocritical," Maira muttered.

Colin raised an eyebrow at her questioningly.

"The boat," she said with a wave of her hand. "I thought their whole thing was 'no more fossil fuels.'"

Colin gave a low laugh. "People like that never have a hard time justifying any means to their ends. Rules for thee but not for me and all that."

They had made it to the front of the cabin. The windows were dark. Colin leaned forward and put his ear to the door briefly. There was nothing but silence. He shrugged and stepped back. He could spend time circling the building and really investigate it. He dismissed the idea. Yeong-Ja's injuries still hadn't been assessed. Time was of the essence.

"Do you think you can break it open?" he asked.

Maira eyed the door. "Probably. Before we do that, though…" She reached forward and tried the doorknob.

With a click, the door creaked open. There was a musty

smell inside. Part of that scent was long disuse, stale air, and dust. The other half, unfortunately, was familiar to anyone who had survived the Green Poison. Someone had died here. He saw the same weary recognition in Maira's eyes.

"At least they're not going to shoot us," Colin offered.

"Small favors," Maira replied.

They stepped into the cabin. It took a moment for Colin's eyes to adjust from the daylight outside. As everything came into focus, he was pleasantly surprised. Far from being some hermit shack, this must have been a ranger station or research outpost. Charts and maps were pinned to the walls. Scientific equipment of a type he didn't recognize was set up around the walls. There were basic facilities: a sink, some cabinets, one bed, and a table.

The previous occupant was sitting at the table. wore a uniform of some kind, though the details were hard to make out at this point. Decomposition had thoroughly had its way with them. There was little more than desiccated skin and a few wispy strands of hair clinging to a skeleton. A few hard-working beetles scattered at their approach.

"Sorry about this," Colin said to the body. "We're a bit on the desperate side. I hope you understand."

He stepped over to the bed and set Yeong-Ja down as carefully as he could. She reached out and grabbed his wrist as he began to straighten back up.

"Leo?" she asked hoarsely.

Colin hesitated and shook his head. The sniper squeezed her eyes shut in regret. He patted her on the hand and pulled away.

"I'm glad to see you talking, at least," Colin said. "You've been out for around an hour, unless I miss my guess. How are you feeling?"

"Hurt," Yeong-Ja said. She reached up and touched her temple with a wince. "Head. Leg. Really bad."

Colin nodded. "It's good that you can feel the leg. Might not seem that way at the moment, but it's better than the alternative. Is it OK if I ask you some questions?"

Yeong-Ja nodded but motioned to her throat weakly. "Water?"

Colin chuckled. "Yeah. Just a little at first, though."

He got her canteen from her kit and gave her a few sips. She accepted them eagerly. Maira shuffled around the cabin in the background. She stopped by the sink and tested it curiously. There was a groan of pipes and then the sound of the faucet coming on. She turned it back off swiftly.

"Looks good," Maira said. "Must be pulling from a tank."

"Alright then," Colin said. "At least we can top up our canteens before we leave. Maybe even have a bit of a wash."

"That would be nice," Maira said.

She went over and opened the cabinets to go through them. Colin turned his attention back to Yeong-Ja.

"Still with me?" he asked.

The sniper nodded wearily. "Not dead just yet."

"You're not going to die. Not from this anyway. You'll be right as rain before you know it."

Colin pulled the bedside table over to him and laid out his medkit. He retrieved a penlight from inside it and checked both of Yeong-Ja's eyes. Both dilated and contracted appropriately. That was good.

"Can you list words that start with an 'E' for me?" Colin asked.

Yeong-Ja frowned briefly. "Early, evening, eventually, elementally, effervescent..."

"Good," Colin said with a smile. "That's really good. Now I want you to repeat a phrase for me, OK?"

"A phrase for me, OK," Yeong-Ja said, with a weak but sly smile.

Colin laughed. "That's good, too. Try this one: the fast little fox jumped over the bumpy log."

"The fast little fox jumped over the bumpy log," Yeong-Ja repeated.

Colin let out a soft breath. "Excellent. I wish I could get a CT scan done, but we can only do what we can do. All right, let's take a look at that leg."

"What if we didn't, and just never spoke of it again?" Yeong-Ja offered.

"You'd have to give up your promising career in track and field," Colin said absently as he looked the limb over.

It was definitely broken. The question was how badly and in how many places. He restored the penlight to its place and got shears out of the kit.

"I'm going to have to cut your pant leg away, OK?" Colin warned her. "I'll be as gentle as I can, but it's going to move your leg some."

Yeong-Ja nodded and took a deep breath. Colin set about cutting the fabric away. Yeong-Ja flinched as he worked. Removing her boot on that leg was a separate ordeal. It dragged a hiss of agony from between her clenched teeth. He found himself admiring her pain tolerance. He'd known strapping Marines who would have been cursing and screaming by this point.

The revealed flesh was puffy and already purple with

bruising. Her leg bent where it shouldn't a third of the way down her shin. There was a tear in the flesh there; the bone hadn't punched through, but it was a compound fracture. Her ankle was swollen by a third over its usual size.

Maira glanced over and hastily turned back to the cabinet, humming to herself. She sorted through items and stowed anything useful in her bag. Colin saw her pause out of the corner of his eye. She was holding up a yellow snack cake in a wrapper. She frowned and put it back.

"Three breaks at least," Colin said quietly. "The tibia and fibula in the lower leg, and another in the ankle."

"That would explain the pain," Yeong-Ja replied.

Colin met her eyes. Steady, he told himself. Project confidence. No one wants to be treated by a medic who seems worried. Sure, he wished he could take her to a hospital and have her treated by proper doctors. But what was it that Maira kept saying? If wishes were fishes. They had to deal with the world as it was.

"So, there's going to be a couple of steps to this, and none of them are going to be fun for you," Colin said.

"Tell me," Yeong-Ja said firmly.

"First, I'm going to have to clean the wound. We can't risk you getting an infection. After that, we'll have to deal with the bones being out of alignment. That means a reduction. Once that's done, I can splint you up."

The sniper swallowed hard. "Do what you have to do. I trust you."

Colin's smile was genuine. "Thank you. I'll do my best to minimize the pain, but I'm not going to lie to you. This will hurt."

"Maira?" Yeong-Ja called.

Maira stepped over immediately. "What's up?"

"Will you hold my hand?" Yeong-Ja asked quietly.

Maira didn't hesitate. "Of course."

She took Yeong-Ja's hand in her own and crouched down beside her so that they were on easy eye level.

"Just look at me," Maira said to her. "And grip as tight as you need to."

Yeong-Ja did as she said, keeping her eyes locked on the other woman's. She took another deep breath before nodding once. "All right, Colin. Do what you must."

Yeong-Ja's hand was hot and sweat-slick in Maira's. She could feel the tremor in the other woman's grip. The sniper always seemed so unflappable, and even now she remained composed. There was real fear underneath, though. Another human being, frightened and in pain.

"Stay with me, Yeong-Ja," Maira said. "You're gonna be OK."

There was the hiss of an antiseptic spray. Yeong-Ja twitched and her grip tightened. It was enough to make Maira's hand ache. She ignored it. Every part of her hurt at this point, so what was a little bit more pain?

Maira could still feel the heat from the C4 detonation and the ensuing blaze. She had never experienced anything like the raw terror she'd known at that moment. Even the radiation scare in St Louis hadn't torn her down like that. Her mind had shut down completely in the face of it. If Colin hadn't been there to pull them out of the literal fire, she felt certain she would have died in Groves.

Like Leo.

Her mind retreated from the thought. It was too painful. Stay in the moment, Maira told herself sharply. Yeong-Ja needs you here and now. Focus.

"Are you OK?" Yeong-Ja asked her.

Maira couldn't help but laugh at that. "I'll get through it. We both will, right?"

Yeong-Ja nodded. There was a wet grinding sound from the direction of her legs. Neither of them looked. Yeong-Ja's already firm grip clamped down like a vise on Maira's hands. Tears welled up in her eyes, but her voice stayed steady.

"This is not the end, Maira. As long as we're alive, we can play another hand. We can do better."

Maira smiled and reached up to brush sweaty hair from the sniper's face. "I know."

"All right," Colin said with a huge sigh.

Maira glanced at him. He was soaked through with sweat, and she didn't think all of it was from the heat. Just because he was a medic didn't mean all of this was stress-free for him. It didn't stop him, though. They would have been lost without him back at Groves, doubly so now. She felt a surge of gratitude toward the man.

"The bone is reset," Colin continued. "You're an absolute champion, Yeong-Ja. Are you ready for me to splint you up?"

She nodded, and Colin started applying a splint that he'd taken from his medkit. A few grunts later, and her grip on Maira's hand finally began to relax. Maira hid relief. She had started to worry that she could hear her own bones grinding together in her hand.

"OK," Colin said. "You're all set."

He held up an injection pen. There was a familiar ruby liquid in it. Maira immediately had to fight the urge to gag just looking at it. She'd had to detox from the combat cocktails during their downtime at the Kansas Core. It was two weeks of hell that she did her best to never think about.

"I'm going to leave this with you," Colin said. "Don't use it unless you have to, but if you absolutely must function…"

He left the rest unsaid. All three agents were familiar with the effects of the cocktail. It would allow someone to go on well past the point of endurance and ignore the worst pains. Unfortunately, that also carried with it the grim possibility of hurting yourself further. The body's warning systems existed for a reason, after all.

Yeong-Ja nodded and pocketed the shot. "Hopefully, I won't. I've never had to take it, but I have known people coming off. I did not know a person could vomit that much."

Maira swallowed hard. "Let's not talk about it any further, OK?"

They both looked at her. Colin winced.

"Fresh memories of your own? Fair enough. Change of topic. We have plenty to discuss, after all, like what the hell we're going to do next."

"Hide here for a few years, hope for the best?" Maira asked with bleak humor.

"Could you really live with doing that?" Colin asked her.

Maira shook her head. "No. I made this mess. I'm going to fix it."

"Hey," the medic said sharply.

Maira's head came up. He glared at her, as heated as she had seen him get in the brief time they'd known each other.

"Cut that shit out, all right? The whole 'Maira has to save the day, she's in this alone, she must do everything', all that crap? That's the actual problem. That's what's dragging you down. You gotta let that go."

Maira blinked and looked at Yeong-Ja, who shrugged weakly.

"Blunt, perhaps, but he's not wrong. You have a habit of playing Atlas. We are all agents of the Division here, Maira. You are not alone."

Maira's first instinct was to get defensive. There was a sharp retort just waiting on the edge of her tongue. Someone had to take charge, right? Was it her fault if no one else stepped up? The words stuck in her throat, though. They were a lie. It was unfair to blame this on the other two.

So, listen to what they said. Was there truth there? Was she in the habit of taking on too much? When everything had fallen apart, her priority had been keeping Kazi and herself alive. Somehow from there, she'd ended up feeling responsible for all of Athena. That burden, that need to seize control of the situation, had cost her brother his life.

Maira had left Athena, of course. It wasn't like she'd just up and disappeared in the night, though. The first time she'd felt like she could walk away was when she'd discovered an even greater responsibility: that of a Division agent. Why worry about one community, when she could try to save the entire Eastern Seaboard? Don't just try to save a life. Try to save the world.

"I..." She took a deep breath. "I'm sorry. You're right. I can't promise I'll change completely this very second. Old habits die hard."

Colin's face softened. "Well, we'll check you if you fall back into the rut, OK?"

Maira nodded. "Thank you."

"We should have before. There were a dozen times any of us could have said something to you. Instead, we let you just keep piling more onto your own shoulders. No more of that."

Yeong-Ja nodded her agreement. "We are a team. We only survived the Groves by working together. That is how we will survive tomorrow, too."

"I just wish it hadn't…" Maira started before she choked up. She fought down the lump in her throat. "Leo tried to talk me down. He tried, and I just couldn't listen. And he's the one who ended up paying the price."

"We don't know that for sure," Colin said.

"ISAC said it couldn't locate him. What else could that mean?" Maira asked.

"ISAC's not shy about saying someone's dead. If he'd flatlined, the system would say so. I think something else must have happened," Colin said.

"Why don't we ask?" Yeong-Ja suggested.

Maira and Colin looked at her in confusion. The sniper shrugged expressively.

"ISAC," Yeong-Ja said. "Can you reconstruct the last data we have from Agent Fourte as an ECHO?"

"Processing," ISAC replied.

"That's… huh. That's a clever idea," admitted Colin.

"Playback initiated," ISAC said.

The ECHO, or Evidence Correlation Holographic Overlay, was one of the many sophisticated applications of the SHD Network. Using data mined from a huge variety of sources, it could reconstruct events and present them as a three-dimensional display on the agents' AR lenses. They would appear as spectral objects in the same orange hues as an agent's watch.

Before the trio's eyes, a scene assembled itself from a thousand sparkling dots. Leo was recognizable in the middle, being dragged by a pair of the Reborn gunmen. A figure on a horse loomed over him. Raffiel, Maira assumed. His details were blurrier, the system trying to compensate for limited input. The pair of soldiers threw Leo down in front of his brother.

"This one surrendered," one of them said.

The voice was tinny, presumably recorded from Leo's radio mic. It was understandable, though.

"Leo," Raffiel said quietly.

Leo raised his head and stared at his brother. "Didn't believe it at first."

"Neither did I. You're not supposed to be here."

Leo shook his head. "Me? You ran away from home. Family thought you were dead. I thought you had died." He sounded genuinely anguished, a startling break from his usual stoic demeanor.

"I had to leave. Father was…"

"No word to Mom? No word to Jaela? No word to me?" The emphasis on the last word was painful. "Two years, Raff! Resigned my commission to look for you, and nothing!"

The words erupted from Leo in a shout. The guards stepped toward him threateningly. Maira flinched and half-rose, like she could intervene. Raffiel held up a hand, and they subsided. She sat back down with a soft sigh.

"I am sorry I hurt you, Leo. That wasn't what I wanted. I just wanted to control my own life. You can understand that, right?" There was a pleading note to the question.

"You call this control?" rasped Leo. "Look at you! Got you on strings like a puppet."

"So you don't understand," Raffiel said softly. He sighed. "We're doing what has to be done, Leo. We're saving the world."

"Murdering people," Leo retorted.

"Are your hands clean, then? You fought overseas before the Rebirth ever happened. Did you pack those skills away when the end came?" The questions were pointed and angry. Leo must have hit a nerve.

Leo stared up at his brother. "Made plenty of mistakes. Wanted better for you."

"Yes. I know you did. You wanted things for me. Father wanted things for me. So did Mother. You all did. Somehow it never mattered what–"

A gunman ran up, cutting Raffiel off. "Sir, the strike team is reporting resistance, but the explosives are planted."

Raffiel nodded. "Very well. Pull our people back. Detonate the storage once they're clear."

"What?" Leo said in shock. "Raff, don't do this!"

Raffiel shook his head sadly. "It's done."

Leo lunged for the radio mike on his shoulder. It earned him a blow with the butt of a guard's rifle. He was knocked to the ground, blood spattering in a burst of orange sparks. Maira raised a hand to her mouth in horror. Raffiel climbed down from the horse and stood over him.

"I'm sorry, Leo. For everything. You have your orders, and

I have mine. Cassandra will want to know why the Division is blundering into our works."

Raffiel crouched down and reached for the ISAC brick on Leo's shoulder. The hologram fizzled out. The playback ended.

"Well." Colin cleared his throat. "He was alive."

"I do not envy him, but yes, where there is life there is hope," Yeong-Ja said.

"We have to get him out of there," Maira said.

"There is a chance he doesn't want to be rescued," Yeong-Ja said thoughtfully.

"What? That's bullshit. Leo can be an ass, but he's neither a quitter nor a traitor," snapped Maira, astonished.

"You heard them. He folded. Does that seem like Leo to you? He didn't resist until he realized the danger that we would be caught in the demolition."

Maira fretted. Yeong-Ja had a point. Leo was many things, but he was not the kind of person to surrender easily. If they had taken him without knocking him out in the first place, it was because he wanted to go with them. It wasn't hard to imagine why. He had wanted to get to his brother.

Could she really blame him? Maira tried to put herself in his shoes. What if it had been Kazi? What lengths would she go to in order to reach out to him, to try to save him?

Any lengths, she realized. She would have done anything.

"OK," Maira allowed. "Maybe he let them take him voluntarily. That doesn't change the fact that they hurt him, and that they've now taken him prisoner. You heard Raffiel. He wants to take him to Cassandra."

"That is concerning," Colin mused. "He went right for the

ISAC connection, too. That's precise knowledge for someone meeting an agent for the first time."

"The way Raffiel kept talking, I don't think this is the first time they've met one. If anything, he seemed surprised we were trying to stop him. It makes me think they want him alive, at least. They could have shot him then and there," Maira said.

The thought made her feel sick to her stomach. Small favors that hadn't played out in the hologram. Watching Leo get executed would have been a bridge too far for her.

"It does seem his situation has worsened," Yeong-Ja said. "You are right. We may have to step in and save him, even if that is not what he would wish."

"We still have the same problem," Colin said. "And we don't need to make the same mistake twice. Namely, we don't know enough about the Reborn. We've seen them fight, and we know who leads them. That leaves a lot of unanswered questions."

Maira nodded reluctantly. As much as she wanted to race after Leo immediately, there was no telling what they'd walk into doing that. It was that kind of recklessness that had gotten them into this mess in the first place. Now the roughnecks would have nowhere to turn but the Molossi for protection. The defeat at Groves could be the first domino in everything they'd built crashing down.

"OK, so we do some recon," Maira said. "We figure out where these assholes are operating from and what makes them tick. And then we use that information to get him out."

"I like it," Colin said. "So, how do we do it?"

Silence stretched with the three of them staring at each other. Maira reached up and rubbed the back of her neck.

She regretted the gesture immediately. She hated the feel of her scars under her fingers. She lowered her hand slowly. Desperation rose in her. There had to be something they could do.

"The radio station," Yeong-Ja said suddenly.

Colin tilted his head. "The what now?"

It clicked in Maira's head. "No, she's right. That's it. The Reborn were broadcasting that signal, and it was strong as hell. We said they must have been using a captured radio station to do it."

Colin's eyebrows went up. "That's not bad. Yeah, that's a start. Are we sure they'll still be there?"

"Sure?" Maira asked. "No. Are there ever guarantees in this business? But I bet they weren't satisfied with one threatening broadcast. There's more refineries, platforms, storage facilities. Plenty of targets."

"ISAC," Yeong-Ja said. "Can we pinpoint where the broadcast was coming from?"

"Processing request," the AI responded.

"Actually a pretty handy program," Maira said. "I have to admit."

"Don't let it hear you," Colin remarked wryly. "It'll go straight to ISAC's head."

"Most likely broadcast source: Lake Charles, Louisiana," ISAC said.

Maira frowned. "How far is that on foot?"

"Estimated travel time by optimal path: twenty-eight hours," ISAC replied.

Maira sighed and rubbed her face. "Just a hop, skip, and a jump away, huh?"

"Ah," Colin said with a grin and a raised finger. "But why walk when we can ride in style in our stolen boat? It's connected by waterways after all."

Maira raised her eyebrows. "I had genuinely forgotten about that damn thing. Assuming it has enough fuel, that's great. Means we don't have to make a sled to drag Yeong-Ja with us, too."

The sniper frowned. "No one drags Yeong-Ja."

Maira grinned lopsidedly. "Needs must? But like I said, we don't have to!"

"It's a start," Colin allowed. "But for right now, we need to do a few other things. I need to check you and me for any injuries, too, and make sure they're cleaned. We could all use some cleaning in general, really. And we need to get some rest."

Maira took a deep breath. "Yes. OK."

She hated to lose time, but at least they didn't have to walk there. There's time, she told herself. We can still fix this. I can still fix this. I can pull this back.

I have to.

CHAPTER 8

Colin guided the fanboat up the waterway and out into the open lake. It was nice being on the move like this. The speed got the wind whipping through his hair and broke the humid heat of the area. It would have been a fun expedition, were it not for everything else involved with what they were doing.

Yeong-Ja sat nearby, her rifle leaned against her. She had her eyes closed and her face turned into the breeze. Colin hadn't wanted to bring her along. By any reasonable estimation she was in no condition for a fight. Her leg could not support her weight, and too much activity risked further harm. The argument was fresh in his mind as he looked at her.

"I am not staying," she had said.

"What if something happens, and we're not there to protect you? You're too vulnerable right now. You can't run–" Colin had said fiercely.

"What happens," she had cut him off, "if you both get killed or captured and I'm stuck here in a cabin on an island in the middle of a marsh?"

Colin hadn't had a good response to that. The reality was

without them she'd be stuck. She would run out of supplies long before she was fit to travel, and she would starve to death. It was a cruel fate to condemn someone to. He couldn't blame her for wanting to stick with the group.

"Let her come," Maira had said quietly. "We finish this together one way or another."

And that was that.

Maira, for her part, sat near the front. The rest at the cabin seemed to have done her a world of good. Some of her broken edges were rounded off. She was calm and steady, engaged with the world again. The shotgun was laid across her lap, ready to go. It was a vast improvement from the nearly catatonic state the destruction of Groves had left her in.

Even at this distance the smoke cloud was visible. The town must still be burning. The surrounding wetlands should keep the fire from raging across the state, at least. It seemed like a very small favor indeed. By now, Colin supposed, the roughnecks and the Molossi must know how the battle had turned out.

What would they do in response? It was easy to imagine the panic among the former. The Division had promised to protect them, only to fail and get wiped out at the first clash. Colin had to assume they would turn to the Molossi for protection. Colonel Georgio would move his troops up and prepare for battle with the Reborn at the next opportunity.

Colin wasn't sure how to feel about that. He had volunteered for this mission for a chance to apologize to Marcus Georgio, for being the one to live when Georgio's son had died, only to get his opportunity in a way he'd never imagined. The worst way possible, that was what it felt like now. Georgio's hatred of the Division had been the catalyst for their blind intervention at Groves, and Colin had done nothing but make it worse.

It had left him in an unpleasant emotional limbo. The mission was still important, of course, but why was he even here if he was himself an obstacle? Still, in the manner of strange blessings, the disaster at the destroyed refinery had clarified things for him. Colin was here because his cell needed him.

Maira, Yeong-Ja, and Leo – each were in trouble in their own way. If Colin did nothing on this journey into the south, he would watch out for them. In that way, he needed them in turn. Maybe the grand goals should have been enough. Maybe the strategic preservation of oil reserves and supply lines should have kept him going. In truth, though, that had never been how Colin's heart worked. He lived for others.

Lost in his thoughts, Colin realized too late that Maira had been saying something. Her voice had been almost lost in the putter of the boat's propeller. He waved a hand so that she would look at him.

"What did you say?" Colin called.

"Pull in just outside town," Maira yelled back. "We don't want to draw too much attention."

Colin nodded in response and steered the boat down one of the side rivers branching off from the lake. She was right. Making a big show of their arrival would end with another human wave wiping them right off the map. Luckily the waterways here connected all along the coastline. The surrounding land varied mostly by water level. Some of it was little more than swamp. In other places, copses of trees stood, spreading shade beneath their branches. Most was just grassland, flat stretches of rich green that waved in the breezes. It was easy to make a landing wherever they needed. Even if they finished it out on foot, the boat must have shaved a day or more off the trip to get here.

Colin slowed the craft as they neared the shore. This had once been a landing point for the locals. It must have been a nice place to spend a day at the lake once. Now it was overgrown, and parts of the docks had collapsed. Colin guided the boat up onto the shore a short way – the light fiberglass construction of airboats made such maneuvers possible.

He and Maira disembarked, landing amidst the tall grass. Colin turned back to where Yeong-Ja peered over the side at them. She was resting her rifle across the edge of the boat's side, casually keeping it pointed skyward from ingrained habits.

"Call if anything happens," he said.

"I would tell you to do the same." Yeong-Ja smiled. "I won't be able to come to help, however."

"We'll try to scream one last time over the radio if we die," Maira said helpfully. "That way you know to take the boat out to sea and hope for the best."

"How considerate of you," the sniper replied.

Shaking his head, Colin waved. The pair of agents strode off up the road east toward the city of Lake Charles.

"And then there were two," Maira said.

"I wish we could bring her along," Colin said wryly. "It'd be nice knowing I had a sniper playing the angel on my shoulder."

"I think you're more worried about her being back there by herself," Maira said.

"That, too." Colin looked back over his shoulder briefly. "I don't doubt her ability to take care of herself…"

"I never thought you did. She's hurt. It's natural to be concerned. But honestly, we'll be in more danger than she will. There's no reason for the Reborn to come hang around a rotted landing."

"True. I'll focus my energy on worrying about us instead," Colin said.

Maira snorted a laugh at that. They continued in silence. The road they were on joined with a highway and curved to the north. Leaving behind the marshlands was a relief. The rotten egg smell had become so omnipresent that Colin had forgotten about it until he didn't have to smell it anymore. The greenery became scrub and grass run wild.

Gray clouds crawled across the sky. They brought relief from the sun, but the air only grew heavier. They paused to rest in the ruin of an old gas station. There in the shade Colin took hearty gulps of water from his canteen. Maira did the same. Both of them watched darker clouds roil in the distance. Occasional rumbles rolled in.

"Don't much like the look of that," Maira said.

"I'm definitely missing Dixie Dog at this point," Colin admitted.

Maira grinned at him. "Ah, don't sweat it. You're not made of sugar. You won't melt."

Colin huffed and put his nose in the air. "You don't know that. I am very sweet, after all."

"I'd accuse you of being a marshmallow, but you have more in common with a candy cane," Maira noted.

"Is that another way of calling me gangly?" he demanded.

"You may interpret it however you wish, sirrah." Maira pronounced her words with a cultivated, pompous air.

They set out once more. Their path, helpfully picked out in orange by ISAC, took them toward the heart of the city and deeper into the worsening weather. There were soon increasing levels of development. Most of it was the cheap commercial places that flooded every city of middling size. Pawn shops, strip malls, outlet stores, and more lined the road and filled little complexes. There were some residential areas, too, apartment buildings and townhouses.

All of it was falling in on itself these days. Roofs had collapsed. Creepers ran up walls. Kudzu, the invasive vine from Asia, climbed every surface it could reach. Some buildings had vanished completely under this green facade. It rendered them little more than shapeless emerald lumps. The sight of it all set Colin to thinking.

"You know I activated in New York first."

Maira nodded. "I recall the tale."

"At first the city was mostly what you'd seen on TV, right? And then over the months it started to crumble. Time keeps passing, and it's only gotten worse. Entropy doesn't take a break."

"That is definitely true," Maira said. "Everything falls apart over time, especially my joints."

Colin chuckled. "You're an old woman before your time, huh?"

"Oh, absolutely. You're the one who told me I carried the weight of the world on my shoulders, right? Do you know what that does to your knees?"

"Nothing good. Especially when you stack it with all that running they made us do in the service," Colin said.

"God, don't remind me. I already have to think about it every morning when I get out of bed," Maira said.

A garbage truck lay on its side in the middle of the road. It had careened into a building a long time ago. Old debris littered the ground around the impact. The rear had spilled its cargo in the fall. The biodegradable parts of the trash were gone, leaving behind scattered chunks of plastic. The two agents cut around the whole mess.

"So, OK, things fall apart," Maira said, picking the conversation back up. "Where's that got your head at?"

"Aside from the inevitability of death and decay?" Colin asked. He shrugged. "I guess I used to think a lot about rebuilding. Getting the lights back on, you know? I think a lot of people dreamed about that."

"Ah," Maira said understandingly. "And it seems less and less likely that that's what the future holds."

"Yeah," Colin agreed. "I guess I'm just starting to accept there's no going back. Whatever form this all takes, it's going to have to involve moving forward instead. Doing something new, not just bringing back the old."

Maira nodded slowly. There was a quiet as they both mulled the thought over. Colin wasn't sure how to feel about it. "Save what remains" had been a rallying cry for the Division. That was just buying time, though. At some point that wasn't enough, was it? They passed a forgotten strip mall. Shop fronts had sunk in as if they were melting. Collapsed awnings littered the sidewalk. Broken glass crunched underfoot as they walked.

"Someone shared with me a vision, once," Maira said. She paused and laughed. "That sounds very metaphysical when I say it that way."

"Was it?" Colin asked.

"Metaphysical? No. Maybe a little philosophical." Maira flashed him a smile. "The key is this: as horrible a form as it came in, we have an opportunity."

"I'm listening," Colin said.

"The world we knew carried the weight of history. Maybe it was easier a lot of the time, but it could also be cruel and unjust. Now it's all wiped away. The slate's clean. The only things waiting for us in the future are what we choose to bring with us."

"That's a heavy responsibility," Colin said quietly.

"Absolutely," Maira agreed. "It's also the greatest privilege I can imagine. More so than any other group in living memory, the world will be what we make of it. Out of all the horror, all the pain and suffering, we get a chance to do things right."

Colin had to take a minute to let that sink in. "Is that why you feel like you're responsible for everything? Because in a way, we all are now?"

Maira gave a wry laugh and a shrug. "I'm pretty sure my issues go a lot deeper than any one easy explanation, but I'm sure it plays into it."

"I like it, though," Colin said. "We're not desperately giving CPR to a world that has already died. We're the midwives of a new one."

"Oh, that's good," Maira said. "Do you think we can get that on a T-shirt?"

He laughed and kicked a pebble in the road at her. "Now you're just being a bully."

"It's true," she allowed. "If there was a toilet nearby, I'd grab a stepladder and pull you down to give you a swirly."

As if on cue, the first heavy drops began to fall. There were only a few at first, but the rain picked up quickly. Soon they were sloshing through puddles, both of them soaked to the bone. The rain was surprisingly warm.

"Did you wish for a shower at any point recently?" Maira asked, spitting water to the side.

"I might have," Colin admitted.

"I'm going to say this is your fault, then."

They continued on. The structures around them grew larger, though that did nothing for the condition they were in. Multi-story buildings had simply toppled in places, strewing the streets with debris. They picked their way carefully among broken brick and rusted metal. To Colin's horror, there was bone amidst the rubble. Bodies that had sat, rotting, until the building itself fell.

"Maira," he started.

"I see them," she said softly.

There was nothing more to be said. These people had been beyond their help for years. When the dead outnumbered the living nine to one, there was no good way to handle it. The biohazard fears aside, the labor of trying to bury so many boggled the mind. This might seem disrespectful, but it was not the worst outcome. At least nature had them here.

"Hostiles guarding location nearby," ISAC announced.

Maira pushed Colin into the shadow of an alley.

"Don't move," she said in a low voice.

ISAC's warning had come only just in time. The rain, unpleasant as it was to have to hike through, may well have saved their lives. The gray deluge made it hard to pick out details at a distance. They had the AI to help them make sense of things. The enemy was not so fortunate.

To Colin's credit, he did not protest. "What are we dealing with?" he asked quietly.

Maira peeked out carefully. There was a large building at the end of the street. It was in somewhat better condition than its fellows. Someone had taken the time to clear away the worst of the overgrowth. That wasn't the most telling detail, however. What gave it away was that they had taken the time to ring it with loops of barbed wire as well.

"They've fortified a building at the end of the street. Must be the radio broadcast station. I see wire. ISAC, can you highlight hostiles for me?" Maira asked.

Several figures appeared in orange outlines. Now that she knew where to look, she had an easier time picking out details.

"At least two of the gunmen. I see five others, the cannon fodder or workers. I'm not sure there's a difference when they're not in battle." All the people were under an overhang in front of the building. It lay beyond the barbed wire and across a parking lot from where they stood.

Colin nodded. "That's fewer than I was worried about."

Maira kept looking the building over. "I think it's more like an armed checkpoint than a fort. The building isn't restored enough to be housing large numbers of people. Maybe they restored functionality and then just garrisoned it with troops to maintain access?"

"Believable enough for me," offered Colin. "So, what's the approach?"

Maira locked eyes with him. "You trust me enough to let me make the call again?"

Colin smiled slightly, rain dripping down his face. "I trust you enough to listen to whatever suggestions you have."

"Fair enough," Maira said. "The gunmen are the biggest threats. I'll move to the other side of the street and–" She reached back to where she usually slung her rifle and froze. "Fuck."

Colin winced. "Yeah. Not gonna be able to pick people off at this distance, I'm afraid. Here, let me take a look, maybe…" He leaned out carefully then pulled back and shook his head. "They're too far apart. By the time I take one, the other will have heard the shot and they'll be on the move."

Maira couldn't lie. Losing Johnny's Winchester hurt her. Somehow the loss hadn't really sunk in until this moment. That was the only item she'd kept in the destruction of the mountain homestead. All that remained now were her memories. She took a deep breath and tried to shake it off. Now wasn't the time.

"All right, new plan. I'll work my way up to the parking lot without getting spotted. Once I've got a good chance with my shotty, I'll signal you, and we'll take them together."

"Shouldn't we offer them a chance to surrender?" Colin asked.

Maira put a hand to the glowing watch on her wrist. Her wet clothes clung to her, rubbing against the scar tissue on her back. It was not a pleasant sensation.

"They charged into machine gun fire at Groves. Do you really think they'll surrender here just because we ask?"

"They had more people with guns standing behind them there. This isn't the same situation," Colin said uneasily.

Maira hesitated and wiped water from her face. "Are you

willing to risk your life to do it? Because I don't want either of us to get hurt."

"I don't want us to be murderers even more," Colin said.

Maira nodded slowly. "All right. When we're in position, you'll call out. We'll give them a chance."

Colin frowned. "I don't like the idea of you trying to sneak up there by yourself either."

Maira clapped him on the shoulder. "I sure as hell don't like it myself. But there's two of us, and I prefer you here, ready to give me covering fire if I need it."

"What if there are more inside?"

"Then you unleash all that deadliness you accrued working with the Marines."

"Great," Colin muttered. "All right. Let's do it."

"We've got this," Maira said. "Listen for the signal."

She set out from the alley. The rain was definitely her best friend now. Without it, her chances of reaching the lot undetected would have been zero. At least this way she had a chance. Maira did her best to stay low and move quickly. She had never mastered the art of stealth, but these people had no reason to expect them. She tried to breathe steadily, calmly.

From alley to alley in quick bursts. They're not even watching for me, she told herself. They're all having a smoke. Laughing about a joke. Talking about what they're going to do for dinner. No, that was a bad train of thought. She shouldn't humanize the people she might have to kill.

Maira slipped into the parking lot. Most of the way there. It was easier now. The rusting cars made for good concealment. She crouched behind the remnants of an SUV to catch her breath. She got the shotgun off her pack. It was slick with rain.

There was nothing she could do about that. Not an inch of her was any drier at this point.

This close she could hear them talking to each other. She couldn't make out what they were saying, just the sound of voices. Everything specific was lost to the rain. One of them was whistling. She could only just hear it.

The last stretch Maira took more slowly, more carefully. The risk was greatest here. She could afford a few seconds to try to do this right. She slid up behind the closest car to them, a four-door sedan. It had been blue once, she thought. She could hear her heart pounding in her ears. It almost drowned out the sound of the Reborn. They couldn't have been more than twenty-five feet away at this point.

Maira checked her shotgun one last time carefully. Loaded, safety off. Nothing crazy going on here. She was going to have to clean it very carefully the next chance she got. The last thing she needed was for the weapon to fail her when she needed it most. She peeked out the side. One of the gunmen was at the far side of the overhang. She tagged him with a nod. ISAC would show Colin that was his target. The other one was closer, leaning against a column and looking out at the rain. His side was to her.

"I'm in place," Maira whispered into the radio.

"This is the Strategic Homeland Division! Drop your weapons and put your hands in the air!" shouted Colin from across the distance.

There was a breathless pause. The Reborn burst into action. They scattered for cover. They weren't complying. The one at the column raised his gun. Fuck this!

Maira stood to her full height, SPAS-12 set, and fired. The

gunman stumbled from the impact. A shot rang out in the distance. Colin. Maira didn't have time to worry about that now. Her target had impressive reflexes. He whirled to face her.

Maira pumped the slide on her shotgun. A shell fell away, lost in the rain. He was firing, but so was she. The windows of the sedan blew out in a spray of glass. The Reborn fell back with a yelp. Maira leapt the hood of the car and sprinted toward him, working the slide once more. He was still on his hands and knees. Dark liquid was spilling from his mouth or his neck, it was hard to tell.

He raised his head. Maira made eye contact with him for a split second. She shot him again from only a few feet away. His face evaporated into a red ruin, and he fell back to the ground, dead.

Maira whirled, ready for a fight. The other gunman was laid out on the ground. His blood mingled with the rain in a widening pool. The lightly clad workers stared at her in unconcealed terror. She brought the shotgun to bear on the closest one, her heart a jackhammer in her chest. The woman had a machete in her hand. If Maira didn't–

The Reborn dropped the weapon. It fell to the ground with a metallic clang. The sound punched through the adrenaline haze of Maira's brain. Maira realized she and her target were both shaking.

"Please," the woman whimpered. "Don't, don't ..."

"Drop your weapons," Maira barked. "All of you! I want them out of your hands, now!"

They did as she demanded. One of them had started sobbing. She could see a dark stain spreading on the front of his pants. A surge of nausea rose in her. Not at him. At this. The entire situation. The overhang smelled of blood already. Suddenly that made her want to vomit.

Maira wiped a hand across her mouth without lowering the shotgun. "Don't move."

"Maira!" Colin came sprinting up. He skidded to a halt, nearly losing his balance on the rain-slick ground. "Are we good?"

"Yeah," Maira said. She spat to the side, trying to get the bad taste out of her mouth. "We're good."

Colin stepped up to the nearest of the Reborn workers. His height really struck Maira at that moment. He had a wholesome, nonthreatening air the entire time she'd known him. Here, confronting an enemy, his face was cold. It was easy to imagine him as frightening, looming a foot taller than them.

"Are there more of you here?" he asked.

It was the woman who had carried the machete. She glanced around unhappily. "I don't…"

"Answer him," Maira said sharply. "Don't bullshit us."

The woman swallowed hard. "Not right now. Everyone went on the march to destroy the unclean place."

The phrasing made Maira shake her head. It really was cultish. Someone was doing their best to indoctrinate people, and it appeared to be working. She wiped her mouth again. Now that she was actually out of the rain, somehow she felt even more conscious of how she was soaked to the bone. Her clothes were plastered to her.

"We need to search the building, see if we can find anything," Colin said quietly.

"What are we going to do with them?" Maira motioned with her shotgun. One of the workers flinched.

Colin studied them briefly. He kept his voice very quiet. "I don't have it in me to be a cold murderer, Maira. I don't think you do either."

She gave him a sad smile. "I definitely don't want to be."

"Then we let them go."

Maira swept her gaze across the group. They were all watching the pair of Division agents with wide eyes. "There could be more nearby. They could run off and get reinforcements."

"True. So, what do we do?"

"We split up," Maira said. "One of us goes inside and sees what there is to see. The other stays out here with them. Maybe even asks them some questions. We meet back up, and we let them go when we're leaving. They can't do any harm that way."

"Sounds smart," Colin said. "Are we going to flip a coin?"

The stink of the blood was still in Maira's head. She couldn't seem to get away from it. She swallowed convulsively, demanding that her stomach not misbehave. She was an agent of the Strategic Homeland Division, damn it. She was not going to vomit in front of these people.

"I'll take inside."

Colin gave her a measuring look. He nodded. "Be careful. They could be lying about more. If anything happens…"

"You'll be the first to hear about it," she promised.

Colin turned his attention fully to the group of Reborn. "All right, you lot. Kick those weapons away and have a seat on the ground. We're going to have a little chat."

Maira stepped to the door of the building. VALET PARKING read a rotting sign. She took a deep breath and headed inside.

CHAPTER 9

Maira vanished into the building.

"ISAC, monitor her vitals. Immediate notification of any serious anomalies," Colin instructed.

"Acknowledged," the AI replied.

Colin turned his full attention to their temporary prisoners. Their fear was palpable. He didn't take any pleasure in that. Beyond his natural distaste for cruelty, fear verged on useless in Colin's eyes. He had known enough bullies and brutes in his life. Their tactics might compel obedience one time, but the next it would drive someone to desperation.

"I'm not out to hurt you," Colin said evenly.

One of them glanced at the nearby body of a gunman. The corpse must seem a compelling argument to the contrary. Colin and Maira had come upon this little group like a thunderbolt from the clear blue sky. Colin chewed his lip uneasily.

"Listen, I'm not going to lie to you. The Reborn and the Division – you know about the Division?" he asked and held up the glowing watch on his wrist.

There were nods and some mumbled affirmations. It did

nothing to decrease their fear. He couldn't argue with that in all truth. When mass media had gone down, the chaos of the early days in New York was the main image in circulation. Few got to see the eventual victories, or survivor communities getting to enjoy a hard-earned peace.

"Well, those two groups are clashing. I don't know what you've been told, but the Reborn have been murdering people. We can't let that continue. The chaos has to stop. But that doesn't have to be a problem between us. Answer my questions, and don't do anything stupid, and you can walk away from this."

They might have relaxed marginally. It was hard to tell. Most of them were still watching his rifle warily. One of the women frowned about what he'd said. Colin focused his attention on her.

"What is it?"

The woman startled. She hadn't expected him to notice, or perhaps she hadn't thought he'd care. She stammered something unintelligible and looked away hastily.

Colin sighed. "Look, I already said I don't want to hurt anybody, right? I'm not going to shoot you for saying something. If you have a question, go on, ask."

She cleared her throat uneasily. "The Voice said that the Division wouldn't care what we were doing. She said not to worry about it."

"The Voice… is that what you call Cassandra Raines?" he asked.

There were nods. Colin restrained the urge to snort. Did Raines believe her own nonsense? Or was she cynical enough to be playing this oracular drivel as a scam? That was a question that would have to wait for the day when he got to ask her himself, he supposed.

"Well, the Voice doesn't speak for the Division. Our goal is to keep this country from falling apart." Colin paused. "Well, fall apart any more than it already has."

"The old world is dead," one of the men burst out. "The Rebirth has come, and the choice is to embrace the future or be left behind." He looked terrified as soon as he was done speaking.

This wasn't exactly the information Colin had been hoping to get, but it was interesting all the same. Understanding what motivated the Reborn might hold the key to getting them to stand down. He was willing to let the conversation go down that road.

"That's certainly one take on the whole situation," Colin said wryly. "Here's another one: murder, arson, and terrorism are all bad things, and we're still going to stop them."

"We don't want to hurt people either," another one of the prisoners said. "But we've seen the fruits of the old ways. It hit us right in our homes. We can't let people trap us in a past that was killing us."

"What do you mean?" Colin asked.

"This is Louisiana," she said. "Even before the Rebirth, climate change was tearing into us. Unprecedented hurricanes, out of control flooding. And the people in power sat by and did nothing. They say that's not murder, but that's only because the same people doing it made all the rules. The same people raking in the profits."

Colin blew out a sigh and leaned against a column. "You're not wrong. I wish I could say the world used to be fair, but it never was, and some people got a lot more of the unfairness than others. But the people you're hurting now, they're not the same people who hurt you before."

"They bled the Earth before, they bleed it now. What's the difference?" the woman said.

"No one's getting rich off what's happening here," Colin said. "I'm not sure being rich is an idea that even applies anymore, but I can tell you that's not what's motivating the roughnecks. There's a lot of people out there counting on them."

"Like who?" demanded the woman.

"Communities running all the way from California to Florida, and north to New York besides. The world hasn't died. There's millions of people living their lives still, and they need food, heat, light, supplies of all kinds," Colin said.

"The Voice teaches us how to subsist in alignment with nature, and not at war with it. We must remember that we are part of the Earth, just another section of the great web."

It was the same man who had made the outburst earlier. The Voice's true believer, Colin mused. The woman who kept talking seemed like she'd been convinced, too, but she wasn't just reciting things she'd been told.

"There has to be a balance," Colin said. "A lot of these people weren't ready to become farmers overnight. Some of them never will be. Demanding everyone change who they are overnight isn't going to work. It's just going to get a lot of people killed."

"Every great revolution has a price that must be paid," the woman replied. Her heart didn't seem to be in it, though.

"Maybe. Is that what's happening here, though? Look, I

don't know what you have been through. How did you end up with the Reborn?"

The group of people exchanged uneasy looks. Was this some kind of verboten topic? Colin couldn't be sure whether it was that or just a certain natural caution about giving information to the man holding you prisoner. One way or another, the woman chose to answer.

"I'm from New Orleans. Did you know we've been hit by a hurricane since the Rebirth?"

"The Rebirth… is that what you call the Green Poison?" Colin asked.

"Humanity has been the poison," recited the true believer. "The Rebirth was the first stage of the cure. Our numbers had to be culled for Earth to have any hope of surviving."

Colin stared at him. "You can't truly believe the pandemic was some kind of blessed event."

The woman shot the man an ugly look. "The deaths were obviously tragic. We all lost people. No one was happy to see it happen."

The true believer glowered. "A forest fire leaves new growth in its wake. What some call a disaster can be salvation."

Colin was starting to grasp it. In a weird way, it wasn't a completely different philosophy than the one that Maira had espoused to him on the walk here. A longing for a future utopia to rise from the ashes of devastation. "The Reborn" indeed. The difference, Colin thought, was that Maira would have stopped the Green Poison given the chance. Cassandra Raines would have caused it without a second thought.

Colin shook his head. "Leave it aside. No, I didn't know there was another hurricane. That must have been horrible."

"It was no Katrina," she said quietly. "Thank goodness. But we didn't have any warning until it was on us, and things were already in a bad way when the rain started to fall. Those who hadn't died from the sickness faced floods. Already damaged buildings collapsed. A lot more people died."

"That's horrible," Colin said. "I'm so sorry."

She shrugged it off. "Sorry doesn't do shit. Do you know what did? The Reborn showing up in the wake of the storm. They brought food, clothes, medicine, and more."

"What did they ask for in return?" Colin asked.

"Nothing." She gave him a challenging look. "Believe what you want, but the Voice didn't round us up at gunpoint. She helped everyone she could, and she made us an offer. We could come with her if we wanted to and start a new life."

Colin could imagine it. The people of a city overwhelmed by successive catastrophes, and the savior that appears among them. The genuine gratitude that would have poured out. Raines wouldn't have needed to conscript people. They would have signed up in droves.

"What then?" he asked.

"She taught us the truth," said the true believer fervently.

The woman looked a little embarrassed by him at this point. "She divided us up to go to different compounds she ran. It wasn't a comfortable life, but it beat starving in flooded city streets by a mile. There was work to be done. In return, all our needs were provided for."

"So why have armed guards with you?" Colin motioned to one of the dead gunmen.

They all shrank a little bit, reminded of how they'd ended up here. Colin winced. Not his most tactful move, perhaps.

"They weren't here to imprison us, they were here to protect us," the true believer snapped. "And you murdered them."

"Well," the woman said uneasily. "They weren't going to let us run away either."

The fanatical man glared at her. "Did you plan to?"

"No!" she responded irritably. "But you and I both know some people have tried to leave–"

"Traitors," the man said contemptuously.

Colin tilted his head. "What makes someone a traitor?"

"Colin." The transmission in his ear cut him off. It was Maira. "I think I've found something."

The inside of the building had a distinctly unpleasant odor to it. Maira had discovered a lot of nasty smells in her life. Rotting corpses, burn pits, and just recently the rotting-egg smell of a marsh. This was a new one. It was like mildew times a hundred. This was wet country, and that dampness had sunk into every corner of this decaying building. Mold had blossomed in its wake.

Even so, it was a relief from the blood-stink of the overhang outside. Maira decided to count her blessings and continue on. Another silver lining: this place wasn't as dark as she had expected. The Reborn had strung up lights along the walls and ceilings. They must have had a generator along with them, because the power grid here was definitely no longer operational. Maira was surprised at the waste. Were they burning the hated fuel just to keep the lights on?

There were signs of occupation all throughout the first level. They must have used this area as their campsite. They had tents set up inside the building. As funny as it looked, it was obviously a necessity. There were crumbling gaps in the walls and ceiling. Water dripped down in a hundred leaks.

Maira followed the lights. She trailed water as she walked, feeling something like a drowned rat lost in the walls. They led her up through the building floor by floor. The elevator was no longer an option, obviously. The stairs weren't in any better condition than the rest of the building. The Reborn had gone to some pains to make them passable again. Boards spanned gaps. Weak points were reinforced. She might not agree with their philosophy, but she admired their carpentry skills.

Maira stayed alert as she moved. The captured Reborn might have said that there weren't any more of them around, but she didn't plan to die gullible. Even so, she was two stories up before it occurred to her that her shotgun only had one shell left in it. She had no further reloads. She contemplated the weapon and then attached it to her pack with a sigh.

The pistol in her thigh holster would have to do. It was nothing fancy. A standard military M9 sidearm, utterly mundane and practical. This one, however, was a comforting presence for her. It was the first weapon she had picked up with the coming of the Green Poison pandemic, and it had been with her ever since. It was also what she'd used to end the life of rogue agent Rowan O'Shea.

That thought made her wince. Sometimes it felt like her brain just couldn't give her a break. There was always some part of her mind clawing around like an animal trying to escape a trap. Had it always been that way, or had it started when the world ended? Maira honestly wasn't sure anymore. This was the way things were now.

Something creaked nearby and tore her from her thoughts. Maira slowed her steps. The sound had come from a side room, away from the trail of lights leading upward. She crept along the wall carefully, pistol ready in her hand. If it was one of the gunmen, she would have to place her shots carefully. The M9 wouldn't be enough to punch through their body armor on its own.

The sound came again. Maira held her breath. Something was definitely moving in the room beyond. She could hear rustling. They were searching for something. Did they have a weapon hidden in there? Or maybe they had some way to signal the rest of the Reborn?

Maira took a deep breath. She stepped out and kicked the door squarely in the center. She was not a large person, but everything here was dilapidated. The entire door tore away from the hinges and hit the ground with a crash. Maira stepped into the gap immediately, ready to shoot.

The wall had collapsed here, leaving a huge hole. She could see the gray sky and rain beyond the opening. It was momentarily dazzling. A bird shrieked at her and took flight. It fled into the outside and was gone. There was nothing else in here.

Maira sighed and lowered her weapon.

"I'm starting to think this lifestyle isn't good for me," she said.

She regretted it immediately. Her voice seemed loud against the quiet. Just because this had been nothing didn't mean there were no dangers. What was the right amount of caution? How did you maintain a balance when the world was like this? As people used to say, it wasn't paranoia when someone really was out to get you.

Maira returned to the hallway and continued up the stairs. The lights led her to a ladder to the roof. The Reborn had been far more active here. Tables were set up with computers on them. Several were on and running. Cables interconnected them and ran through the roof's access hatch. Maira was drawn to the electronics with the inevitability of a moth approaching flame.

When Maira was just a child, her father had brought a behemoth of a desktop home. He had brought the family around to look at it. This is the future, he'd said to them. Her brothers hadn't paid much attention, but Maira's imagination had been captured. She would sit in his lap while he used the device, watching avidly no matter what he was doing. It seemed like a tiny miracle, a keystroke here or a mouse click there conjuring results on the monochromatic screen.

That had been the beginning of a lifelong fascination. Maira had learned to write little games with Visual Basic. C++, Python, and more followed. The endless possibilities of the internet had fired her imagination. She had chased those dreams into the Navy and beyond, pursuing cybersecurity and a life on the digital frontier.

Then the world ended.

Computers hadn't vanished overnight, of course, but they faded into the background. Especially once the internet crumbled, there were simply more important things to worry about. Where her next meal was coming from was more important than whether wireless connectivity was available. The fascination had never died, though.

And here they were, humming their comforting electrical hum, as if nothing had happened. Maira ran fingertips across keyboards. Part of her longed to dive immediately into figuring out what exactly they were doing here. It seemed incongruous. The Reborn had a primitivist fervor to them. Why cling to these relics of the old world?

Part of it must be linked to the radio broadcast, but that didn't seem enough to explain this elaborate setup. Before she could worry about that, however, Maira decided she needed to follow the lights and cables to their end. She had a suspicion what she would find, but there was no excuse to not be thorough with this much on the line.

She climbed the ladder and pushed the hatch completely open. Rain immediately spattered on her face. The gray sky was as overcast as ever, and the storm showed no sign of relenting. Maira scrambled up and out to find herself standing on the roof. The city was laid out around here in all its decaying glory. Nearby the lake it took its name from shimmered under the clouds.

The cables ran past her and socketed into a number of things on the roof. One of them she had anticipated: the great broadcast tower that was the building's raison d'etre. That was why the Reborn had sought out this particular place, so they could salvage it. Small ones might be easy enough to jury-rig your own, but to be able to reach across hundreds of miles? Easier even now to find an antenna of that scale than to try to make one.

The other cables connected to solar panels that had been laid out on the roof. That explained how they were powering this entire operation. The panels would be of little use during low light times like the current storm, but with batteries added into the system they could keep this place running indefinitely. Was this a real glimpse of the future that Raines imagined? Or was this merely a grudging concession to need?

The answer to that might lie in what the setup was actually accomplishing. Maira climbed back down the ladder to the floor below, glad to leave the rain behind once more. The computers still hummed happily. She walked among them and spent a minute or two examining what the active ones had running.

It swiftly painted a picture of a far more sophisticated operation than she had expected. They weren't just setting up to send a few threatening radio broadcasts. This was something more long-term and involved. There were encryption programs and more. Eventually, unless she missed her guess, they would be able to take messages here, encode them, and send them out to anywhere within broadcast range. With a similar station on the other end waiting...

This was the beginning of a Reborn communications network. A system like this could broadcast anywhere in the world, depending on the conditions.

Maira sat down in a nearby chair. The idea itself was a big deal, but the implications could be even more important. If Raines was setting up something like this, she anticipated the need for communications with that kind of reach. This wasn't a matter of purging a few offensive oil drillers near her stomping grounds. It was the beginning of an empire.

Maira turned her attention back to the computers. There were already files in place, ready for use. They were encrypted, of course, but that wasn't a problem. Maira took her pack off and rummaged through it. Amidst MREs, spare clothes, and other necessities, she found the thumb drive tucked away safely.

The drive had all of her "special use" programs from her old life loaded on it. Most of the time, the little device amounted to nothing more than a keepsake of a lost past. Just occasionally, though, it came in handy. Maira socketed it into one of the computers. A few minutes of finagling later, and all the secrets the Reborn thought safe were at her disposal.

Maira paused to appreciate the moment. She had been good at this. Sometimes that was nice to remember. She turned her attention back to the files. Most of it was of limited interest right now: supply requests, propaganda broadcasts, that kind of thing.

Curious, Maira started one of the propaganda recordings.

Cassandra Raines popped up on the screen. She stood proudly, hands on her hips and chin raised. She was dressed in all green with the symbol of the Reborn marked out in silver on her chest. It seemed very on the nose to Maira, but cults had never been known for their subtlety.

"Friends, family. I am the Voice of the Reborn, Cassandra Raines, and I have come to deliver you exciting news.

"In the months we have labored together, you have learned of the rightness of our cause. You have come to understand that a new way of life is needed. Our way of life. Until now, our work has been focused inward. We have been building the foundation. But you know the truth: it is not enough for us to do what is right. Everyone must learn what you have learned. The world must be Reborn."

She paused. An offscreen crowd applauded wildly, mixed with cheers.

"Now is the time for action. We march forward into a brave future, free of the sins of the past. Not everyone will understand at first. Some will even fight us. We will save those we can, but we cannot let the recidivists stop us. We must be prepared to do anything, to fear nothing, because if we do not, we will lose everything."

Another round of applause. Maira was forced to concede it didn't sound like a track. The woman really did have these people in the palm of her hand. Cassandra turned to the side and motioned. A man joined her on the stage. Maira recognized him instantly as Raffiel. Leo was more stoic than his sibling. Raffiel was smiling broadly, obviously proud to be here.

"You will also know well by now Raffiel Fourte, one of my longest followers and most trusted advisors. Here and now, before you all, I pronounce him the Hand of the Movement. As I speak for you, he shall fight for you. He will lead our heroic forces out into the world, and his guidance will ensure they overcome all obstacles.

"We stand before you, but our efforts rest on your shoulders. Work hard. Every one of you, guardian, farmhand, or otherwise, is indispensable. Without you we fail.

"Embrace greatness! Accept nothing less! For we have seen the face of the future and have been Reborn!"

The video ended. Maira shook her head. Raines was undeniably charismatic. The Reborn were a cult of personality in many ways. They had an ideology, but she wasn't sure how many of them grasped the idea, and how many of them were just following the woman. She saved all of it to review later just in case there were hidden gems.

There were three things that held her attention for right now, however. One was a map of Freighty routes with convoys and their travel dates notated. Maira frowned at that. Vastly more worrisome, the image bore all the hallmarks of a SHD creation. That would explain how the Reborn kept catching them so completely off guard; they always knew where their enemies were going to be and when. Unfortunately, it did nothing to explain where they'd gotten the map from.

The second was a travel itinerary. It showed when and where a specific person was planned to be for the next several weeks. Included were messages that should be broadcast to that location prior to the VIP's arrival. The luminary in question? None other than Cassandra Raines, the Voice of the Future.

The last item was important – or useful, at least – only in conjunction with the second. It was nothing elaborate. What had caught her attention was who it was coming from and who it was going to. The sender was Raffiel Fourte, and the message was intended for Raines herself. The contents were a single sentence.

"I've captured a Division agent, and he has no idea about the deal you cut. Something is wrong. I will bring him to you."

Maira ran her hand over her face. This was too much to tackle alone. She queued her radio. "Colin, I think I've found something."

"Do you need me to come to you?" he asked.

"No," Maira replied. "I'll be down shortly."

She looked back to the computer, mind still racing. A new possibility occurred to her. With her current access to the system, she wasn't limited to just reading their decrypted

files. Maira could send a broadcast of her own. With ISAC's
assistance, she could very likely get a message out to the
Division. It was unlikely they'd be able to respond, but at least
she could update them as to what was going on.

It seemed well worth doing to Maira. She spent a minute
typing up a report. Part of her wanted to censor it heavily, but
she fought that urge. She wasn't motivated by security, she
just wanted to save face. She told the whole truth, instead.
Leo's capture, Yeong-Ja's injury, and their current dire straits.
She appended all the files she'd just stolen, too. At least if they
got wiped out the next cell would be better prepared.

"Maira?" Colin asked on the radio.

"Sorry," she replied. "Just a few last second tasks. On my
way soon. No worries."

Before she could second guess herself, Maira interfaced
ISAC with the system.

"Send that message to the attention of Agent Brenda Wells,"
she said. "Standard encryption, tagged high priority."

"Acknowledged," ISAC said.

It would be unlikely to get through immediately thanks to
the weather, but the program would keep trying. The only
downside to this plan was she couldn't spike the whole setup
without destroying her message. Instead, she locked the
Reborn out of their own system. As one final trick she set up
a contingency program: the whole system would wipe itself if
they did manage to regain access.

Maira had done what she could here. She rose to her feet
and retrieved her thumb drive. Once that was tucked back
into safety and her pack was back on her shoulders, she
headed down the stairs. The information she'd gathered had

more than justified this side trip. It might change the course of their entire mission in the south.

Colin waited with the prisoners out the front. He looked up as she approached and gave a relieved smile.

"You made it."

"Well, I stopped for ice cream on the way, but yeah, I'm here now," Maira quipped. She turned her head to survey the Reborn sitting on the ground. "They didn't lie."

"Yeah, we've had an interesting conversation out here. Anything worth the trouble inside?"

"We'll talk about it soon," Maira said. "Let them go."

Colin nodded and turned to the prisoners, motioning with his rifle. "Off you go."

The people stared at him in a mixture of confusion, disbelief, and fear.

"What, seriously?" a woman asked.

A sour-looking man shook his head. "It's a trap! Don't fall for it."

"A trap…?" Colin shook his head. "Are you insane? I have you on the ground, disarmed, with a gun in my hand. If I wanted to execute you, I could have done it, no problem. Instead, I'm letting you go, scot-free. Do you really want to give me a chance to change my mind?"

Hesitantly, they got up. One quickly made a break for it. When he wasn't rewarded with a shot in the back, the others followed. Soon only the woman remained. She had a frown on her face.

"You're going to keep fighting them, aren't you?" she asked.

"As long as we have to," Colin replied. "The moment they stop being a threat to others, we'll stop being a threat to them."

"I don't think she'll ever stop," the Reborn said quietly.

"You don't have to go back," Colin said. "There are other places. Other survivor groups. You can still choose a different path than the one she's on."

"She's still the one who saved my family," the woman said. She squared her shoulders. "Thank you for not killing us."

She turned and hurried away without another word. Colin watched her go and shook his head. Maira thought his shoulders slumped the slightest bit. He had a soft heart, she thought. He really did hope he could save one of them.

"I feel like being a Division agent gets people to thank you for the strangest things," Colin said.

"You're not wrong about that," Maira said. "At least it's less blood on our hands."

"I will drink to that," Colin said and got his canteen out to take a swig of water. "We should probably get on the move just in case there are more nearby they can warn."

Maira nodded and the pair of them hurried out into the rain. It was starting to thin, she thought. Maybe the storm would be over soon. Perhaps that was just wishful thinking.

"Yeong-Ja," Colin said into his radio. "You reading us?"

"Loud and clear," came the prompt reply. "How goes the expedition into enemy territory?"

"It went well," Maira replied. "Aside from the odd spot of homicide."

"On our way to you now," Colin said. He turned off his radio and studied Maira thoughtfully. "You're surprisingly chipper. What did you find that improved your frame of mind so much?"

Maira gave him a tight smile. "I'll explain in detail once

we're back with Yeong-Ja, but I think I've figured out what we need to do next."

"OK…"

They walked on a short way in silence. It swiftly became too much for Colin, however.

"Maybe give me the short version?"

"Sure," Maira said. "We need to assassinate Cassandra Raines."

CHAPTER TEN

"Every group has its leaders. That's who we target."

David had his boots up on a desk. His air of insouciance was at odds with the gravity of his words. The rest of their cell sat in other places in the abandoned office. Colin was sitting in a chair turned backward, his arms crossed against the top of the back for support.

"That's not funny," Colin said.

"I'm not joking," David said. "Have you looked outside lately?"

Colin glanced toward the window. Snow was falling again, a white curtain fluttering against the cityscape. Huge chunks of the city were dark. They had always called New York the City That Never Sleeps. Unfortunately, this wasn't just a nap. These were death throes, and they were becoming increasingly violent with every passing day.

"I've seen. I know things are bad," Colin said.

"Every day there's rioting. Worse, even. People getting dragged into the streets and burned alive because they might be carrying the virus. Lunatics dressing up in costumes and beating people senseless. It's a madhouse."

"So, your solution is to just start killing people?" Colin said sharply.

"Not randomly. I'm saying we specifically target the worst of the malefactors. The organizers, the instigators, the rabble rousers. We put them down," David said.

"What do you hope that will accomplish?" asked Jason, another of the agents.

"Two things. One, we cull the shit-starters and the rest lose their nerve. Most of these people just want to hide. It's the handful pushing them out, telling them they have to do something that are the problem. With them gone, we get quiet nights again. Two, even if someone is still feeling froggy, now they've seen an example of how it will go. Jump, and you get cut down."

Colin felt nauseous. "These are American citizens. They have rights."

"Not any more they don't. This is martial law, and we answer to nobody but the president. We can do whatever we have to. Whatever we want," David said.

"You're talking about hurting people. Killing them. You get that, right?" Colin demanded. He always knew David had been brash, but this kind of talk was appalling. In the midst of the Green Poison epidemic, it seemed people were changing, even those he now fought beside.

"You should understand better than anyone, Colin. Surgery hurts someone to save them. This is no different. These ringleaders? They're poison. They're tumors. And we have to cut them out."

"I am afraid I am not following your logic," Yeong-Ja said after they had regrouped and Maira had explained her plan.

Her voice shook Colin from his memories. He nodded, deeply relieved at Yeong-Ja's reaction. "Thank you! Maira, this isn't a solution. We can come up with a better plan."

Maira frowned at them both. "You said it yourself, Colin. Cassandra's got these people revering her like she's some kind of sacred oracle. You can't reason someone out of a belief they didn't reason themselves into. She has to be taken out of the equation."

Colin crossed his arms over his chest. Maira still had him worried. She might not have wound herself to the breaking point yet, but it seemed like that was only a matter of time. There was already something of the same feverish light to her eyes he'd seen before the battle at Groves.

"Maira, I need you to listen to yourself. Seriously, take a minute and go through what you're suggesting. Do you really want to be an assassin? To set out specifically to murder someone? We're federal agents, not a hit squad," Colin said.

"We killed the guards at the broadcast tower, didn't we?" It was a quick rejoinder, but she dropped her gaze. "Obviously, no, I don't want to kill people. But let's not pretend any of us is a pacifist."

"Killing one time doesn't mean we never have to justify it again," Colin said. "You're right, we've all taken lives. But we weren't there for the purpose of killing them. Death was never the goal."

"The authority to use extreme force must be treated as a heavy responsibility," Yeong-Ja said, and Colin remembered how she had butted heads with Maira's decisions during the events at Groves. "It is not enough to say that we can do a thing. We must always ask why, and exhaust other possibilities first."

"In the time it takes you to do that, Cassandra is only going to do more harm! I'm telling you what I saw in there. They were laying the groundwork for expansion. Even once she's wiped out the roughnecks, that's not going to be enough. She'll keep going until someone stops her. You know how many people are just barely hanging on as it is. What do you think is going to happen to them after she kicks away all the support we've put in place?"

Frustrated, Maira walked over to stand next to the boat, looking away from them.

"I could show you the video I saw in there. This shit is a cult, and Cassandra is the center. They hang on her every word. Even if she wasn't the one controlling their food, their shelter, everything, she'd still be inside their heads. She's not wrong about everything, but they're treating her like she's divine. You can't reason people out of a position they didn't reason themselves into."

"OK," Colin said and took a deep breath. "Let's say we did manage to find her and kill her. What then?"

"What then what?" Maira asked irritably. "They'll lose direction without her. We can contain the rest of them."

"Will they?" asked Yeong-Ja. "Cassandra Raines may be the one who started the Reborn, but it is a large movement now judging by what we've seen and heard."

"She's the head of the serpent," Maira said.

"Or the head of a hydra," Colin countered fiercely. "She's not the only capable leader they have. Raffiel was in charge of their invasion force, and he dealt with us handily. If she's dead, what stops him from taking charge? Or someone like him?"

Maira turned at that, brow furrowed. Her hands were

flexing again. The motion confirmed some of Colin's concerns. She was falling into a familiar behavioral pattern. They had to break this cycle somehow.

"None of them will have the same cachet she has," Maira insisted.

"Again, you cannot be certain of that," Yeong-Ja said. "We have learned much, but we do not know enough to pretend to have all the answers. It seems equally possible to me that killing Raines would make a martyr of her."

Colin nodded agreement. "What if it just kicks the hornets' nest and makes things even worse?"

"I can imagine a future where they have set aside their environmentalism for vengeance," Yeong-Ja said. "Imagine the Reborn pushing into every territory we have secured and supplied. Hunting every agent they get wind of, and punishing those who have dared to cooperate with us."

It was a grim conjecture. Colin blew out a sigh and sat down on a nearby bench. The aches and fatigue were catching up to him. One night of rest at the cabin had not been enough to recuperate. Maira, to her credit, was taking time to think about it. She frowned deeply, staring into the distance.

"All of that assumes we even succeed," Colin said wearily, his thoughts drawn inevitably back to New York.

"What?" Maira asked in surprise.

"Look at us, Maira. All of us are tired. Yeong-Ja is badly hurt. We're low on ammunition. We don't have any turrets, any drones, any fancy tricks to dazzle and confuse our enemies. If you take us into the belly of the beast…"

Yeong-Ja nodded stiffly. "The odds would not be in our favor of coming back out."

Maira licked her lips uneasily. She raised a visibly trembling hand to her forehead, her gaze still focused on the horizon. "Sometimes sacrifices have to be made."

"Does that include Leo?" Colin asked.

Her head snapped around at that. Colin felt a flicker of regret. Perhaps it was cruel to push this particular button. He buried the reaction. If nothing changed, he felt like she'd set off by herself and do something suicidal. Something had to shake her out of this.

"Leo is..." Maira swallowed hard. "He..."

"Leo is still held captive as far as we know. If we show up and try to assassinate Raines – succeed or fail – what do you think they'll do to him in turn?" Colin demanded.

Maira slid to the ground. It wasn't a graceful movement. Her legs just folded under her, and she dropped to the dirt. She sat there with an exhausted look on her face and studied her hands.

"What will they do to him if we do nothing?"

Colin moved to sit next to her. He was past caring about the wet ground that squelched underneath him. "We don't have all the answers, remember? But I promise, we aren't going to do nothing. Maybe we can negotiate for his release, or maybe we break him out. We'll figure it out."

"We have a great deal more information now than we did before. The kind of knowledge that we lacked. We should make contact with the roughnecks and share what we know," Yeong-Ja said.

"That would give us a chance to regroup and rearm, too," agreed Colin. "No matter what we do next, improving our own status will give us a higher chance of success."

Maira sat there for a while. Colin started to wonder if she had even heard what they'd said. The trauma she was carrying around had its claws in her deep. Was she going to be able to listen?

"I'm doing it again, aren't I?" Maira said quietly.

Colin felt a surge of relief. "Yeah, maybe a little. You asked us to check you, Maira. Listen to us now. Please."

Maira lifted her gaze to his and took a deep breath. "All right. We fall back to Houston and make contact with the roughnecks. We resupply and get our strength back."

Colin rested a hand on her shoulder. "Thank you."

"Indeed," Yeong-Ja said. "If you had tried to set off on a solo mission, I would have had to chase you down and bring you back. I was not looking forward to it."

Even now, Colin wasn't sure. The sniper said it so matter-of-factly that she might well have meant it seriously. He narrowed his eyes at her. One day, he would figure out if Yeong-Ja was a joker. Probably not today, though.

"All right," Colin said. "Let's load up and get out of here. And hope the boat has enough gas to actually get us where we're going."

Thankfully, the fuel tank held out on the trip along the coast back to Houston. Maira knew she should have taken the chance to rest, but it was impossible. Instead, she sat in the bow as had become her habit and watched the water whip past. The wind did feel good, at least. It was amazing how fast the fanboat could move once it got going. It ate up the miles with alacrity.

Maira's thoughts swirled just as quickly, if with far less

direction. There was part of her that still chafed at this decision. Viewed through that lens, it all seemed so painfully clear. Raines had become a threat. The only way to save the things Maira cared about – the only way to justify the things she'd already done – was to answer that threat without hesitation. Would anyone really miss Cassandra Raines?

And yet, thanks to her cell, there was just enough doubt now. The lens had cracked. What if they were right? What if all she would do with her reckless charge was get people hurt, killed, all over again? That was the pragmatic level, of course, but it went deeper than that. Maira had taken the life of Rowan O'Shea, a confirmed mass murderer and war criminal. Her face haunted Maira even so.

Did she really want to add to that? Did she really want to be followed around by the ghost of Cassandra Raines, too?

Maira sighed and pressed her face into her hands for a few seconds. The skin of her palms was rough and dirty. Even so, they blocked out the world for just a moment, and that was a blessing. Maybe she could just hide her face for a few months and let this whole thing blow over. Surely no one would mind that.

Maira let her hands drop with a snort. Even if she stole the boat and struck out for the Bahamas, she couldn't escape all of this. She couldn't run away from her problems when they came from inside her. This pain that was eating her up, the memories and the fear, she had to face it head-on sooner or later. She had to learn to live with it before it ate her alive.

For now, she needed to live in the moment. Maira turned her attention to the other two agents. For her part, Yeong-Ja had promptly gone to sleep the moment they set out. It was a feat that filled Maira with the deepest and darkest shade of green envy. Sleep had never come that easily to her, even when she had been young and carefree. Since she'd joined the Division, insomnia had become a constant companion.

Colin was piloting the fanboat, as usual. Maira wished she could take over for him. As tired as she was, he looked worse. There were dark bags under his eyes, and the starch had gone out of his spine. The fact that he had appointed himself the cell mom was not lost on Maira. Maybe they needed one. But she worried that his drive to take care of others was going to push him to his physical limits sooner rather than later.

The medic must have felt her looking at him because he glanced over. He offered her a tired smile. "Everything OK?"

Maira nodded. "As much as it can be. Are you OK?"

Colin seemed surprised by the question. It made Maira feel worse. She'd obviously been too wrapped up in her own problems lately. She was impacting the mission and letting her cell down. That would have to change now.

"I'm holding on," Colin said. "I think all of us are wearing thin. It's been a lot to deal with coming at us very quickly."

"It has," Maira agreed. "Does it help if I offer the old standby of 'one way or another, this, too, shall pass'?"

Colin grinned. "Not really, considering I would also like to live to see the other side."

"*Pff.* Now you're just asking too much," Maira said.

"I do have a problem with consistently demanding too much. It's very bothersome I'm told."

Maira laughed. "Yeah, bothersome is definitely how I would characterize you."

Colin frowned, and her laughter died. He motioned ahead

of them, and she turned to look. There was a column of smoke in the distance. Maira's heart sank immediately. That had yet to be a sign of anything good on this entire mission. Somehow, she doubted that was going to change here and now.

"Please tell me that's not Houston," Maira said. That was where they had met Rychart when they'd arrived in this area.

"It's the right direction," Colin answered grimly.

Maira stood unsteadily and went to wake Yeong-Ja. A quick shake of her shoulder, and the sniper sat up blinking.

"What? Are we in danger?"

"Not sure," Maira said. "There's smoke up ahead. Take a look through your scope, and tell me what you can see?"

Yeong-Ja nodded, and Maira got out of her way. She lifted her rifle and peered through the scope in that direction. She spent a few seconds just looking and tinkering with the settings. Maira fought the urge to impatiently hurry her. They had enough problems without her going off again.

"There is good news and bad news," Yeong-Ja said.

"Bad news first," Colin said.

"It is definitely coming from the location of the central processing facility."

Maira winced. "What about the good news?"

"The facility appears to be largely intact still. Judging by the fate of Groves, I doubt that would be the case if the Reborn had control of the area," Yeong-Ja said.

"Anything else?" Colin asked.

"Not at this distance," Yeong-Ja said.

She put her rifle back down. Maira walked back up to the bow of the boat and leaned against it to frown at the smoke.

"I guess we'll have to wait until we get there to find out what's going on."

The minutes that followed were tense. Maira felt like her brain was a rat in a maze, and even feeling that just made her worries worse. She tried to focus on pragmatic concerns, but there was nothing she could do to change them. She had one shotgun shell and one and a half magazines of 9mm bullets. Her body armor was damaged, and she had no replacement plates. So on and so forth, repeating in her thoughts.

They crossed Trinity Bay and passed Morgan's Point. The signs of fighting became clearer as they approached their destination. The facility that the roughnecks used as their headquarters was definitely damaged, but it was largely still intact. Some towers had fallen, and several buildings had collapsed. It was nothing like the apocalyptic destruction that had been visited upon Groves, however.

"What do we do?" Colin asked.

"Yeong-Ja's right. If the Reborn were here, they would have laid this place to waste," Maira said. "Take us right in."

Yeong-Ja nodded agreement. Colin did as asked, and the boat puttered toward the docks. There were the marks of a battle here, too. Bullet holes abounded, and one of the docks was sunk into the water. Yeong-Ja pointed out the side of the boat.

"Look," she said.

There were dead bodies floating in the water. Several dozen of them, in fact. Maira leaned over to try to get a better look. They were dressed as Reborn, mostly the dark-clothed enforcers. That seemed like good news on the surface. It was better that the Reborn had died in the attempt than succeeded. Even so, she couldn't shake a chill.

Someone was running down to the dock to meet them, waving their arms. Maira squinted, but she couldn't make out who it was.

"Are they waving us off?"

"I don't think so," Colin said. "I think they're just trying to get our attention."

The person was a bit stocky with a baseball cap on. They were dressed in rugged everyday wear. Recognition came to Maira as they closed in, and she stood and waved her own arms back wildly.

"Dixie!"

The boat drifted to a halt next to one of the docks, and Maira hopped off. Dixie immediately pulled her into a tight hug. His face brushed hers, and his cheeks were wet. She said nothing of it. Her own eyes were not dry.

"I thought you were dead," he said in a muffled tone before stepping back.

"There were several moments where we were pretty sure we were dead, too," Maira replied.

Colin helped Yeong-Ja onto the dock and followed behind. The sniper had to lean heavily on him to avoid putting any weight on her leg, but she managed slow progress. They both looked pleased and surprised to see the Freighty driver, too.

"I'm so glad… Where's Leo?" asked Dixie.

"Taken prisoner," Maira said. "We're going to get him back, mark my words. We came back to check in and assess the situation."

Dixie started nodding but half a second later was shaking his head. "No, can't do that. You have to get out of here."

Maira blinked. "What? Why? Dixie, what happened?"

He glanced over his shoulder worriedly. "Well, we saw that Groves was burning from a distance. None of you made contact. There was no sign of you at all. A lot of arguing followed, as I'm sure you can imagine."

Maira recalled the simmering factions among the roughnecks. "All very civil, I'm sure."

"Well, nobody got shot, that's something at least," Dixie said. "Then the scouts came back. They told us that the Reborn force that had destroyed Groves was still alive, and they were headed in this direction."

Colin flinched, immediately understanding the consequences. "These people were already terrified when we left."

"Yeah. It seemed pretty clear at that point that you'd been killed. Even if the Division somehow knew and were sending more people, they weren't going to get here in time to make a difference." Dixie grimaced. "And, well ..."

"The Molossi stepped up," Maira said quietly.

"You guessed it. Apparently, the moment he saw the smoke from Groves, the colonel sent for reinforcements. A few hundred of his closest friends showed up the next day. Georgio announced martial law."

"Under what authority?" Maira asked in surprise.

"Under the authority of 'we have a shit ton of guns and people willing to use them,'" Dixie replied. "A lot of the locals were relieved if anything. They were scared, and he said he was going to protect them."

"Can't blame them too much for that," Colin said. "The Reborn annihilated Groves. They blew the oil reserves."

Dixie nodded. "It's still burning."

"There seems to have been a battle here as well," Yeong-Ja prompted.

"Yeah," Dixie said. "The Reborn showed up in force, and there were a couple of hours of about a thousand people doing their best to kill each other."

"Since you're here and the refinery is intact, it appears the Molossi won," said Yeong-Ja.

Dixie nodded again. "It wasn't pretty, but they did. Truthfully, it was a slaughter. The Reborn weren't a match for them. It was like watching someone feed themselves into a woodchipper. Finally, the last ones ran for their lives."

"The Molossi live up to their opinion of themselves, apparently," Maira mused. "I suppose that's good news, considering."

"Better than the alternative, maybe," Dixie said. "But he hasn't released martial law either. They've spent the time since hunting down the Reborn strays."

"Any sign of Raines or Raffiel?" asked Colin.

"Raines, no. I guarantee they'd be crowing about it if they'd caught her. Who is Raffiel?" Dixie asked.

Colin shook his head. "Never mind. It would take too long to explain."

Maira frowned. "Why are they hunting down the stragglers?"

Dixie winced and rubbed the back of his neck. "They keep giving them what they call trials. In actuality they line them up, read a list of crimes, and…" He swallowed.

"Fuck," Maira said.

Colin ran a hand through his hair anxiously. "You've got to be kidding."

"I wish," Dixie said. "I tried to leave, too, and they stopped me."

"You're a prisoner?" Maira asked.

"Officially, no," Dixie said. "But they took my keys and told me my vehicle was temporarily commandeered in support of their mission here, and that they would return them soon."

Maira felt increasingly sick to her stomach. The whole situation was spiraling out of control. At this rate, the entire region would turn into a battleground. They had to do something. Or was that just her being crazy? How could she know the difference? The situation was already bad, they couldn't afford any more mistakes.

"We cannot let them continue to execute people in cold blood," Colin said flatly. "We–"

"Shit," Dixie said. He was looking over his shoulder. "Shit shit shit…"

They followed his gaze. People in black uniforms and carrying guns were approaching. Maira took half a step back. This went beyond bad. A frisson of real fear ran through her, standing her hair on end. She had no desire to end up in front of a firing squad.

"Do we run?" Maira asked. "Do we fight?"

Colin looked over the group approaching them warily. Maira tried to do the calculations in her own head. There were around ten of them, and all wore combat armor. Each one carried an assault rifle. There was no easy cover around. Even if they fled on the boat, it was fiberglass. They wouldn't make it.

Colin shook his head. "We cooperate. Maybe we can talk to the colonel. Salvage this situation somehow. It sounds like he has ended the immediate threat. If we can convince him to stop there…"

"Maybe we can keep this from becoming a bloodbath," Maira finished.

"Agent Kanhai and company. What a relief to find you alive."

The blonde woman speaking was familiar. It took Maira a few seconds to place her as one of the aides that had come to the meetings with Georgio. Her tone was cool, but not overtly hostile. The soldiers with her held their guns ready, but they did not aim them at Maira or her comrades.

Maira kept her hands well clear of her weapons. If they weren't going to make this ugly, neither was she.

"It was closer than I'd like, honestly," Maira said. "I'm afraid I didn't catch your name before."

"I am Lieutenant Colonel Patricia Clark. I'd like for you to come with me, if you'd be so kind. The colonel would like to speak to you."

It didn't feel like a request. Maira's jaw tightened.

"Cooperative," Colin said quietly.

Maira took a deep breath. "Very well. Please, lead the way."

Yeong-Ja leaned on Colin to keep the weight off her bad leg. They walked past Dixie. She could see the fear and worry writ large on his face. He seemed like he wanted to say something to her. Maira gave him a subtle shake of her head. There was no escaping him being linked to them, but they didn't need to give the Molossi any excuse to crack down on him further.

The soldiers fell in around them as they walked to the entrance of the main facility building. They didn't crowd them, but the encirclement was a statement unto itself.

Attempts to deviate from the path chosen for them would not be appreciated. There was no sign of the locals about their work. The entire place had something of the air of a ghost town. This, no doubt, was the martial law of Colonel Marcus Georgio. Everyone locked away, for their own safety of course.

They were brought into the administration section of the building. There were a number of offices here. All of them were dark save one. Maira couldn't help but notice that it was the largest of the group. Maybe it had been available, but she didn't think so. She had a feeling Georgio had promptly taken it when he seized power. She wondered where Rychart was, and hoped the man was OK.

"I'll need your weapons," Lt Col Clark said.

Maira narrowed her eyes.

Clark showed no reluctance or remorse. "They'll be returned to you when you leave."

Maira glanced at the other two. Yeong-Ja gave her a very small, reassuring smile. Colin nodded. Maira looked back to Clark and suppressed her irritation. She removed the pistol from her thigh holster and held the grip out. Clark took it, then removed the shotgun from her pack as well. Other soldiers relieved Colin and Yeong-Ja of their weapons.

"Thank you for your compliance," Clark said. It did not sound sincere. "You may enter the office."

Maira stepped inside. It was much as she'd expected in layout, a standard corporate manager working space. The trappings had changed, however. Now there were military maps and personnel charts up everywhere. This was becoming the nerve center of a war campaign. Maira couldn't hide her frown.

Colonel Georgio sat behind the desk. He was looking at documents when they came in. He only looked up once they'd arranged themselves before him. It felt like a power play to Maira. He was trying to assert the authority he'd claimed here. Unfortunately, the truth of the matter seemed to be that she didn't have the means to contest it.

"The Division agents once more, miraculously alive. Well, most of you. I see your number is reduced."

Maira gritted her teeth. She kept her voice calm. "We haven't given up on him."

"Admirable. Never leave a man behind, hmm? That must be a new policy." Georgio sat back with a creak of his chair. "So, tell me, Agent Kanhai. Why did you return here?"

She raised an eyebrow at him. "We were sent to protect this place. Once we managed to extract ourselves from the events at Groves, why wouldn't we come back?"

"'The events at Groves'. I assume you mean the disastrous defeat you suffered, after promising you could contain the threat of the Reborn?" Georgio's gaze was dark and hard. He scarcely seemed to blink.

"I admit I made hasty choices that did not obtain the best results in that confrontation. I consider it fortunate that the civilians were removed from the situation, and that the only loss was in property," Maira said.

"Yes, I'm glad they were not present to suffer the consequences of your failure," Georgio said. "Luckily for everyone, the Molossi were present to keep the Reborn from inflicting any further harm."

Maira nodded stiffly. "Yes, I heard of your victory. It sounded like you had more soldiers than you had planned to have at Groves. I'm glad you were able to make use of the additional reconnaissance time. I can only imagine how helpful they would have been if we'd stood together."

Georgio smiled. It wasn't a kind expression. "I am not one to waste any resource. I am confident we would have won regardless, but it was a relief to be able to make the victory a decisive one."

"Congratulations, then. The threat appears to be handled. When will you be standing your men down and returning to Dallas?"

It was Georgio's turn to narrow his eyes. "I have no plans to do any such thing."

"Why? With the Reborn defeated, what need is there for you to stay?"

He snorted. "I am sure you possess many skills, Agent Kanhai, but you do not have a military mind. We defeated one force. We don't know if it is within the power of the Reborn to raise another. For all we know, they could come back with ten times the numbers."

Maira shook her head. "So, you plan to stay forever, is that it? There could always be a new threat."

"I will continue to secure this region until such time as I encounter a legitimate authority to cede control to," Georgio said. The emphasis on the word "legitimate" was unmistakable. "However, do not worry. I do not plan to let the Reborn threat persist unchecked."

"What?" Maira said. "What do you mean by that?"

"Once we have policed the remainder of their forces here, we will go on the offensive. I will remove the Reborns' ability to wage war, and thereby ensure peace in this region."

The way he said it sent a shiver down Maira's spine. "How, exactly, do you plan to do such a thing?"

"As I said, you lack a military mind. I will locate their strongholds and eliminate any remaining hostile forces. If needs be, I will garrison those areas as well." The colonel said it with absolute calm.

"I've heard some of your methods in this area," Maira said. "The 'trials' you've been holding. Tell me, will those extend into your newly conquered territories?"

"Conquered territories? How dramatic."

"I call a spade a spade," she said flatly.

"Call it what you wish. I will use any means necessary to ensure that the law-abiding citizens of this region can sleep safely in their beds at night. If the only way to do that is to remind people what justice looks like, so be it." Georgio sat forward again and steepled his fingers. "You, however, will not be here to see it happen."

Maira tensed. She could feel the other two agents do the same alongside her. "And what does that mean?"

Georgio smiled with a certain dark humor. "That you will depart at your first convenience, of course. You will be released, and you will head north immediately. I already told you, agent. The Division will not be welcome in any locales under my protection."

Maira couldn't deny a moment of relief. He was not about to take them out back and shoot them in the head. That, at least, was something of a small favor. The import of his words sank in a moment later, and she stepped forward.

"We can't leave," Maira said. "The Reborn have one of our people."

"Can you be certain of that?" he asked curiously.

"We saw him captured," Colin said, apparently unwilling to leave Maira to face Georgio alone any longer.

Georgio gave the medic a look of undisguised withering contempt. "Then he is most likely dead by now. I imagine they have questioned him and disposed of him."

"Maybe, maybe not," Maira said, fighting to keep her voice even. "I refuse to give up on him."

"You are not being given a choice, agent. You will leave and return to your headquarters. Once there, you will inform the Strategic Homeland Division that any further intrusion in Molossi protectorates will be treated as hostilities and met with all due force."

Maira's hands closed into fists. Her knuckles stung. The damage was mostly healed, but the pain was still faintly there. "I can't do that."

He studied her over his joined hands. "Just to be clear, Agent Kanhai, you are refusing to depart? In absolute terms?"

Come on, Maira, she told herself. Pull this back. She was losing it again. She was going to get them killed.

Yeong-Ja spoke before she could. "We will not abandon our own to the enemy."

Colin nodded firmly. "Nor, for that matter, will we abandon the citizens of this region to your arbitrary idea of justice."

Maira glanced at them with some surprise. Colin's jaw was firm. Yeong-Ja gave her a subtle wink, as though to say, you're not always wrong. This time, all of them saw the necessity. They were going to make a stand.

"I see."

"I couldn't be there to save David," Colin said. The words

sounded like they hurt. "I won't let that happen again. Surely you can understand that?"

There was a flicker of something in Georgio's eyes. A mirror of Colin's pain, but something more. Fear? Maira couldn't place it.

"I understand very well what must be done in David's name."

The colonel's face was hard to read. There was a certain cold satisfaction to it. To Maira's surprise though, there was also an element of frustration and regret. It reminded her of his strange reaction when she'd committed to the battle at Groves. On some level he didn't want it to come to this. She wondered why, if there was more to this than met the eye.

Either way, it did not seem to impact his resolve.

"Lieutenant Colonel Clark. Please take the agents into custody."

CHAPTER 11

No sooner had the colonel spoken than the Molossi soldiers flooded into the room. Colin could see the tension in Maira's shoulders. She was half a second away from trying to punch her way out of this. He stepped close to her and lowered his voice so that only she could hear him.

"This isn't the moment. Our chance will come."

Maira glanced at him with wild eyes. He could see the struggle in her. A certain measure of calm asserted itself, and she gave him a tight nod. They were pulled apart brusquely by the soldiers, who proceeded to cuff each of the agents one by one. Colin turned his eyes on Georgio.

"If you think doing this is honoring your son, you're wrong."

The colonel's jaw tightened. Fury flashed in his eyes. It was gone as quickly as it had shown. "Leave him. Take the rest. I want to talk to him alone."

Clark frowned. "Sir, are you sure…"

"He is one man, and he is handcuffed. I will not be in any danger. Now go."

The other two agents filed out of the door. Yeong-Ja caught Colin's eye on the way out, and he gave her a slight smile. I'll be fine, he tried to convey. Within seconds they had all left and the door was shut behind them. Colin was left standing in front of the desk, facing the colonel alone.

"You are bold, I will give you that much credit," Georgio said.

"Boldness has nothing to do with it. I would be letting David down if I didn't speak up in the face of all this," Colin said sharply.

"Is that so?"

The colonel stood and walked over to the window to look out. Colin could see the fading evening light beyond him. The leftover smoke from the battle still stretched skyward. He wondered what those sights meant to the older man. Did he feel pride at having saved this place from destruction? Or was he capable of trepidation at the war to come?

"How well did you know my son?"

Colin frowned. "We fought together in New York. He was part of my cell."

"That isn't what I asked you. How well did you know him? Did he tell you about his past? Did he tell you what he wanted from his future? I have served alongside men for years and never knew them." There was a pensive tone to Georgio's voice. Colin didn't know what to make of it.

He contemplated how to answer. "There wasn't a great deal of time for personal bonding. We were activated directly into a crisis situation. Our attention was focused on what we had to do moment to moment."

Georgio nodded. "So, you did not know him well, then."

"I saw who he was in the heat of battle. I saw him put everything on the line to help people. Surely that tells me something about him," Colin said. David was part of the Division, after all. If he could have, Colin would have done everything to save him, just like his current cell would do everything to get Leo back.

"Perhaps. It is like a snapshot, wouldn't you say? No one moment can tell a whole story. There will always be … context loss."

"Are you getting at something, colonel? Because I have to admit, I'm at a loss. I don't know what you want from this conversation," Colin said.

"Clarity. I want clarity," the colonel said.

Which, of course, clarified nothing at all, noted Colin wryly. He kept the observation to himself. Directly antagonizing the man would serve no purpose whatsoever. It was wiser to keep the conversation going. If nothing else, perhaps he could gain some insight into the person who had decided to take them captive.

The colonel seemed to take his silence as acceptance. He turned to face Colin again, his gaze searching. "What if I told you he was a troubled youth? That he spent his childhood doing regrettable things?"

Colin blinked. "I don't know. What sort of things? Lots of people make bad decisions when they're young. It doesn't define who they are for the rest of their lives."

"That's true," Georgio conceded readily. "But then, there are bad decisions, and there is vicious cruelty."

"Cruelty in what form?" asked Colin.

"I truly wish I could say it only took one form, as that would be an isolated incident. He killed a neighbor's dog. Kicked its head in. He claimed it had attacked him. No one else was there to see it," the colonel said. His gaze had shifted off Colin and into the middle distance.

"That is disturbing, but—"

"That was when he was twelve. At fourteen, he broke a child's arm at school. The reasons were never clarified. David insisted it was an accident, and the hurt child agreed."

Colin shifted uncomfortably. "Is there more?"

"Oh, yes. When he was seventeen, he assaulted an old man leaving a gas station. Beat him with a bat so badly that the man lost vision in his left eye. I was told he was lucky to survive."

There was a strange tonelessness to the way the colonel laid these facts out. Colin had heard similar diction from those who had survived severe trauma. People had a way of disassociating themselves from horrible things, given time. It was a survival mechanism. Was that what was happening here?"

"That's horrible," was all Colin said aloud.

"It is. That time, of course, the victim survived. He said…" Georgio took a deep breath. His eyes focused on Colin again suddenly. There was a sharpness to the gaze, almost an anger. "He said that David had demanded his wallet. He had surrendered it, and then David attacked him anyway."

Colin flinched. Part of him didn't want to believe the man. But the stories… hadn't Colin seen the same darkness in David? Hadn't he worried? Georgio did not seem like a kind man, but he also didn't seem like a liar. "Did you believe the story?"

"There was corroborating evidence." Georgio made a dismissive gesture. "It does not matter. I was not there to do anything about it. I was not home on any of these occasions."

"What?" Colin asked.

"I was a Marine. Did you not know?" Georgio asked.

"David did mention something about following in his father's footsteps," Colin recalled. He shook his head ruefully. "So you spent your time deployed."

The colonel nodded. "I missed all but four of my son's birthdays. Quite an accomplishment, wouldn't you say? A track record to be proud of." He did not bother to hide the bitterness in his voice.

Colin studied him. "You blame yourself for the things David did."

Georgio smiled humorlessly. "As I should. If I had prioritized my family as I should have, if I had been there, then perhaps things would not have ended as they did."

"What happened?" Colin asked quietly.

"He was tried as an adult and went to prison. I was furious with him. I came and spoke to him while he was serving his time only once, and that was to tell him he was no longer my son."

Colin stared at him in surprise. "You disowned David? He never mentioned…"

"As I said, it seems you did not know him. I do know that upon release he went through the various steps necessary to join the Marines. Perhaps he hoped that in this manner he could prove himself to me." Georgio sighed and shook his head.

"You don't know?" Colin asked.

"I had broken off contact. Much of what I know now, I pieced together after New York. What happened to him there… yes, that is what motivated me to take up arms again."

Georgio locked his eyes on Colin with laser focus. "I tell you all this so you will understand: whatever you may believe, everything I do now, I do in his name."

"I'm sorry, colonel, but I don't accept that. The brutality you're engaging in, there's no excuse for it. There are better ways. Whatever mistakes your son made as a child have nothing to do with this, here and now."

Georgio frowned and looked down briefly. When he responded, however, it seemed to have no connection to what Colin had said.

"Did you see my son die, agent?"

Colin hesitated, then shook his head. "No. I saw him badly wounded, but I'm afraid I wasn't able to be with him in his final moments. I was knocked unconscious."

Georgio nodded. "I see. That, at least, makes sense."

Colin furrowed his brow. "Sir–"

"That will be enough, agent." Georgio picked a radio up off his desk. "Clark. I am done with the prisoner. You may retrieve him and place him with his comrades."

Colin tilted his head. The entire conversation made no sense to him. He wasn't sure why Georgio was disclosing all of this to anyone, much less him. Was it because they were the only ones who had known David? It didn't seem like reminiscing, though. It was like Georgio was trying to tell him something.

The door opened. It seemed he might have a lot of time to think it over in confinement.

The Molossi escorted Maira and Yeong-Ja through the building. Maira kept Yeong-Ja's arm around her neck and helped her walk. Not only did the other woman need the assistance, but it gave them an excuse to stick close to each other. Maira was on edge and knew it. She couldn't stop from eyeing each of the guards in turn, wondering if she could get a hold of one of their weapons.

"Poker face, Maira. Patience is a virtue," Yeong-Ja whispered.

"Not for Leo it's not," muttered Maira, but she nodded unhappily. "I know. No point in picking a fight we can't win."

"No talking," Clark snapped.

She was walking ahead of them. Maira narrowed her eyes and glared between her shoulder blades. If there had been any justice in the universe, she would have spontaneously gained laser eyes and carved the Molossus in half. Maira had some idea of why Georgio hated the Division, but as far as she knew this woman had no excuse.

"Enjoying yourself, lieutenant colonel?" she asked snidely.

Clark glanced back and glowered. "What, you think I want to have to frog-march you idiots around? We have actual important things to be taking care of, but here you are wasting our time."

"Ah yes, your glorious war. Do you know who the people you're killing are?"

"Traitors and terrorists," Clark said flatly.

"Convenient labels," Maira said. "Actually? They're desperate people from areas devastated by the Poison and natural disasters. Ordinary civilians who turned to Raines because she was the only one there in their hour of need."

"How sad," Clark said disinterestedly. "In my experience, everyone has a sob story, Agent Kanhai. That's no excuse for the things they've done."

"Of course it's not!" Maira barked. One of the soldiers turned his head toward her, and she struggled to restrain her anger. "It's no excuse for yours either. You think compounding their crimes with your mass executions and total war bullshit is going to make things better?"

"We didn't start this war," Clark said. "We will, however, finish it."

"And how much blood will be on your hands before you decide it's done?" Maira asked fiercely. "I know I'm tired of how much I have on mine."

"That's because you're weak."

They had reached the room where they'd stayed previously. One of the soldiers opened the door. Maira and Yeong-Ja were pushed inside. Yeong-Ja nearly fell, but Maira was able to stabilize her. Maira whirled back to glare at them.

"Being reluctant to kill doesn't make me weak. Being eager to kill doesn't make you strong."

"Tell yourself whatever you like," Clark said. "At the end of the day, you had your chance to do things your way, and you failed. Lucky for you, we're here to clean up your mess." She turned to the soldiers. "You two. Stay here. Lock the door. If either of them tries to leave, shoot them."

They shut the door. Maira stood there, furious and breathing hard.

"Goddamn them," she said.

The room was as simple as they'd first found it. All the gear and supplies they'd left behind had been confiscated, but the Node was still up and running in the corner, which surprised Maira.

Maira helped Yeong-Ja over to a bed to sit down. The sniper

looked tired, her face drawn with pain. Maira crouched in front of her, concerned.

"Are you all right?"

"Moving around like this, even with help, is painful. It is of no great concern. I will manage," Yeong-Ja said.

"Maybe that will be the bright side to all of this. We'll sit in here for a few months, and you'll heal up," Maira said.

Yeong-Ja snorted. "I believe you would say 'like hell'. We have work to do, and I will not be what stops us, I assure you."

Maira smiled and patted her good leg. "I'm glad you're along for the ride."

"Strangely, even with all that has happened, so am I. I want to rescue Leo. Not because that is the mission, but because I want to. That's… It is nice."

"At this point we have a lot of reasons to need to get out of here. It's like everyone has gone crazy." Maira stood and paced around the room restlessly. "Would have been nice of them to leave us at least one crate of toys to blast our way out with."

"Unfortunately, we are not lucky enough for them to be that stupid," Yeong-Ja said.

"ISAC," Maira said. "Any connection to Kansas available? Or to any Division safe house or cell, for that matter."

"Processing request," the AI said.

"Sooner or later the Division will send someone else," mused Yeong-Ja.

"I'm just worried about that later possibility," Maira said. "I'd rather they didn't show up to find nothing but scorched earth and dead agents."

"No connection detected," ISAC said.

"Shit," Maira said. She sat down on her bed wearily. "Any brilliant ideas?"

"You will be the first to know if I devise anything clever," Yeong-Ja assured her.

"I hope Colin is OK," Maira said after a moment.

"I don't think the colonel will hurt him. If he's going to execute us, he'll want to make a spectacle of it."

"I'm not sure that was as comforting as you wanted it to be," Maira said.

"My apologies. I've never been very good at telling people pleasant lies," Yeong-Ja said.

The door opened. Maira sat up straight. Her hand automatically went to her empty holster at her thigh, and she glowered as her fingers closed on nothing. Colin was shoved through a second later. He was no worse for wear, to Maira's relief. He glanced back with irritation as the door slammed behind him.

"I told you he would be all right," Yeong-Ja said.

"Yeah, because you said they wanted to kill us flashily later," Maira said. She looked at Colin. "You are OK, right?"

"Yeah, they didn't do anything to me," he said.

Maira looked him over just to be sure. He did indeed appear intact. Barring the tiny bruises, cuts, and scrapes all of them had accumulated, that is. His expression, though, was concerned. His brow was furrowed, and his lips pressed into a thin line.

"I kind of thought he was going to beat your face in for being a smart ass," Maira said.

Colin shook his head in confusion. "He just wanted to talk for some reason."

"About what?" Maira asked in surprise.

"About David."

Colin went and sat on his own bed. He scrubbed a hand over his face wearily. His entire posture spoke of exhaustion at this point. Maira watched him in concern.

"Was it to blame you for what happened?"

"Not that either, surprisingly," Colin said. "I don't know. It was like he was trying to tell me something, but he couldn't get the words out. He just kept going on about how I'd never really known David, because I didn't know all the messed-up things he'd done."

"Not a knight in shining armor after all?" Maira asked.

Colin shrugged. "Who really is? I knew him for a short time, but he was brave during it. I'd like to think I saw the good in him."

He seemed like he was holding back. Maira didn't have it in her to demand the truth. They had all been through so much. Who was she to claw at old wounds?

"Was that all?" Yeong-Ja asked.

Colin shook his head. "At the end he asked if I was with David when he died. I had to say I wasn't."

"Maybe he just wanted to think someone was there," Maira said. "I can understand that."

"Maybe," Colin said.

"We may as well rest while we can," Yeong-Ja said. "I think we all need it, and it would be wise to be at our best should the time for action arrive."

"I don't know if we're punching our way out of this one," Colin said.

Neither of them had a good response to that. Each of them

stretched out. Maira lay on her back for a few minutes staring at the ceiling. There was a vent up there. If this had been any proper universe, she told herself, we could climb through that and escape in a daring manner. Unfortunately, it was the size of a cat rather than the size of a human.

Sleep claimed her before she could think more.

Maira woke to the sound of raised voices outside their door. She lifted her head, bewildered. One of the voices, though muffled, was familiar. There were no weapons to get ready. Maira climbed out of bed uneasily. The other two agents were stirring as well. If she had to, she was going to go down swinging her fists. She promised herself that.

Suddenly there was an odd *fwump* noise outside the door. Maira took a step back in confusion. The door burst open, to reveal none other than Dixie Dog standing in the frame. His eyes were wide with some combination of exhilaration and terror. The Molossi guarding them were behind him, ensnared in some strange, hardened foam.

"I can't believe that worked," he said.

"What?" Maira asked.

"I grabbed one when they came for y'all's stuff! It was a crate that said riot foam grenades. And, like, I could kind of picture that, but at the same time I wasn't a hundred percent on what it would do," Dixie rambled.

Maira blinked rapidly. "What?" She paused. "No, what?"

"Whatever this is, let's not waste it," Colin said and hurried past her.

Maira couldn't deny the wisdom of that. She turned to help Yeong-Ja limp out of the room. The two guards were firmly ensconced in the grenade material. They couldn't even struggle as far as she could tell. She couldn't help but laugh at the sight.

One of their handguns was held in the guard's hand – he must have been menacing Dixie with it when everything happened. Colin crouched next to him and carefully plucked it from his grasp.

"Thanks," Colin said.

The guy made muffled angry noises. Colin checked the chamber and then nodded to them.

"We need to move, like, real fast," Dixie said. "Sooner or later someone's going to walk through, and this is pretty noticeable."

"OK, how are we getting out of here?" asked Maira.

"I've got your boat all ready to go. Refueled it on the sly earlier today. If we can get it going with a head start, you should be good to escape," Dixie said.

"Hot damn," Maira said. "You really outdid yourself this time, buddy."

"A remarkable effort," agreed Yeong-Ja.

Dixie blushed. "Well… hell. Just remember to rate me five stars on Yelp when you get a chance, all right?" He grinned and motioned. "C'mon!"

They hurried through the building. They could only move so quickly thanks to Yeong-Ja's injury, but thankfully the area was just as deserted as earlier in the day. The entire way to the front of the building, Maira kept waiting for the shout behind them. That, or would they just open fire? She itched anticipating the bullet she wouldn't see coming.

Voices came from ahead of them instead. They slowed,

and Colin crept forward to get a better look. He flashed hand signals back to them in rapid succession. Two guards, facing outward. One to each side of the door on the outside. That made sense. Maira assumed there would be other lookouts posted around as well, but they'd just have to do their best.

Colin gestured a suggestion: a silent takedown of both. Maira nodded and gently handed Yeong-Ja off to Dixie. He supported her with an expression somewhere between embarrassment and terror. Maira couldn't suppress a grin as she turned back to the door. She put it out of her mind. There was work to do.

Maira slipped up next to Colin, and they advanced as quietly as they could. The guards were making idle chitchat with each other as they approached.

"–not convinced that it was the right choice, is all."

"How can you not be convinced? It's the M16. What else are we going to use?"

"Well, AKs, obviously."

Maira silently willed them to keep on. Don't look back. Don't pay any attention. Any threats will come from the outside, she tried to send telepathically.

"OK, smart guy. Leaving aside the issues of supply and logistics, why would we do that? You want us to use an objectively inferior weapon?"

"I don't agree they're objectively inferior. For one thing, rate of fire. Fully automatic–"

Colin motioned that he was ready. Maira nodded. Five seconds, she held up. Counting now.

"In exchange for a loss of muzzle velocity and inferior range! It's not worth it."

"If you look at the math–"

Maira leapt on her target's back as Colin lunged to the side. She put her arms around his neck in a sleeper hold. The Molossus started thrashing desperately in terror. He beat her against the wall over and over again. Each time, lights flashed in front of Maira's eyes and the air was driven from her lungs. Maira clung to him with all the tenacity of a starving tick.

The guard weakened rapidly from there. He slid to the ground and with a raspy grumble lost consciousness. Maira held him for a few more seconds just to be sure. Then she released him and stood with a wince. She wouldn't be surprised if she had a bruised rib from that. Colin was standing over his own target, and he gave her a thumbs up.

Maira shook her head down at the two Molossi. "Fucking morons."

She plucked the two M16s from the ground. Each one had a full mag with a round in the chamber. Their situation was improving by the minute. At least now they could actually shoot back if someone tried to kill them. Yeong-Ja hobbled up leaning on Dixie, and Maira handed her one of the rifles.

They hastened the rest of the way to the docks. The boat was where they'd left it, and thanks to Dixie they were all set for a new voyage. Colin and Maira worked together to get Yeong-Ja on board. Colin climbed in as well. Maira turned to Dixie.

"All right, let's go, man. We owe you one for this."

Dixie gave her a broad grin. "Let's be real, you owe me way more than one at this point. But I'm not going with you."

"Dixie, these people aren't fucking around. They will kill you if they find half an excuse."

"They still have my rig, Maira. I'm not leaving without it," Dixie said.

Maira stared at him. "That's crazy. Get in the damn boat."

"I'm a Freighty, Maira. You know how you need to go save Leo? Well, I'm not losing my truck. You know that supply route you're fighting for? The trucks are what make it happen. People aren't making more of them. But go! You're wasting time, and you need to have already been gone," Dixie said.

As if on cue, there was a shout from back in the direction of the facility. Maira looked that way anxiously. Lights were coming on in the building. Someone had discovered something. Dixie was right, they were out of time and then some.

"Shit. Be careful, man. If you die, I'm going to kill you."

Dixie waved it off. "I'll be fine! Good luck."

Maira scrambled onto the boat. Colin started the engine immediately. It pushed the water away from the boat in waves. They sloshed against the docks, then pulled away. From there they picked up speed quickly. Maira glanced back one time, worried. Figures were pouring on to the docks. Dixie was already nowhere to be seen. She smiled a little. He was smart enough to not be linked to their escape.

He'll be OK, she told herself. He has to be. And if not, well, we'll come back and save him, too.

Once they were several miles away from Houston, Colin killed the engine and left them drifting on the water. Waves could be heard slapping against the boat, which rocked gently. Both of the women looked at him with questioning expressions.

"It seems like we made it. At least, I think if they had pursuit boats or something we'd have seen them by now. So now, well…" Colin said.

"Now we need to figure out what our plan is," Yeong-Ja said.

Maira took a deep breath. "Rather than suggest that we all lemming ourselves off the nearest cliff, I'm prepared to hear both of your ideas. What do we do?"

Colin made a face and scratched his jaw. "I think…"

"Don't be shy," Maira said. "You can't come out with anything worse than I've managed so far."

"I think we're going to have to do something very stupid. Something that will, even in the context of this mission, qualify as not one of our best ideas," Colin said.

Yeong-Ja raised an eyebrow. "I have my own thoughts on the matter, but I'm not ready to lay my cards on the table. You go first."

Colin took a deep breath. "Well. Maira, I know how you're going to react to this, but hear me out. I think we need to figure out where Cassandra Raines is and go there."

Maira stared at him. "You have got to be kidding me."

"I agree, actually," Yeong-Ja said.

Maira sat there silently for several seconds. Colin could see the entire gamut of emotions run across her face. Frustration, anger, even amusement. She scrubbed her hands on her face vigorously for a few seconds.

"I'm going to throttle you both," she said.

"That's fair," Colin said. "But in fairness to us, the situation has changed. Or rather, what we know has changed."

Yeong-Ja nodded. "The fact that the Molossi plan on pursuing a strategy of total war against the Reborn, including invading their compounds and policing their population… it changes things dramatically."

"OK," Maira said. "Let's say that I let you guys talk me back into what you talked me out of. Why are we going there? Are we eliminating her?"

"In all truth, it may now be necessary," Colin said. "If Georgio spoke true – and I don't think he's a liar whatever else he is – then Cassandra has refused to surrender. From what we know of her, it fits the profile. She's an ideological diehard. She'll fight to the end."

"If she is, in fact, refusing to stop her invasion… if she is prepared to drag her faction into annihilation rather than face defeat… then we don't have a choice," Yeong-Ja said. "We have to prevent the slaughter between the Molossi and the Reborn."

Maira sighed quietly. "I have to admit, I was hoping it wasn't going to come back around to this. Once you had me questioning it, I hated the idea more and more." She paused. "It's funny, I once demanded Brenda tell me if she'd dragged me along on an assassination mission. I was so angry."

"It's a grim thing to contemplate. I'm still hoping that another option will present itself," Yeong-Ja said. "That is a small difference at least; I still suggest we be extremely thorough in our approach. See what hand we're dealt, then decide how to play it."

Colin nodded. "I'm happy to agree to that."

"Me, too," Maira said. "There is something else to consider, though. We know that Raffiel was bringing Leo directly to her. Judging by the fact that the Molossi didn't have Leo, he must have left the force to do that. So, if we go where she is, we have a chance of finding Leo there as well."

"Absolutely," Colin agreed. "If he is on location, that's our top priority. We'll get him out and figure out our next move after."

Maira took a deep breath. "All right. We've got two rifles, a handgun, no backup, no tricks, and a tankful of gas. Let's go."

CHAPTER 12

"Are we sure this is the camp she's going to be at?" asked Colin.

Maira shrugged. "It is according to the information I pulled from their system at Lake Charles. Beyond that, who knows? If they've realized we hit that place, they may have changed their plans."

"It hasn't actually been a long time," Yeong-Ja said. "A lot has happened, but our foes are not supernatural. They're not any more omniscient than we are. It'll take time for them to learn things and react to them. Our chances are still good."

Colin nodded and steered the boat in toward the coast. They were lucky in that the Reborn camps had been established as far from population centers as possible. It made sense, Maira supposed. They were not actually a product of the Green Poison. Raines had been establishing them years beforehand, when having such a thing close to a city would have drawn a lot of unwelcome attention to her operations.

It had taken them until the afternoon to get the boat to this point. Once they got onto land, they would only be a short way away from the camp itself. Maira was intensely curious as to what they would find there. Even now she found Raines's mindset a curious thing. What sort of life was she providing to these people who had gathered around her?

The boat slid up onto the coast. Colin killed the engine, and the group climbed out onto mucky ground. Mud squelched under Maira's boots. She was glad she wasn't wearing any kind of loose footwear. Terrain like this would have snatched it off in an instant. She turned to help Yeong-Ja onto the ground.

They had stopped at a wooded area on their way here and gotten a long branch. With that they had been able to fashion a makeshift crutch for Yeong-Ja. She still needed their help, of course, but she was better off than she had been. It gave her a certain limited mobility without needing someone to lean on all the time.

The sniper flashed Maira a friendly smile once they had her on her feet. The trio set out inland. The sun was overhead, and this place had a high water table just like so many locales in this region. An abundance of stagnant water had mosquitoes and other insects out in huge swarms. There wasn't a lot they could do to get rid of the irritating situation. Maira did her best to put them out of her mind. Her success was limited.

"I am really starting to hate swamps, marshes, and any other type of wetland that we may or may not be traversing," Maira said.

"They're not what I would call the most hospitable locales in the world, no," Colin agreed.

He slapped his neck and winced as he spoke. Maira was starting to question whether she was actually going to make it to their destination with any blood left in her veins. That would be quite the epitaph on this whole adventure, she mused. The cell had braved gunfights, imprisonment, fire, and injury only to be overcome by the world's hungriest mosquitoes.

"We'd make a pretty good tourist attraction," she said.

Colin gave her a curious look.

"Oh. Uh. Sorry, I guess you missed most of that thought train," Maira said.

"Leo did warn me that you were a talker," Colin said.

"Me, too," Yeong-Ja said.

Maira blinked at them. "I beg your pardon? He warned both of you that I am a 'talker'? When, exactly, did that happen?"

"Oh, it happened separately," Colin said. "He told me on my way into the briefing."

"Yes, he caught me upon my arrival and pulled me aside. Said he had to warn me," Yeong-Ja said.

Maira frowned at them. "You are both fucking with me."

Colin held up three fingers solemnly. "Scout's honor."

"I have never told a joke," Yeong-Ja said.

Colin turned to stare at her when she said that. Maira felt her own eyebrows go up against her will.

"There's no way that's true," Maira said. "I have definitely heard you tell at least one joke."

"Prove it," Yeong-Ja said. "I would like you to cite what I said and when."

Maira was flustered. "I haven't been keeping a journal or anything. I don't have that information at my fingertips."

"Ah, then I suppose you'll have to fold this hand, won't you?" Yeong-Ja declared with satisfaction.

"I don't know. What I do know is, never play cards with her," Colin said.

"I resent the implication of that," Yeong-Ja said.

"Is she a cheater?" Maira asked.

"I would like proof if you make that accusation as well," Yeong-Ja said primly.

"Proof I do not have," Colin allowed. "Nevertheless, I don't need to see a legless body to know better than to go swimming with sharks."

Maira laughed. "He's got a point."

"I see no reason to concede anything in this conversation," Yeong-Ja said.

Maira was impressed that the sniper seemed only slightly out of breath. Between her leg, her height, and the wet ground, she was having to work much harder than both of them were to stay moving. Maira kept an eye on her nonetheless, ready to step in whenever she needed help. Occasionally the crutch did get stuck in the mud, and Maira had to assist with pulling it loose lest Yeong-Ja topple into the slime herself.

They continued on. The ground, blessedly, started to firm up some. Maira took the first opportunity to wipe goop off the bottom of her boots. It was making her footing unsteady. All she needed was to get into a firefight and do a half gainer because her feet slipped right from under her while she was on the run.

"I know you don't have your rifle anymore," Maira said. "But what kind of shot do you think you could pull off with the M16?"

Yeong-Ja frowned. "There is no substitute for proper equipment. I fully believe I could land a shot a mile away, but seeing my target at that distance would be problematic."

"I'm still impressed by your confidence," Colin said.

"It may end up being our best bet at taking her down even so," Maira said.

"If it's necessary," Colin said. "Like we said on the boat, let's not just commit wholesale to assassination before we exhaust every option."

"Of course," Maira agreed hastily. "I promise, I'm not off the deep end again. I'm just trying to think ahead."

"Speaking of ahead, I believe I've spotted our destination," Yeong-Ja said.

They pulled up out of respect for her keen eyes. Maira searched the horizon herself. It took her a moment, but there did indeed seem to be structures at the very edge of what she could spot. She flexed her hands uneasily. The pain focused her thoughts. The Reborn might have been butchered at the hands of the Molossi, but it didn't make them any less dangerous to three battered agents on their own.

"So how do we approach this?" Maira asked.

"Carefully," Yeong-Ja said.

Colin retrieved some binoculars from his pack and spent a few seconds looking the area over. Then he handed them to Maira. She peered through. Unsurprisingly, the binoculars helped a lot. Buildings sprang into focus, and people among them. Maira swept her gaze slowly across the area, collecting as much information as she could.

She wasn't sure exactly what she had been expecting. There were a lot of mixed images in her mind at this point. Something medieval? Something Amish? Something weird and otherworldly to line up with a compelling vision of the future? In the end, it was none of these. The camp reminded

Maira of nothing so much as the mid-1900s fortifications she'd seen in history books.

Most of the buildings were concrete. There was nothing beautiful about them. Each one was just a squat gray box. At this distance there was no discerning what purposes they served. There was nothing to set them apart. The other few looked more like shantytown constructions, all plywood and scrap. Perhaps they had been set up to absorb overpopulation, Maira wondered. There was no way to be sure.

The vast majority of the people visible had all their energy focused on one thing: agriculture. The grounds around the community had obviously been dedicated wholesale to growing crops, and people were tending those fields en masse. Some appeared to be harvesting crops, some were planting new ones. Maira knew next to nothing about farming, so the specifics were lost on her. What she did know was that she could easily see more than two hundred people working just from this vantage point.

An interesting caveat to that was the dearth of the enforcer types they had encountered at other Reborn locations. She did spot a couple. A few were keeping a watch on the fields. Others were walking around in the heart of the community. It couldn't have been more than two dozen of them in total from what she could see. That was a relief on one level, but a worry on another.

"Not a lot of their gunmen around," Maira said.

She handed the binoculars in turn to Yeong-Ja. The sniper nodded once she had finished her own lingering examination.

"It does seem to be surprisingly few of them. Any guesses what that might mean?"

Maira held up three fingers and counted down her ideas. "One, they don't police their populations as closely as I thought they did. Two, they stripped their garrisons to supply the military force we encountered at Groves. Three, they're here, they're just all hanging out somewhere we can't see them. Inside one of those buildings maybe."

"It would make sense there's at least a few more in a barracks somewhere," observed Colin.

"Sure, so let's say offhand there are at least half as many again as we can see. That still would put us at less than forty," Maira said.

"Forty is plenty to kill us and have a second shift available to dig our graves," said Colin wryly.

"Yes," Yeong-Ja said thoughtfully. "It is not, however, enough to keep an eye on the perimeter of this entire place. One other thing I noticed is that not all of them are wearing the homespun. It isn't a uniform."

"Yeah, I think it's more pragmatic than that," Maira said. "They must just replace clothes as they get worn out."

"And after all, we are past the age of mass media," Yeong-Ja said. "It is not as though they have wanted posters with our faces down there."

Colin looked between them. "You're suggesting we go down there and investigate in person?"

"There are hundreds of people here, maybe thousands," Maira said. "There's no way they know everybody on sight. So yeah, I think that if we are serious about trying to find a solution other than killing Raines, we need to get down there."

"I was just really hoping not to die today," Colin said wistfully.

"No one chooses the day they will pass," said Yeong-Ja. "All we can choose is the manner in which we face it."

"That is exceedingly deep," Maira said. "I'm gonna be thinking about that one for a while."

"I got it off the side of a bathroom stall," Yeong-Ja said.

"See, that has to be a joke," Colin said immediately.

"Prove it," Yeong-Ja replied.

Colin waved her off. "Bah. At any rate, that will mean ditching our gear. Everything. We can't exactly wander around with rifles and ISAC bricks and hope not to draw attention. We go in there geared up, we're starting a firefight. If we want to avoid killing, we don't have a choice."

Maira nodded. "You're right. We'll hide our gear out here and come back for it later. Come on. Let's mosey on into town, what do you say?"

It was one thing, Colin thought, to say they were going to do something. It was quite another to actually have to do it. He was fully ready to admit that he was not excited to give up the pistol he had gotten in Houston. That brief stint in Molossi custody, unarmed and helpless, was not something he wanted to repeat. Still, the essence of their job lay in doing what had to be done.

They walked toward the town, carefully easing toward the least populated areas so as to draw minimal attention on their approach. It was going to demand something of a careful balancing act, Colin said to himself. On the way in or out, they needed nobody looking. But as quickly as possible once there they needed to just be part of the crowd. In both cases, whatever would draw the least attention to them would be best.

The fields definitely had a scent to them. That scent was manure. They must be keeping animals as well. It would only be smart then to turn around and fertilize the fields with the waste. Colin eyed the various buildings. Was one or more of them a barn, then? Cows? Goats? Sheep? He supposed it didn't matter to their own objectives here.

"Hey!"

The voice rang out as they neared the center of the community. Colin tensed. He saw a flash of his own fear mirrored in Maira's eyes. In spite of their hopes and best efforts, it hadn't taken them long to get spotted after all.

"We make a run for it on my signal," Maira said softly, for their ears alone.

Colin turned to face the person who had called out to them. It was one of the enforcers. She didn't seem to be in any hurry, strolling over toward them. Even so, she had a rifle worn on a strap and held across her body. If they bolted, it felt painfully certain they were just going to get bullets in the back for their efforts.

He noticed a frown on Yeong-Ja's face. "What is it?"

"Her rifle. It is a FN SCAR-H. That is an unusual weapon," Yeong-Ja replied. "Many of them carry such odd models. I would have expected to see more military surplus, perhaps."

"We never did find out where they're getting all these armaments from," Maira muttered. "The tools, sure, fine, well enough. A lot of the guns, maybe they bought them before the Green Poison hit or stole them after. But they have things like RPGs and C4, too."

"It is definitely weird," Colin said.

"It's a mystery," Maira said. "And I don't like that."

The woman was close enough now that they had to let their conversation die out. Instead, they waited for her to approach. Colin wondered if he could take her down in a grapple. The idea died instantly with a look around. There were tons of people in sight now. Anything unusual they did would draw attention.

Colin put on what he hoped was his most charming smile. "What can we do for you?"

The Reborn guard looked them over carefully. Colin knew his smile was fading in spite of himself. His eyes kept darting to that gun. I'm about to get us killed, he thought. She is going to paint these fields with our brains and then we'll just be fertilizer, too.

"You folks coming off a work shift in the fields?"

Colin experienced a sudden moment of absolute clarity. He saw them through her eyes. This was not a threatening assemblage. Three people, one of them injured. All of them covered in sweat and bug bites and utterly filthy. His fear evaporated in a heartbeat.

"Yeah," he said. "We are worn the hell out, to be honest."

"Good of you to be out there working with that bum leg. Takes all of us pulling together to make this place work. I'm always glad to see newbies embrace the spirit," the guard replied.

Yeong-Ja nodded politely. "I am always delighted to be of service. As you said, we must all work together for the common good."

"Attaway. Well, if y'all have worked up an appetite, you should head over to the mess. They have some leftovers from lunch, I'm pretty sure."

Colin glanced at the others. "That is… an excellent idea. Thank you so much. That will be where we head."

The woman nodded. "Pleasure. I'll see y'all around."

The trio of agents continued on their way. Once they had managed to get out of hearing distance of the guard, Colin let out a low whistle.

"I nearly blew that for us by being afraid it was already blown, I think," he said.

Maira blinked at him. "That was quite a sentence. Do you think you could say that three times fast?"

"Smart ass," Colin replied. "At any rate, I think the mess she mentioned may actually be a great idea. People love to gossip over food, and that could contain the information that we need."

"This place is not what I expected, if I am honest," said Yeong-Ja.

"No," Colin said with a look around. "It could be nice here, as long as this is the life you want and choose. The problem is, of course, that in the end, Raines doesn't plan to give people a choice."

The mess hall was a large concrete building. It had windows, on close examination. Or, to be accurate, it had holes in its walls. There was no glass. Maira wondered if that was some sort of statement.

The sunlight coming through the gaps kept the interior from being as crushingly depressing as it might have been otherwise. Everything was just concrete. Walls, ceiling, floors. It was bare. No decoration, no comfort. The actual dining hall took up most of the building. The back area was closed off, presumably a kitchen or storage or both.

The tables, at least, were wood, even if they were still rudimentary things. Several of them ran the length of the chamber, with benches alongside to act as seating. At the far end another table had been set up perpendicular to the others, this time to act as a serving area. Maira could see the immense bowls and platters from here.

The chamber was only about a third occupied. A few people sat off by themselves. Most, however, were gathered in groups here or there. They ate and talked and laughed, the same as she would expect a gathering of people to do in any environment. It made her sad, obscurely. These really were the same people as anywhere. The bloodshed was all such a stupid waste.

In all honesty, though, it actually smelled pretty good here. She supposed that was fair. These people were devoting massive efforts to agriculture. They would at least enjoy the fruits of that labor, often the literal ones. The food would be fresh and plentiful. In that regard, they were better off than a significant number of the survivor enclaves that Maira had encountered. Some day she hoped that all the enclaves they knew could be so self-sufficient.

"We should probably eat," Maira said. "You know, for the sake of blending in."

Yeong-Ja nodded solemnly. "Our cover is very important. It'd be dumb to avoid it and would draw too much attention."

Colin shrugged. "I'm not going to argue. I'm hungry. Let's eat."

They walked together to the end of the room. The food provided was simple fare, but Maira didn't consider that a mark against it. Peas, carrots, fava beans, asparagus, radishes, artichokes … it was a vegetable cornucopia the likes of which she hadn't seen since the Green Poison hit. There was even honey-tossed rhubarb as a dessert. They must keep bees somewhere nearby, or perhaps at a different camp. Her mouth was suddenly full of saliva to a rather embarrassing extent.

Each of them filled a plate. Maira searched the room for a likely group. One in particular was engaged in lively chatter. She led the other agents toward that one. They settled in at the edges and received a few amiable nods at their presence. Maira immediately took a mouthful of food, but she kept listening as she ate.

"He shouldn't have said it, it's that simple." This speaker was a burly, bearded man.

"It is his job to advise her. If he hadn't, he would have been derelict in his duties." A thin woman with a prominent nose was the one arguing with him.

There was a pause that seemed like a good chance to jump in. Maira hastily swallowed so that she didn't spray half-chewed vegetables across the table by asking a question. "What's all this?"

They turned to look at her in surprise. For a moment she wondered if she'd made a critical error in speaking up at all. It wouldn't be the first time that her mouth got her in trouble.

"You must be new here," the man said.

"Oh, yeah," Maira nodded rapidly. "The three of us just came in from New Orleans last night."

"Well, I'm glad to hear there are people there still coming to their senses," the man said proudly.

"At any rate, the subject at hand is the rather swift fall of the Voice's right hand," the woman said.

Colin made significant eye contact with Maira at that. She nodded. It seemed very likely they knew who "the Voice's right hand" was. They had definitely snared an interesting topic.

"A well-deserved fall," the bearded man clarified.

The thin woman sniffed. "All he said was that we would be wise to seek peace terms, considering–"

"Fah!" the man growled. "One defeat and he was ready to give up. Make peace? These people are at war with the Earth itself. What's there to make peace with?"

Maira had by now eaten half her plate. She had few regrets. "The Hand... I think I've heard of him. Raffiel Fourte?"

"The one and only," the woman said admiringly.

"His brother was a Division agent, but was working with the enemy," the man said significantly. "It makes sense Raffiel wasn't as committed to the cause as he pretended to be. Cassandra knew this, despite Raffiel's position in our community."

"You can't judge someone by their relatives," the woman muttered.

"And he wanted to make peace with those roughnecks?" Maira said.

"Yes, exactly!" declared the man, banging on the table. "See, even the newbie gets it! We're not judging him by his relatives, we're judging him by his decisions."

"I just believe that imprisoning him may have been an extreme resolution," the woman said.

"Well, keep your opinions to yourself, unless you want to join him," the man said. "You know there's no room for malcontents."

The woman looked around nervously. "My loyalty to the cause and to the Voice are absolute. I certainly didn't mean to suggest otherwise at all. Of course it's her decision in the end."

The conversation seemed likely to die out at that point. Maira finished up the rest of her plate. She noticed the other two agents had as well. She ate the last bite of rhubarb with a soft sigh of regret.

"So, uh, what's going to happen to the Hand now?" Maira asked.

"Oh, he'll be shipped to the prison camp for re-education, obviously," the man said with a shrug. "Him and his brother both."

Leo, Maira thought. She glanced at the other agents and saw similar thoughts in their expressions. They rose, their meal finished, and deposited their plates in a communal tub where the dirty ones were gathered to be cleaned. From there the three Division agents hurried outside to where they could talk without any risk of being overheard.

"So, Raines is here," Maira said. "We confirmed that. She could be in any one of these buildings."

"That's true," Colin said. "But now we know Leo is indeed here, too. Like I said on the way, that means our priority is saving him now."

Yeong-Ja shook her head slightly. "This place disturbs me. It seems so pleasant, and there are obvious benefits to their lifestyle. Then you hear of the authoritarian judgments handed down, and there is talk of arbitrary punishment for contrary opinions."

"And a re-education camp," Maira said grimly. "You're

right, obviously. I'll be damned if I let Leo end up in a place like that."

"The actual taking him there seems like a good opportunity, though," Colin pointed out. "Do we know where this 'prison camp' is?"

Maira pondered. "I imagine we can figure it out. If we get back to our gear, I still have all those files. I can access them on the tablet, and we can parse out a layout of their camps. Something there will give it away, I think."

Colin nodded. "So we figure out where they're going to take him. Then we watch the route there carefully. We wait until they're good and clear of this or any other camp or large gathering, and that's when we hit them. No matter how heavily they guard him, it can't be as many as they'll have in total here or there."

"It's our best chance of actually rescuing him," Maira agreed.

She couldn't help but feel more hopeful than she had since the destruction at Groves. It was a tremendous relief. Leo was not dead, and they even had an opportunity to save him. It went beyond just a rescue operation. It felt like a chance at redemption for her.

"And Raffiel as well," mused Yeong-Ja.

"Yeah," Maira said. "Interesting, that. A leader with at least some popularity among their number even now. One who wants to make peace."

Colin nodded. "It seems like we're going to be rescuing him accidentally anyway, if he and Leo will be traveling together."

"That will depend on the actual situation. Who knows how they'll be moving them, in what organization. I'm not risking

Leo to save Raffiel, I don't care how reasonable of a Reborn he might be," Maira said.

"No, absolutely not," Colin agreed.

"Yet if we can get them both, it may be worthwhile to consider what advantage it could offer us," Yeong-Ja said. "Even if he could only divide the Reborn to some extent, that could still be a useful advantage. He'd also be a goldmine of information we still need."

"Maybe," Maira said with a frown. "But let's not lose sight of the fact that the Molossi pose a huge threat of their own now. Just turning him loose on these people isn't acceptable either."

"Yeah," Colin said with a sigh. "It's quite a mess, and it's not even all our fault."

Maira gave a soft laugh and clapped him on the shoulder. "At least we have a goal now, and the beginnings of a plan. Let's slip out of here and get back to where our gear is. I want to figure out where the prison camp is. The Reborn had so many successes ambushing the Freighties on the road. I'd say it's about time we returned the favor."

CHAPTER 13

The prison camp turned out to be very literal. This, at least, was not something that Raines had created before the Poison brought everything crashing down. According to the data that Maira had captured, they were using a pre-existing facility abandoned in the pandemic. That made a certain amount of sense to Colin. In the world as it was, such a thing would have drawn far too much attention still. People volunteering to move out onto your cult ranch was one thing. Kidnapping people to brainwash them was another matter entirely.

Of course, once all authority had dissolved, it was anyone's game. The Reborn had seized control of the derelict city of Lafayette and all the surrounding lands. That had included the Vermilion Parish Jail. Rather than let such a thing go to waste, Raines must have seen the potential. Now that was where all the malcontents of the Reborn ended up.

There wasn't a lot to go on about what actually happened there, based solely on the documents that Maira had seized.

Mostly what they had were the supplies that were redirected to the area. Most of it was innocuous. Food, clothing, things like that. Some of it was more revealing. All the captured supplies of medical grade sedatives were redirected to that site. So, too, were any stashes of LSD and mescaline that were located. The combination made Colin's skin crawl. It was exactly the sort of things the government had once used in the MK Ultra projects. They were trying to brainwash people.

"Someday, when we aren't spread as thin, we're going to have to do something about this place," Colin said.

Maira nodded grimly. "It worries me how often we have to say that. 'This is bad, but we have bigger fish to fry'. The more we peel back the curtain, the more horrors we're going to discover."

"We can only do so much," said Yeong-Ja. "It almost makes me sympathize with Colonel Georgio's methods, however."

"Almost," Colin said. "Except that the same people he's lining up are the ones being kept in line by fear of places like this. They're victims coming and going."

"Atrocities committed at the demand of others, and more than enough blame to go around," Maira said. "A familiar theme from history. I hope we can handle it better than they did."

"For now, if we can stop the outright war on our hands, I'll call it a start," Colin said. "Show us the map again, ISAC."

A graphic of the area, collated from archived satellite photos, appeared on each of their HUDs. It showed up as a grid in glowing orange with a variety of geographic information available. Colin indicated the place where they were, down toward the Louisiana coast. The spot shimmered in the vision of the other two agents. He did the same for the location of the prison camp, northeast of there. This was the terrain the people transporting Leo and Raffiel would have to travel across.

"This is where the site we just visited is, and here's where they're going to be taking Leo. Luckily, the terrain narrows down transportation options a lot," he said.

"If they stick to land transportation, they're going by Highway 82," Maira said.

Colin nodded. "Or they can do what we've been doing and take a fanboat across the wetlands. Either option will get them to where they're going."

"It would be much more difficult to prevent them from getting there by boat, it seems to me," Yeong-Ja said.

"Almost certainly," Leo said. "But I don't actually think we have to worry about that too much."

Maira looked at him curiously. "Why not?"

"Well, think about it like Raines. Every time they use the fanboats, they're violating their own tenets. They have been willing to do so in extremis, when it seems like that could be the key to defeating their foes. Other than that, though, we haven't seen them using vehicles at all," Colin explained.

"That's true. No tractors, no cars, and thankfully no tanks or APCs. Considering how much of the terrain here is dominated by wetlands, the boats may be a concession to necessity as much as anything," Yeong-Ja said.

"OK," Maira said. "So we assume they go by land. No cars – they'll go by foot or horse based on what we've seen them use."

"I did note a carriage," Yeong-Ja said thoughtfully.

Colin tilted his head. "When?"

"It was behind one of the buildings back at the camp. I did not mention it at the time because it didn't seem important."

"Could it be Raines's personal transport?" offered Maira.

"Could be," allowed Colin. "But if they've got one they could have more. We'll have to at least be ready for that possibility, too."

"Right," Maira said. "On foot, riding horses, or in a horse-drawn carriage. Welcome back to the nineteenth century."

"Pretty inevitable considering their leanings. It's not impossible to do things in a more modern way free of fossil fuels, but it's harder. They haven't shown that kind of industry anywhere I've seen," Colin said.

"No," Maira agreed. "Maybe that's Raines's grand plan for her empire, but the current set up is primitivist and agrarian."

"Simple enough. We should pick a good location for an ambush along the highway and wait for them to attempt to complete their journey," Yeong-Ja said.

"My thought is here," Colin said. He tapped the spot. "82 forks into 35 going north, and 82 going northwest. If they're traveling by foot, fine. If they're traveling by horse or carriage, they'll still have to slow to make the turn."

"Terrain around there is some trees, small houses, and grassland," Maira observed. "There was a gas station right there at the turn."

"That might be the key then," Colin said. "We use that structure to launch our attack."

Yeong-Ja and Maira both nodded their agreement.

"We can head there at any rate," Maira said. "If a better option presents itself, we stay flexible. Regardless, we have to keep in mind what we're here to do."

"Save Leo," Yeong-Ja and Colin said at the same time.

Colin laughed. "Jinx."

"You're going to feel bad when my luck runs sour now," Yeong-Ja said.

"Oh, c'mon, that's not going to happen." Colin looked at Maira plaintively. "Is she messing with me? She is, right?"

Maira shrugged. "Don't ask me. Figuring Yeong-Ja out is going to be just as long-term a project as getting their region back to good."

Yeong-Ja simply smiled enigmatically.

"All right," Colin said with another laugh. "Let's get moving. We wouldn't want to miss our rendezvous. We can take the river up to there, and then walk the rest of the way."

Maira realized she was starting to enjoy these rides on the fanboat. They hurtled along the brown water at high speeds, and the wind never failed to be a joy. She turned her face into it and shut her eyes with a smile.

"Do you think we can just keep this when everything is done? Load it up into the back of a semi and take it everywhere with us?" she asked.

"It's possible we could," Colin answered. "That's a bad idea though."

Maira blinked her eyes open and focused on him. "What? Why?"

"The Division has some things in common with the military, and you know what one of those things is?"

"What?" Maira asked.

"If you get the right tool for a job, you're doing that job from now on. Do you want to get sent to nothing but marshes, swamps, and bogs from here on out?" Colin asked.

Maira laughed. "No, thanks. I guess you're right."

"I would say that if you want a boat, you should check the nearest marinas wherever you go," Yeong-Ja said. "In theory, there are a tremendous number simply sitting."

"Nah, no good," Colin said.

"Okay, Buzz Killington, why can't we do that either?" Maira asked.

"Too late. Maybe you could have snagged some soon after the Poison hit, but now? You better know how to fix a rusted-out hull," he answered.

Maira sighed dramatically. "I guess my dreams of nautical freedom are dashed all around."

Colin grinned. "My apologies for being the bearer of bad news."

"I'll never forgive you," Maira said.

"Approaching target destination. Arrival in five minutes," ISAC said.

"All right," Colin said. "Heads on a swivel. We're deep into Reborn territory now. They could have waypoints, farmsteads, any number of things scattered around."

Maira nodded and turned to keep her eye on the surrounding terrain. Evening had come, and the sky was a dark gray. The landscape was much as the map had indicated. They were far enough out of the wetlands now that the ground could support substantial copses of trees. The rest was dominated by grasses. Small houses dotted the landscape, and likely much of the grassland had been kept cut short once upon a time. Now it grew tall and wild.

Yeong-Ja was holding the injector pen in her hand. Maira saw and leaned over toward her.

"Has the time come?" Maira asked.

"I know we're going to get pretty close to the ambush site just by the boat, but it's still a several minute hike. I just don't think I can do it with my leg like this. Just hobbling around the central facility wore me out." Yeong-Ja sounded tired even thinking about it.

"It's your call," Maira said.

Yeong-Ja took a deep breath and pressed the pen to her leg. She flinched, then pulled the now-extended needle out. For a few seconds she sat there shivering and breathing hard as the complex mixture of drugs did its work. The combat cocktail made it possible to function in spite of grievous wounds, with the delayed cost of terrible withdrawals. There was also a constant risk that, with pain dulled, the user would hurt themselves worse and not even realize it.

Maira rested a hand on her shoulder. "You'll be OK."

Yeong-Ja nodded and gave her a grateful smile. "Thanks."

Colin parked the boat, and they climbed out. It would take them about fifteen minutes to walk from there to the road junction they had decided to use. Maira carried both of the rifles on the way so that Yeong-Ja could focus her energy on walking. They stuck to the road to avoid having to wade through the tall grass. The pavement here was in no better condition than it had been in Groves; it was gray and cracked, marked by green sprouts pushing through every gap.

"Some Roman roads made it all the way to modern times,"

Maira commented. "I doubt ours would last another few decades."

"Sometimes I think that was the sickness at the heart of our civilization," Yeong-Ja said. She was puffing a bit but was easily understood. "Everything we did was disposable. We couldn't plan past the present."

"You might have a point," Colin said. "But nobody expected the Poison. How do you plan for something like that?"

"Realistically, I don't think you can," Maira said. "You can try to mitigate the damage some, but some things will always be devastating."

"They'll have to start repaving the major roads the Freighty supply lines depend on," Colin said.

"Make sure to note it in your reports," Maira said drily. "Famine, war, plague, also roads getting pretty bad out here."

They passed a number of small buildings on the way. All were shuttered and dead. Even the people who survived the terrible culling of the plague days tended to have fled. Thousands survived in the big cities and banded together. If a small community got hit, you might have only a handful of people left. Even if they could figure out a way to get what they needed, humans were social creatures.

Maira squinted at the sign out in front of one place. C N DIN was what remained legible of the original text. She puzzled over that. As they drew near she walked over to peer through the dirty windows. There were a couple of tables visible, and a counter behind which lay a kitchen. She smiled sadly and walked back to the side of the others.

"What was it?" Colin asked.

"Cajun Diner," Maira said. "Looked like a little hole in the wall place. I bet it was delicious."

"Probably," Colin said. "All the best places are."

It was not much further on to the junction itself. Little clumps of trees grew all around. None of them were particularly huge, but it was still a nice break from swamp plants and grass. There were signs that some repairs had been done at the gas station on the corner. Maira motioned a warning to the others. She gestured that she would investigate. Colin nodded, and Maira broke away from the group.

It looked like the awning over the gas pumps had fallen in. Someone had then propped it back up, removed the useless pumps, and replaced them with plastic barrels, held up from the ground on stools. Maira examined them curiously. Both had little taps available. She held out her hand and hit one. Clean water flowed out. It splashed against her dirty skin, removing the outermost layer of grime.

By everything that is holy, please let me get a bath sometime soon, Maira thought.

The doorway to the building was propped open. It had received minimal maintenance. The interior had none of the shelving one associated with gas stations. It had been cleared out to just leave an open room. There were footprints in the dust, though none of them looked recent. Big rectangular marks, too. Maira eyed them and decided they were where sleeping bags had been laid out.

She emerged back out into the evening air. Crickets chorused amongst the tall grass. Maira gave her friends the all-clear signal and they approached the building. Yeong-

Ja wasted no time in finding a bench to sit on over by the building. Colin came directly to where Maira was standing.

"Anything interesting?"

Maira shook her head. "They've turned it into a waystation, that's all. A place to refill your canteens, a place to sleep out from under the sky. There's no sign of anyone here at the moment. We should be good."

"Might as well top off our own water while we're at it," Colin said. "Then we can get set up for what has to be done."

Maira took a deep breath. "Another fight."

"Probably," Colin said. "I've been wondering if we can risk giving them a chance to surrender."

"The moment they connect who we are to who he is, they'll realize they have a hostage right there in Leo," Maira said.

"Him and Raffiel both. That's what I'm afraid of, too," Colin said. "This whole situation is enough of a mess without a gun to his head."

They stood together in silence for a few minutes, watching the grass wave in the breeze. Croaking frogs had joined in on the growing night's chorus of animals. Maira's inner turmoil was not as great as she had feared it would be. Her refusal to listen to the screaming nerves in her body that demanded she recklessly take action seemed to be making them quieter as a side effect. Instead, what she felt was a terrible weariness, not just of the body but of the soul.

"I wonder, sometimes, how long we can do this for," she said.

"Do what?" Colin asked.

Maira gestured around. The motion encapsulated where they were now, but also far more than that.

"Everything we do. This life as Division agents. Do you know I've lost track of the number of people I've killed since I started traveling with Brenda? Isn't that insane on some level?" she asked.

"It's not as if we're just engaging in wholesale slaughter with no rhyme or reason," Colin said. "We're always trying to save lives. We're always trying to protect people, ultimately."

"Sure. And there was violence in my life before. We would have to fend off raiders at Athena from time to time. But that was always direct. They were coming after us, and we were fighting back against them." Maira sighed.

"This is more abstract?" Colin said.

"Yeah, I guess. More abstract and more constant. I sometimes feel like I'm losing sight of the goal. Like it's boiling down to just this is what I am, this is what I do. And I don't like that."

"I could try to talk you around, but are you sure you want me to?" Colin asked. "You don't have to do this, Maira. You could walk away right now, I wouldn't stop you. Yeong-Ja wouldn't either."

"I'm not going to abandon you two, much less Leo, right in the middle of all this Charlie Foxtrot. Especially not when I caused some of it," Maira said.

"OK, so say you stay until we've somehow resolved this. You could leave then. You could ride with the Freighties, or drill with the roughnecks, or even go all the way home back to Athena. You don't have to torture yourself," Colin said.

Maira looked into the distance. The evening gray was growing ever darker. Night would be upon them soon. Distantly she wondered if the prison transport would come tonight, or if they'd be stuck here until tomorrow.

"I think I'm caught between feeling I have to do something, and not knowing if I can stand what I have to do," Maira said.

"That's hard, Maira. I wish I could resolve it for you. I like fixing things. But this one, this one you have to figure out on your own." Colin squeezed her shoulder companionably.

Maira gave him a smile. "Thanks for listening to me prattle on about it. It helps."

"Any time. Even for those of us who aren't as conflicted, I think that's one of the things that keeps us sane. None of us are in this alone. Don't forget that, OK?"

"You got it." Maira turned back toward the building. "All right, let's set up to catch these bastards off guard and save Leo."

In the end, there wasn't very much prep they could do. There was a rickety, abandoned little house on the other side of the junction. Colin took up a position in that. The door was already rotting off the hinges, so it was easy enough to get inside. He moved over to sit against a window looking out. Maira and Yeong-Ja had remained at the waystation, spread out to avoid concentrating counterfire. They all had a clear view up the road.

All they could do then was wait. Colin did his best to stay awake and alert. It was getting harder by the day. They had gotten some occasional rest, but it was always uncomfortable or cut short. Fatigue was a growing concern. In the deepening darkness, with nothing to do, his eyelids were becoming heavy. He resorted to pinching himself occasionally to stave off sleep.

A glance at the vitals of the other two agents revealed they weren't doing any better. Both would occasionally slope off toward the signs of a sleeping person, then jolt back to alertness. It would have been funny if it wasn't a potential disaster in the making. Colin leaned to glance down the road again. Nothing.

The stars filled the night sky. Light pollution was all but nonexistent nowadays. It was a new moon, too, which didn't help with the dark or the sleepiness. For all the other downsides, it did make for a beautiful display. Colin spent a few minutes finding constellations to keep his mind occupied. Here was the Big Dipper, and there was Orion forever on the hunt.

Colin jolted. He wasn't sure if he'd fallen asleep. He started to ask ISAC what time it was to see if he'd lost any, but the sound of hooves on the road cut him off. With a sharp curse, Colin searched for any sign of what he'd heard. He spotted it quickly. Coming up the road was a carriage, drawn by a pair of horses. A lantern swung at the front of it, and there was a person driving it with another sitting next to them.

"We have them," Colin said into the radio.

"Spotted," Maira replied. "Can either of you tell who those two are?"

The fear was obvious. None of them wanted to shoot Leo by accident. Colin peered to see if he could spot any details. It was hard to make anything specific out, even with the enemy lantern helping. He grimaced, sweat dripping down his forehead. The carriage closed in on the intersection.

"They're Reborn," Yeong-Ja said. "Take them."

A ping immediately showed that Maira was going to take the man in the passenger seat. Yeong-Ja claimed the driver.

Colin left it to them. The handgun he'd taken from the guard back at Houston was better than nothing, but it wasn't suited to feats of marksmanship.

A pair of shots rang out simultaneously. The Reborn in the passenger seat fell forward to be rolled over by the carriage and crushed into the road. The driver cried out and fell to the side. They hit the ground in a heap. The horses stopped and reared, terrified by the sudden sound and loss of guidance. Colin came through the doorway of the house sprinting.

The door on the side of the carriage facing him opened. A Reborn stumbled out, swinging a rifle this way and that. They spotted Colin. Their weapon flashed in the dark. The gunshot echoed. All Colin knew was it didn't hit him.

He leaned against a telephone pole. His target fired twice more. One was close enough that Colin heard it crunch into the other side of the pole. Colin refused to let it rattle him. He chose his shot with care, aiming with both hands, and squeezed the trigger. The pistol bucked in his grip.

Colin didn't wait to see if it had hit. He corrected his aim and fired again as rapidly as he could manage. Somewhere in there the Reborn staggered back against the carriage, then slid to the ground. Colin put two more shots into them just to be on the safe side. He paused and tried to listen through the pounding of his heart.

Silence. There had been other gunshots in the mix there. That was all Colin was sure of.

"ISAC, agent status?" he whispered.

Their vitals popped up on his HUD again. Nothing was wrong. He released a breathy sigh of pure relief. Something was happening at the carriage. The door on his side burst open. A man fell out and hit the ground. He was just a shadow at this distance. Immediately he began to scramble back to his feet.

"Freeze!" Colin barked. "I will shoot!"

The man went still as a statue. Slowly he raised his hands above his head. Colin carefully stepped out from the cover of the telephone pole and approached. He kept his handgun aimed at the target the entire time.

"Colin?"

It was one word, but Colin recognized the voice immediately. The speaker had never been given to volubility. Colin's face immediately broke out in a huge grin, and he lowered his gun.

"Leo! Hot damn, we got you!"

Colin rushed forward. As he got closer, he could see his identification was correct. It was Leo, and he was manacled hand and foot. Chains clinked in the night's darkness. Colin pulled a flashlight from his kit and held it up.

Leo was staring at him as if he was a mirage. The man looked worse for wear, if better than Colin had feared he might. He was clearly tired and battered. They might have roughed him up, but they had at least not beaten or maimed him.

"It's me. Us," Colin said quickly. He turned the light so that Leo could see his face as well.

Leo relaxed just a little. He took a deep breath. "Everyone OK?"

"Yeong-Ja has a broken leg, but other than that we're not any worse off than you. Do they have a key to your chains?"

Leo nodded and pointed to the driver lying in the dirt. "He did."

Colin went over and fished through the dead Reborn's

pockets. Aside from a small collection of items he had no interest in, he did manage to find the key. While he was retrieving it, Maira came around from the other side dragging someone with her.

"Look what I found. The Hand of the Reborn himself. It seems the rumors were true about his fall from grace."

Raffiel's face might as well have been carved from stone. He kept his chin high in spite of the fact that he, too, was bound. In all honesty, Colin found it kind of admirable. This must all be very strange for the man on a number of levels. Colin wasn't sure he would have kept his composure nearly as well.

"Colin?" asked Leo and held his wrists out.

"Oh, right, sorry," Colin said.

He unlocked both of the sets binding Leo. The other agent rubbed his wrists with clear relief. He stretched his legs, too. They'd left him in the clothes he'd been wearing, Colin noted, but there was no sign of his gear. That was unsurprising. They'd have been foolish to leave him wearing a radio.

"Are you here to kill me for what I did?" asked Raffiel.

Leo looked up immediately. Colin saw the distress in his face. There was no telling what had passed between them in the interim, but Raffiel was still his brother. Leo clearly did not want to see him die. Luckily, Colin had no reason to do anything but shake his head.

"Catching you as well was nothing but a lucky chance, Raffiel. We came here to save Leo," Colin said.

Raffiel nodded slowly. "My brother made wise choices in allies, if you have gone to all this trouble to get him back." He looked down at the shackles he still wore. "Perhaps better choices than I made."

Yeong-Ja limped around the front of the carriage. Maira came over and stood in front of Leo. There was an awkward pause between the two, as if neither was sure where this was going. Suddenly she lunged forward and hugged Leo. She squeezed him tightly. The taciturn agent looked startled, but his face then softened. He awkwardly patted her on the back.

"Glad you're OK. Missed you." Leo looked around at the others. "I missed all of you."

Maira pulled away. "Don't ever go scaring me like that again."

Leo gave a slight wry smile. "I won't."

Colin stepped over to look Raffiel in the face. He was significantly taller than the former Reborn commander, but you wouldn't have known it by the bound man's bearing.

"As for you, we might not have come for you, but that doesn't mean you can't be useful. I'm not one to look a gift horse in the mouth. We need to talk."

"Cassandra is working with the Division," Raffiel said.

They were gathered in the waystation building. Colin had taken the lantern from the carriage and put it in the middle of the group. It amused Maira, if she was honest. All their faces underlit like this gave the assembly the feel of children telling ghost stories. That didn't distract her from the impact of what Raffiel had said.

"That's crazy," she said sharply.

Raffiel shrugged. "You would know better than me, but she believes it. I did, too, until I talked to Leo and he had no idea about it. For all our differences, there's no reason my brother would lie to me about that. When I confronted her about this, she didn't believe me and thought I was betraying everything we'd fought for. The thing is, this alliance is more than just a figment of her imagination. For one thing, while she is driven beyond anyone I've ever met, she is not insane. For another, there is physical proof. Her allies are providing her with war materiel."

"Shit," Maira said.

"The C4, the rocket launchers... That's where she's getting them from," Colin said.

Raffiel nodded.

"Can't be the Division," Leo said flatly.

Maira frowned. "I know you don't want to believe that, Leo, but... it's not like the Division never makes mistakes."

Leo hesitated and nodded. "Not why it's impossible. Why did the Division send us? Why not tell us?"

"There is a lack of centralized leadership by design," mused Yeong-Ja. "It may be that the left hand simply does not know what the right is doing."

"Maybe," Leo said. "Doesn't feel right though."

"Do you know anything else about these mysterious allies?" asked Maira.

"Yes," Raffiel said. "There was a time when Cassandra trusted me as she trusts few others. For one thing, I know they demanded any captured Division agents be turned over to them. For another, I have been with her to help retrieve arms shipments. They had the same taste in accessories that all of you do."

Maira held up the watch she was wearing questioningly, and Raffiel nodded.

"Fuck," Maira said. "That is maybe a little damning."

"Orange? Not red?" asked Leo.

Raffiel nodded. "We may have lived largely disconnected from the world, but we kept up with the news. We saw what happened in New York, before mass media died out."

Implying, Maira realized, that they had seen rogues in action. Did that mean these were indeed Division agents in good standing? She wasn't sure. Maira had started this mission needing the Division to be the most important thing in the world. Without that, she had to question the choices she made. Now she was starting to question things again. She had a dollop of skepticism in her soul about the Division and its methods, in spite of joining them. Was it really impossible that the rot went deep enough for this to be true?

"All right," Maira said. "That's not great, I'm not gonna lie. What do we do about it?"

"Stop them," Leo said without hesitation.

Maira looked at him in surprise. "Leo, you're a company man."

Leo frowned a little and looked away. "I'm proud of the Division. Proud of…" He glanced around at the cell. "Of you. But wrong is wrong."

"Maybe these other agents are under cover," Yeong-Ja offered. "The FBI used to have people embed with all kinds of unfortunate organizations. Sometimes it's the only way to figure out what they're up to."

"Maybe," Leo said doubtfully. "But those arms? They've used them for murder. We can't let it go on, or else there's nothing left to be proud of."

"I would be grateful if you did stop them," Raffiel said.

All of them now looked at the other Fourte brother in shared surprise.

"You want us to stop them from resupplying the Reborn? Why? You that pissed about getting clapped in irons?" Maira asked.

"I'm not delighted by it," Raffiel said drily. "But no. You have to understand, I only disagreed with Cassandra at all to try to save the Reborn from destruction. I do not believe we can win this war against the Molossi. When we got reports about the battle…" He looked away.

"Your being there wouldn't have changed the outcome," Leo said gruffly.

"You don't know that. Neither do I. That's the problem, I'll always have to wonder. Either way, I don't want to see more of our people butchered fighting a superior foe."

"So?" asked Colin. "It won't go better for them with less weapons."

"No, but I think that's why Cassandra thinks she can't lose. She thinks they won't let her. That the Division will keep sending these shipments, and keep propping her up, and eventually even step in on her behalf."

"You want to make her desperate," Yeong-Ja said. "You believe that, with the prop kicked from beneath her, she may be shocked to her senses."

Raffiel nodded soberly. "If that does not do it, I do not know what will."

The quartet of agents and their prisoner sat in uneasy silence for a few minutes.

"Do you know where the next shipment is supposed to come in?" asked Maira.

"Yes," Raffiel said.

"And you'll take us there?" she asked.

"Yes," Raffiel said again.

"That sounds an awful lot like a trap in the making," Colin noted. "Maybe Raffiel thinks handing four agents over will get him back in the good graces of his boss."

"It is not impossible," Yeong-Ja said. "So, the question must be, will we trust him enough to see this through? You know him best, Leo. He is your brother, yes?"

"He is," Leo said.

Leo looked Raffiel in the eyes. The younger brother squared his shoulders but did not plead his case further. There was almost a defiance to his mien.

"Telling the truth," Leo said. "We need to help him."

"Because he's your brother or because it's the right thing to do?" asked Maira.

"Yes," Leo said. He looked around at the group. "Please. Help me."

Maira glanced at the other two. Both nodded firmly. She took a deep breath.

"All right. Deeper and deeper into the rabbit hole we go, where it stops nobody can know. Let's go fight the Division."

CHAPTER 14

The location of the arms shipment ended up being out in the middle of nowhere, even by Reborn standards. These allies that Raines was so dependent on had prized their secrecy, it seemed. The rendezvous was set on a location known as Marsh Island. It had, in the old days, been a wilderness refuge. It was located beyond Vermilion Bay, out to sea. It was exactly what it said on the label: a sodden mass of marsh with nothing to recommend it.

The secrecy was one of the things that still confused Maira. If someone in the Division had thought that backing Raines was the best way to restore civilization in this area, why not be public with it? Surely the official imprimatur of the SHD could only have given her movement a greater legitimacy.

So, were they playing her, then? How? To what end? There were too many unanswered questions for Maira's comfort. It felt like they'd been wading through a swamp, just like the ones everywhere down here. It had already been messy and mucky and dragging them down. Now they'd taken a step on what they thought was solid land, and instead sunk up to their neck.

In this metaphor, they were precisely one wrong move away from drowning.

Maira sighed. That didn't change what they had decided to do. She just hoped it wouldn't come down to shooting. She felt bad enough killing random misguided jackasses across the continental United States. If she had to start cutting down Division agents, too, she would just be another rogue. She was pretty sure that would snap her like a brittle twig.

It was time to get out of her head. She looked around the boat. Leo was back with them, and that felt good. They were a quartet again. Plus, having retrieved the arms from the Reborn they'd killed at the junction, they were better equipped than they had been. Each of them had a rifle now and a sidearm besides. They even had some extra ammunition.

Of course, there was the oddity of the fifth wheel on their car. Raffiel sat beside Leo in the middle of the boat, still in manacles. More accurately, Leo had sat beside Raffiel. They hadn't said a word to each other, as far as Maira knew. The entire trip she wasn't sure if they'd even looked at each other.

Perhaps feeling her gaze, Leo raised his head. "You knew where to find us." It wasn't a question.

Maira nodded. "We hit the Reborn radio station and infiltrated one of their sites. Between the two it was enough to piece things together about where they were taking you and intercept you on the way."

"Where were they taking me?" Leo asked curiously. "Didn't tell me much."

Maira winced. The bruises on his face did suggest he hadn't been the one asking the questions. "They have some kind of re-education camp set up southwest of Lafayette."

"They have a what?" Leo frowned deeply. "What do you mean by that? What kind of place is it?"

"We don't know for sure," Maira admitted. "We didn't get to go."

"I saw the drugs they were shipping there," Colin called. "That's brainwashing stuff, all the way back to the experiments the US government ran during the Cold War."

Leo absorbed that in silence. His expression darkened. Maira could see the anger rising in him. She wasn't sure how to stop it, or if she should. It had to be a grim thing, to know that such a fate had awaited him. Surely, he deserved to be angry about it.

"You knew," he said, his tone accusing.

"Excuse me?" Maira asked in surprise.

Leo had disregarded her completely, however. He turned to face Raffiel finally. "You knew," he repeated.

Raffiel glanced at him and looked away with a frown of his own. "I had heard–"

"You knew!" Leo barked. "I saw the way those people treated you. You were one of their leaders. Do not pretend now that you only suspected."

Raffiel's jaw clenched. He didn't respond for several seconds. "I knew."

"How could you?" demanded Leo. "How did you sleep at night?"

"I am not proud of it, but it was a necessity," Raffiel said. "Some people aren't ready to let go of the past. We had to show them. We had to help them–"

"Help them?" Leo stared at him and then scoffed. "And you had the audacity to call Papa controlling."

"Ce n'est pas pareil," Raffiel growled back in a low tone

before taking a breath. "Cassandra has been forced to make hard choices."

"You're right, it isn't the same." Leo's tone made it clear he wasn't conceding anything. "For all his faults, Papa never tied you down and force-fed you drugs to keep you in line."

"No. Instead he forbade me from leaving, and when I did anyway, he called you home to send after me. And you came, like un bon garçon."

"Attention à tes mots," Leo snapped. It was the angriest Maira had ever seen Leo. Angrier even than his argument with Brenda, when Maira herself had been exposed to chlorine gas. "You assume too much."

"Do I? You were always the good one, Leo. Ready to do as you were told, ready to–" snarled Raffiel.

"Papa told me not to come," Leo said flatly.

That stopped Raffiel in his tracks. He sat for a moment, mouth agape. "Hein?"

"He said you were a lost cause, that I would be wasting my time. He told me I should not throw away my career to chase you down." Leo was undeniably still furious, but his words were now cold and flat.

Raffiel shrank down in the face of Leo's rage. "Non."

"Oh, mais oui," Leo said. "I came because I feared for you. You are my brother, and I love you. It was my decision."

Raffiel looked down at the deck. He scrubbed both hands over his face. "I was fine," he muttered finally.

"The fact that you still believe that is the worst thing yet," Leo said quietly.

The silence between them returned. It was heavy to the point of painful now.

"Family reunions are going to get complicated," Maira muttered when the argument didn't continue.

"What did you say?" called Colin.

Maira flushed and shook her head. He hadn't heard what she'd said, and hopefully no one else had either. Those two definitely had enough to chew on without her making things worse with a smart remark.

She turned her attention to the last two occupants instead. Colin drove the fanboat with a worried expression. She couldn't blame him for that. They all had a lot to worry about, and he was predisposed to it. There was an element of the mother hen to Colin, she decided. He'd probably just started feeling right with all his chicks back in a row, and now they were all running off toward the slaughterhouse again.

Farm metaphors didn't suit her, Maira decided. She shouldn't let the one trip to the Reborn camp go to her head. She just wasn't cut out for the agrarian life at the end of the day.

As for Yeong-Ja, she was Yeong-Ja. Maira wasn't sure how else to define her at that point. Any normal person would have tendered their resignation by now. The leg had to be a source of constant throbbing pain. No one would have blamed her if she'd wanted to leave. Instead, here she was, riding with them and ready to risk it all again.

What if, Maira wondered, this is the part that I really can't let go? Not the Division itself, no. The organization was a bit of a mess. Plagued by rogues and secrets, disorganized and out of its depth. The people it had gathered, though, were something special. Sure, some of them went bad, but they really had bottled lightning in so many of the others.

Yeong-Ja turned to face her with raised eyebrows. Maira realized she hadn't actually looked away from the woman and flushed again. She gave a weak smile and a tiny wave. Yeong-Ja motioned for her to come over. Maira shrugged. There wasn't anything else to do until they got to Marsh Island.

"How are you, Maira?" Yeong-Ja asked.

"Worried that I'm going to come unglued?" Maira asked. "Run onto the scene screaming about how I have to do something, guns blazing?"

Yeong-Ja blinked. "I wasn't, but now I am. Comfort me quickly."

Maira laughed wearily. "No. Not this time. Not ever again if I can help it. I have caused enough chaos for one lifetime. I'm cool as a cucumber now."

"Would a cucumber not be room temperature?"

"Well." Maira tilted her head. "Yes. I mean, if you let it sit. It's just a saying."

"Ah. That makes sense. I'm glad I have you here to tell me these things, Maira Kanhai." Yeong-Ja looked out to sea as she said it. Maira could have sworn there was a tiny smile that flashed across her face.

"You are messing with us, aren't you? I think you're even getting worse with time to see how far you can go with being a weirdo before we call you on it," Maira said.

"If that were true," Yeong-Ja said thoughtfully, "and please understand, I am merely speaking in a hypothetical sense."

"Sure, sure," Maira said. "We're just playing devil's advocate here."

"Yes. Well, if that is what I was doing, I think you could take it as a sign of genuine affection. Is that not what people often say? That to be teased, that is the sign of being loved?"

Maira thought that over. "I do know people who say stuff like that. I myself have occasionally noted that I especially give shit to my friends."

"There you have it then. You have to interpret it how you want to." Yeong-Ja shrugged. "Oh, and if that were what I were doing, I think that I would appreciate if you didn't call my bluff in front of Colin."

Maira stared at her, then let out a laugh. "He's an earnest guy, Yeong-Ja. Very sincere. You could probably drive him batty."

"Hey, I love bats. Vital to the ecosystem. I think they get a bad rap. I think, especially in these trying times, we could all do with being a little batty."

"Fair enough," Maira said. "If that were something that you did, and this conversation were not completely hypothetical, then I think you could probably count on me to keep your secret."

"I am sure that this imaginary version of Yeong-Ja would be very grateful for your discretion," Yeong-Ja said.

Maira shook her head, laughing again.

The boat continued on, slicing through the waves.

"All right," Colin called to the group. "We're getting close to our destination."

This entire situation had him more anxious than a sheep in wolf's clothing. They might have rescued their missing member, but their condition had not changed substantially. They were still effectively running on fumes as a group. Colin had spent the entire drive here wondering if he could somehow call a halt to this nonsense.

It wasn't that he disagreed in theory. If the Division was somehow propping up the Reborn, that was a mistake and it needed to be rectified. He would be happy to help get it taken care of. He just didn't want his friends to get hurt doing it, and it felt increasingly inevitable. How many times were they going to scrape by? Sooner or later, if they pushed their luck too far, it would give out on them.

Colin understood, though, that these weren't the kind of people to see a problem and back down from it. Perhaps that was why he was growing so fond of them. They were kindred spirits in that way. They would fight until the end to see things put right. He promised himself this wasn't going to be said end. This wasn't going to be New York.

Night was giving way to morning now. The sky was still mostly black as velvet, but the very far eastern horizon was just starting to show signs of a rosy glow. According to the timetable Raffiel had given them, they weren't going to have a lot of time to set an ambush as they had before. They would end up arriving at the coordinates at the same time their opponents were supposed to.

They still shouldn't be expecting us, Colin told himself. He would have to hope that would be enough. He could see the dark mass of the island up ahead. It didn't really rise that far out of the sea. Whole sections must flood over with the changing tides. Not the kind of place he would visit given a choice.

"We're getting close," he called to the others in case they didn't see it.

Each of them acknowledged him in turn. A wink from Maira. A smile from Yeong-Ja. A nod from Leo. Nothing from

Raffiel, of course. They had not let him out of his manacles. Colin and the others might be prepared to see this through, but their trust wasn't blind. No one had even suggested giving him a gun. Colin was grateful for that.

Daylight grew and the island grew with it. It was a green shape now. Colin steered them on, keeping alert for any sign of their quarry. He was curious what method they would be using to get here. The waves were unpleasantly choppy this far out from the coast. The fanboat would be fine once they were on the marshy island, but it was not meant for operating in deeper waters.

"Unknown network detected," ISAC said.

All the agents looked at each other in confusion. Colin hadn't heard that in a long time. Judging by the surprised looks all around, none of the others had either. ISAC wasn't sentient and asking for clarification wouldn't obtain any results. Still, someone must have anticipated this scenario for the response to be encoded. What did that mean?

"Up ahead!" called Yeong-Ja.

Colin's attention snapped back into the moment. They had slid up onto the wetlands of Marsh Island as smooth as a knife spreading butter. The ground here wasn't sturdy enough to support large growths like tall trees. The biggest plants were squat shrubs. Most of what could be seen was little more than a dappled mixture of brown water and green sludge.

In the distance, however, was something remarkably incongruous. Colin blinked and shook his head, at first thinking perhaps his eyes were confused. They weren't. Someone had placed a temporary floating helipad out here on the island, and there were several fanboats pulled up to it.

The most startling thing sat in the middle: a helicopter, rotor slowly spinning up.

"They killed them!"

It was a startled cry from Yeong-Ja. Colin squinted but couldn't see what she was talking about. There was red on the platform, he could make that out. He was confused. He slammed the throttle to full. Whatever was going on, they needed to get there and figure it out.

The helicopter was about to depart. The platform was growing rapidly in their view. Colin could now make out there were figures sprawled all over it. One different figure was walking over to the helicopter. They stepped up onto the landing skid and looked back at the oncoming Division cell. To his absolute bemusement, the figure raised a hand in a jaunty wave. Something flashed in the light of the rising sun.

Leo rushed forward to the front of the boat and stood next to Yeong-Ja. She crouched with her rifle braced against the boat's prow, her eye to the scope.

"He's wearing an orange watch!" Yeong-Ja yelled. "He's Division! What do I do?"

"Take the shot," Maira said.

Colin stared at her in surprise. Leo turned to look at her, and Colin could see it on his face as well. This was no casual matter. If they did this, and they were wrong, there would be no going back. They would have gone rogue themselves. Maira didn't look like she was making a joke though. Her face was as grim as Colin had ever seen it.

"The network, the network!" she called amidst the roar of the boat and water. "Shoot him!"

The helicopter had started to rise into the air. The figure

stayed clinging to the door of the aircraft, watching them come. His clothes fluttered in the wind of the rotors. Time was running out fast. There would be no room for second guessing.

Leo nodded. "All right. Do it."

Yeong-Ja did not wait for it to be unanimous. Her rifle spoke. Colin was no expert marksman, but he had been through plenty of training. To be on a moving vehicle, aiming at a small target also on a moving vehicle, with a rifle not even designed with sniping in mind ... that was an incredibly difficult shot. Yeong-Ja was not superhuman. She was not perfect. He had seen her miss before.

The figure thrashed. They were close enough that Colin could see where the side of the helicopter was now sprayed with crimson. The mystery figure fell like a puppet with their strings cut. To Colin's surprise, the helicopter did not even hesitate. It continued to rise and peeled away, zooming off into the sky.

"Rogue agent eliminated," ISAC declared.

That only seemed to raise more questions as far as Colin was concerned. He pulled the boat up right to the edge of the helipad, next to where the other three fanboats were parked. He turned off the engine with a click. The fan died away. They were left standing in silence, save for the lap of water against the hull of the boat.

Maira was the first out of the boat and onto the helipad. She had her rifle ready, but there didn't seem to be any active threats. Unfortunately, instead there was a morgue's worth of dead bodies. She counted swiftly. Nine of them were the dark-garbed Reborn enforcers all of them were familiar with at this point. The tenth body was a woman dressed in green, laid out on her back. The Reborn symbol on her chest was spoiled by a collection of ragged red patches on her chest. The eleventh and final body was the man Yeong-Ja had shot on their way in.

He was dressed in combat armor of a very familiar style. The same style issued by the Strategic Homeland Division. It might have protected him, if the bullet hadn't hit below his left eye socket. As it was, the bullet had continued on through his cranium. It should be simple to get his thoughts on the matter, Maira thought with distant dryness. After all, they were spilled all over the concrete.

He even had an ISAC brick on his shoulder, Maira noted. She frowned at it, though. Most people might not have noticed, but computers were Maira's whole thing. ISAC was just as interesting as any of them; she had spent a fair amount of time messing with bricks while she was stuck recuperating at the Kansas Core. This one was modified. She couldn't be sure how with just a visual inspection, but...

The woman coughed.

"Oh god," Raffiel said behind Maira.

He hobbled forward in his chains, climbing off the boat and onto the helipad clumsily. Colin came up behind as if to stop him, but Leo held up a hand haltingly. Raffiel continued on, blind to the interplay, and fell to his knees next to the woman in green. A low cry of sorrow escaped him. Maira stepped up behind him and looked down. The features on the woman were familiar. She had seen them once on a mugshot.

This was Cassandra Raines.

"What happened?" whispered Raffiel. He cradled her head in his lap.

"Betrayed," Cassandra managed. Blood bubbled on her lips. She reached up to touch Raffiel's cheek. "Raff…"

"Shhh, shhh, it's okay," Raffiel said. "You're going to be OK."

Colin had stepped next to her as well. He was examining the gunshot wounds that perforated her abdomen. He looked up and met Maira's gaze. His face was grim, and he shook his head slightly.

"Mistakes," Cassandra said. There were tears in her eyes. "So many. Sent you away. Didn't believe you. Mistake…"

"You were the only one who saw, Cass, the only one. Everyone stumbles. Everyone."

Cassandra was gone. Her glassy eyes no longer saw anything. Raffiel's words fell away into silence. He sobbed, rocking slowly back and forth and holding her. Leo took a step toward him but hesitated. In the end, he completed the motion and rested a hand on his brother's shoulder. Raffiel reached up and gripped that hand tightly.

Maira looked to the others. Yeong-Ja had stayed in the boat, but she was clearly shaken. The wholesale slaughter was not an easy sight. Colin worked his way from body to body, checking each of them with a medic's care. He shook his head each time, finally crouching next to the dead man with the Division watch that Yeong-Ja had taken out. There was no need for a check there.

"ISAC said he was a rogue agent, didn't he?" asked Colin.

"I thought that's what I heard," Maira said. "ISAC, confirm identification."

"Authenticating SHD credentials," the AI said. "Identity

confirmed. Name: Benjamin Marsh. Agent Status: Rogue. Known Associates: Javier Kajika. Theo Parnell. Aaron Keener. Current Status: KIA."

"Wait." Colin rose to his full height and stepped back. "This is one of Keener's rogues?"

"That's how it sounds," Yeong-Ja said. There was a certain relief to the words that Maira understood. It would mean she hadn't actually shot a Division agent.

"But his watch was orange... it still is," Colin protested.

"Huh," Maira said. "About that."

She stepped up and knelt beside the body. The brick that had caught her attention was on the man's shoulder. It was easy to detach it from the harness and get a closer look at it. It was as she'd suspected when she first noticed them on the fanboat – it was modified in a number of very intriguing ways.

"For one thing," Maira said. "This thing isn't even plugged in to ISAC anymore."

"What?" asked Yeong-Ja.

"I don't know. It's rigged to access a different network. That's not all though. It's putting out a local signal of its own using this little widget." Maira pulled a screwdriver from her kit. "I bet that if I..."

"Maira, be careful," warned Colin.

"Me? I'm never anything less. Ha, got it!"

The nodule came loose in her hand. It was intact, but she'd managed to remove it. Immediately, the watch the dead man wore flashed and turned red. Each of the agents fairly radiated surprise. Maira, even having suspected it, had to admit she was still shocked she'd been right.

"He was spoofing his own watch? Somehow had it convinced he was legit?" asked Colin.

"Apparently," Maira said. She retrieved the watch itself, too. "Give me a second. I bet I can access whatever information is stored locally."

The others had enough faith in her to leave her to it. Or perhaps they just didn't have any better ideas, Maira mused. Regardless, she retrieved her tablet from her gear and interfaced with the watch. There were firewalls in place, of course, but Maira had spent a great deal of time familiarizing herself with how Division technology worked. There was only so much that could be done on certain hardware.

Maira bit her lip, concentrating.

"Aha."

"New information uploaded. ECHO available for playback," ISAC said.

"Play it," Leo said.

"ECHO playback starting now."

A scene coalesced in the familiar glowing orange. It showed the dead agent, Marsh, standing and waiting on the helipad. The trio of fanboats were pulling up. Each had a couple of enforcers on it, with room left over. Raines stepped off one in particular. There was curious dignity to how she walked.

"You're late," said Marsh. "I was starting to worry you weren't coming."

"My apologies," Raines said. "It has been a tumultuous few days."

The way she talked struck Maira. This was, in theory, a more casual version of her than the broadcasts, but she still spoke like she was addressing an audience. Some of that had rubbed off on Raffiel, Maira thought.

"No worries. Just glad you managed to make it." Marsh looked around thoughtfully. "This everybody you brought with you?"

"It is. They will help me load up the cargo. Where is the cargo, by the way?"

There was an edge to Raines's voice. Some fear. Maira could imagine. If these people stopped supplying her, she was going to be almost helpless before the Molossi onslaught. Her dream would be as good as dead right then and there.

"Oh, yeah. No worries. We got it aboard the helicopter right here. One sec."

Marsh turned away. Maira frowned. He had something in his hand. It was familiar. He pressed a button and–

Bullets blasted in from every angle. Multiple sources. Maira didn't need to see them to know what she was looking at. The usage was familiar. SHD striker drones being unleashed. They must have been hovering down by the waterline. They could be nearly silent when they wanted to be, and in the dark would have been nearly invisible.

It was over within seconds. The orange shapes had collapsed to overlap with their real-world counterpart corpses. Only Raines was still moving. She was staring around in complete bewilderment, untouched by the drones. Marsh turned to face her again.

"Sorry about all this, for what it's worth."

Raines crouched down to touch the nearest dead enforcer. She looked up with wide, stricken eyes. "Why?"

"Nothing personal. You were very useful for a while. Thanks

for that. But you wanna know the secret?" Marsh pulled a pistol from his thigh holster. "Nobody stays useful forever."

"Please, d–"

He shot her in the chest six times. She fell where her body now lay, gurgling. The sound died away with a last choking rasp. Marsh holstered the gun and shook his head with a click of his tongue.

"Pity. Ah well. It'll be my turn, too, someday, I'm sure," Marsh said.

Marsh's hologram then raised his eyes to the horizon and he frowned. "Who?" He turned to call back to the helicopter. "Hey, there's another boat coming! Spin it up!"

"She must have lied," someone answered from out of view in the helicopter. "She's not alone."

"Oh my god," Colin said. "That can't be…?"

The playback continued without pause. Marsh stepped to the edge of the platform and frowned. "No, hold on, these ain't Reborn."

"What?" the offscreen man demanded.

"Nope, nope. I can see the fucking glow from here. It's our long-lost kinfolk come to visit," said Marsh. "Now ain't that a hell of a thing?"

"ANNA, confirm. Do we have Division agents incoming?" demanded the offscreen voice.

There was no audible answer, but he cursed sharply. The rotors were spinning up already.

"How'd they even figure out we're here?" asked Marsh in bemusement.

"I don't know, and I don't care!" barked the other voice. "Quit fucking around and get over here!"

Marsh walked back over to grab on to the helicopter. The rest of the recording played out as Maira expected. The helicopter started to take off. Marsh's head rocked under the impact of a bullet. He spasmed and fell to the landing pad where his real-world body waited. The helicopter lifted out of view and dissolved. The playback ended.

Colin stood standing in the middle of where the scene had played out. He looked stricken. Maira took a step toward him in concern. Raffiel stared at all of them like they were crazy. Maira realized, lacking their lenses and earpieces, he had seen none of that.

"Killed her and her people," Leo said quietly. "Her allies did. Gunned them down. Said they weren't useful anymore."

"Colin," Maira said. "What's wrong?"

Colin's gaze slowly refocused from the middle distance and onto her. He swallowed hard, but still looked sick to his stomach. "We need to access all the files in his system. I need to know everything we can find out."

"Why?" she asked.

"Because I recognized the voice of the other rogue. It's impossible, it can't be, but that was David Georgio."

The sun was fully up by the time they'd gathered as much information as they could. Everyone sat around on the platform with dark expressions. Colin knew he was shaking, but he couldn't make himself stop. It was like someone had taken ice and injected it right into the core of his body. He felt cold all the way through.

The files of the rogues had revealed a number of horrifying things. The first and most obvious was that they had been using the Reborn for some time. They had made contact with the faction months ago, under the guise of being agents in good standing. The materiel they had been able to offer Raines had been more than enough to convince her to accept their help. It had jump-started her entire plan to move on the surrounding area, accelerating her timetable by months or even years.

Raffiel was understandably hit hard by this revelation. Out of all of them, he was the one who looked as heartsick as Colin himself. He sat now at the edge of the landing pad with his legs hanging over the side. His gaze was locked on the Louisiana coast in the distance.

The second thing was what had gotten to Colin in his turn. It was a set of missives that had been sent to the leader of the Molossi, none other than Colonel Marcus Georgio. These missives had informed him that the rogues had captured his son from New York and had him in their grasp. They had not minced any words. If Marcus refused to do as they told him, David would pay the price.

From there, the rogue agents had given the colonel a series of instructions. First, to move on the refineries along the Texas coast and seek to take them under his protection. Protection from what, the colonel had apparently demanded. The rogues had promised a worthy threat would manifest itself. It was a procession of dancing puppets from that point.

On the one hand, there was the Reborn. Assailing the Freighties and launching their offensive, they brought terror to the entire region. The Molossi moved in counterpoint to them. Under the threat of Reborn invasion, local communities who would normally have had no interest were desperate. They invited the Molossi inside one by one.

The arrival of the Division cell was somewhere between irrelevant and a bonus. The rogues had instructed Marcus to provoke them into taking the Reborn on. The rogue seemed to believe that would be plenty to wipe Colin and his cell off the map. In all honesty, they hadn't been far off. Colin knew luck had played a part in the fact that they had survived at all.

"And now," Maira said quietly, "their plan has come to fruition. The Molossi are poised to destroy the Reborn. In the process, they have soldiers inside every community from Dallas to Houston. The rogues have control of the Molossi, through their leverage on the colonel."

Leo nodded slowly. "And once the Reborn are destroyed, they will have tacit control over this entire region, along with the majority of the oil production in this half of the country."

"He was dead," Colin said. The words felt heavy coming out of him, like he had to force each one. This simply wasn't possible. "How could he not be dead?"

Yeong-Ja rested a gentle hand on his arm. "You were not there. You fell. How could you have known?"

Colin shook his head. "The reinforcements. They must have dragged me out and just left him. I knew quarantine was fast on their heels, but… surely…"

"They had no reason to believe he was alive either," Maira said sadly. "It was a miracle that you were after what happened."

"And the rogues moved into the quarantine on purpose, and they found him," Leo concluded.

"But that ECHO, that was his voice," insisted Colin. "He wasn't a prisoner. He sounded like he was flying the damn helicopter."

Maira shook her head. "I don't know. I don't have an answer to that part. There is one more piece of information, however."

"I don't know that I can take any more shocks to my system," Colin said wearily.

"No more big surprises," Maira said. "But an important fact all the same. I know where the rogues are operating out of."

That got everyone's attention. Even Raffiel turned his head to look at them from where he sat. Colin wasn't sure what the surge of emotion in his chest was. There was anger and confusion and fear and guilt. He shook his head. There was no picking it apart. It was like a congealed mass, threatening to choke him.

"Where?" asked Leo.

"They were right near us the whole time. Right in the heart of Houston. The Battleship *Texas*," Maira said. "That's the source of their network signal. It must be where they're headquartered."

"The old museum?" asked Yeong-Ja. "I had hoped to visit it once."

"Not a museum anymore. There's no one to visit," Maira said. "Now it's the local operations center for this branch of Keener's merry band of assholes."

"OK," Colin managed to rasp out. "OK."

"Easy," Yeong-Ja said.

He shook his head sharply. "I'm fine. We know where they are, right? So we go after them. We nail them to the wall for everything they've done here. For orchestrating all of this and playing us in the process."

Maira looked worried. "I don't know."

Colin blinked at her in surprise. "What? Why not?"

"Colin, we're used up. Have you seen us? All we have are stolen small arms, a boat, and bad attitudes. Rogues... look, I'm no expert, but I've met one. They're like us, right? Highly trained, well equipped, even the tech to judge by that holo," Maira said.

"A rogue agent is easily among the most dangerous of foes we could encounter," Yeong-Ja said.

"Yeah, and if these files are anything to go by? I mean, I can't be sure, it's not like there's a list, but there's more than one. Could be as many as four. They'd be a match for us on a good day," Maira said regretfully.

Leo crossed his arms over his chest. "What other option? Just run?"

"We've cut to the heart of this," Maira said. "We fall back now, and we get reinforcements. With a few more cells to help us, we can smoke them out no problem."

"If we leave," Colin said heavily, "they will have won by the time we can get any help. They're this close, Maira. If we don't take them down now, we might never get the chance again. You didn't want the Molossi with their hand on the Division's throat. How much worse will it be if that hand actually belongs to people like Aaron Keener?"

Maira took a deep breath. "Look–"

"Network access detected," ISAC announced.

"Fucking shit," Maira said.

All the agents scrambled to be ready. They scanned around the horizon frantically. Colin clutched his rifle so tight it was digging into his hands. His emotions felt like the needle of a compass in the middle of a magnetic storm, spinning wildly with no direction.

"What does network access mean?" Yeong-Ja asked.

"I don't know," Maira said. "Wait, there–"

A drone was flying overhead. It was so high it was just a speck. Yeong-Ja immediately began to try to line up a shot. Colin stared at it with cold fury. Was this one of the rogue drones they'd used in the hologram? Why only send one? It didn't make sense.

"SHD broadcast detected," ISAC said.

"What the hell?" Maira said, blinking.

"What does it say?" asked Leo in surprise.

There was a pause.

"This is a message from Agent Brenda Wells to the attention of Agent Maira Kanhai, or any member of her cell. I received your broadcast. I'm doing what I can to arrange for help, but it's going to take time. For now, though, I've sent this drone to find you. I can't help directly, but I might be able to point you to something that can."

CHAPTER 15

Coordinates.

In the end, that was what Brenda had been able to provide them. The drone had only given them a recording, so there was no way to ask her questions. Or, for that matter, to tell her what they were really up against at this point. Maira and the others just had to head to the location she'd indicated and hope for the best.

The coordinates took them south of Houston, into what had once been known as the Brazoria National Wildlife Refuge. The fanboat howled along as fast as Colin could get it to go. Each of them slept along the way as best they could. It was not what Maira would have called the most restful trip she'd ever taken, but her exhaustion was sufficient that she got some shut-eye all the same.

When she woke, Leo was driving the boat instead. Colin had stretched his long body out on the deck. He was lying there with his mouth hanging open, snoring away. Maira smiled faintly at the sight.

She stood and walked over to stand next to Leo. "I'm glad you were able to give him a break."

Leo nodded with a flicker of a smile. "Driven all kinds. Wasn't hard."

"So do we know anything about this place we're going to?" Maira asked.

"ISAC?" Leo said.

"A combination of freshwater and saline environments, Brazoria is home to a diversity of coastal wildlife, including more than three hundred and twenty species of birds, ninety-five species of reptiles and amphibians, and one hundred and thirty species of butterflies and dragonflies. The estuary provides ample food resources for large populations of wintering waterfowl, shore and wading birds that are easily seen from the auto tour at Big Slough," ISAC provided.

Maira nodded slowly. "Well. That's delightful. Do you think there's time to get a ticket to the auto tour?"

Leo cracked a grin. "Might have to miss it."

"Shit," Maira said with a sigh. "I guess there's always next year."

Maira glanced over to where Raffiel was sitting. Even he had fallen asleep, curled up against the side of the boat. He looked very young lying there. Maira supposed he wasn't even past thirty after all. The way the world was now, no one got to stay young. It wasn't fair, but it was the facts of life.

Kazi had never even gotten a chance to reach twenty, Maira thought. It hurt just to have to hold that in her head. She pressed a hand to her chest and sighed.

"Wasn't a bad kid," Leo said.

He must have noticed where she was looking. Maira smiled at him. "He didn't annoy the shit out of you?"

"Of course. Little brothers. No other choice." Leo gave her a sad smile. He knew what she'd lost. "But a good kid anyway. Good grades. Clean room. No trouble. Not like me."

"Oh, you were the black sheep of the family?"

Leo nodded. "Told you. Bad youth. Lots of trouble. Joined the service to get away from it. Then I had to leave the service to try to find him."

"Raffiel seemed to think otherwise," Maira said. "Though I admit I don't follow French."

Leo laughed quietly. "Raffiel was born eight years after me, Maira. When I was causing trouble, he was just a little boy. By the time he was ten I was trying to straighten out. The version of me he thought he knew was one that had already made those mistakes."

"I guess it's funny, how all we ever know is a part of a person," Maira said. "No wonder he never imagined you'd come after him on your own. That must have been hard, to be activated before you'd found him."

"It was." He swallowed hard. "Almost didn't go."

Maira could only stare at him about this revelation. "You almost ignored your activation?"

Leo nodded. "Proud to be Division, but... family is family. Made my choice in the end, showed up, did what I was supposed to. I spent the last year and a half wondering if I'd made the wrong choice."

"He's here, Leo. You found him in the end," Maira said.

"Yeah, but tied up in this..." Leo growled and gestured, "... Reborn horseshit. I should have been there. Should have kept him out of this nonsense."

"It's a lot to take in," said Maira. "So, what's the plan now?"

Leo took a deep breath. He glanced at her out of the corner of his eye as if afraid to look at her directly. "Want to let him go."

"What, now?" Maira asked.

"Stop off, yeah. Unchain and cut him loose," Leo said.

"OK," Maira said. "Why?"

"Not his fight now. If the rogues see him with us? They'll kill him if they can. Don't want that."

She mulled it over for a few seconds. "Why tell me? What's stopping you from just doing it?"

"He's my brother, but I know what I would think if he wasn't. He's a Division prisoner. High profile. Useful. Also maybe dangerous, free. Nearly killed us before. Nearly killed you." Leo did not bother to hide his shame on this subject.

"Ah," Maira said. She blew out a deep sigh. "Yeah. I mean, that's a tough one. He's not a choir boy, Leo. But then, who on this boat is? I've made choices I regret, but I've lived to get a chance to make new ones."

Leo's gaze was hopeful. Maira smiled at him.

"Yeah. Cut the kid loose. Maybe he can make a difference with the Reborn now that he knows what they are doing wrong. Hey, wake up, everybody!"

Colin sat up, snore ending in a startled choke. He wiped spit off his cheek blearily. Yeong-Ja lifted her head with a tremendous yawn. Raffiel himself jerked awake as if stung. He looked around wildly, then frowned and sank back.

"What's up?" asked Colin sleepily.

"We gotta make a little pit stop," Maira said. "Turn the second Fourte loose on the world once more."

To her surprise, Yeong-Ja simply nodded as if this made

complete sense. Colin frowned for a few seconds as he let it work through his brain. This took longer than it might have otherwise, purely due to fatigue, Maira imagined. He shrugged and reached into a pocket. He pulled the manacle key out and tossed it to Maira. Raffiel watched this entire exchange uneasily.

"All right then." Maira turned to Leo. "Bring us in."

Leo smiled as broadly as Maira had ever seen him. He steered the boat in toward the coast. They were soon stopped a short way onto the shore. The ground was predictably very swampy. There was nothing to be seen just looking around. Maira stepped over to stand in front of Raffiel.

"On your feet."

The former Reborn commander stood clumsily. The look he gave her did not suggest a massive surplus of trust.

"Why are you doing this?" he asked.

"Because Leo wants to. And because even you deserve a second chance. Maybe you'll be able to turn the Reborn around now that you know what's wrong and what's right. Hands?" Maira said.

Raffiel held them out uneasily. Maira unlocked the manacles on his wrists, then crouched and did the same for his legs. He stretched experimentally, then stepped toward the edge of the boat. He threw one leg over the side. Only then did he look back.

"Leo," he said.

"Yeah?" Leo asked.

"Thank you. For this. For… coming after me. Will I see you again?" It was a small question, asked with an almost funny casualness considering the scenario.

"If I live. If I don't, I'll haunt you instead," Leo said matter-of-factly.

Raffiel smiled at that. He glanced around to the rest of the group and just nodded. He leapt from the boat to squelch onto the ground. With no further ado he walked away. Leo didn't watch him go. He steered the boat back onto the water and they were on their way again to their mystery destination.

"He'll be OK," Maira said.

"Course he will," Leo said. "He's a Fourte."

"Quite a family," Colin said. He stretched back out and was soon snoring once again.

Colin woke to a hand on his shoulder. It was Yeong-Ja. It took him a second to process that fact. He must have slept for a few hours, but even so all he wanted to do was stay down for a few thousand more. Perhaps simply expire.

Instead, he got up with a sigh. "What's the situation?"

They were among the wetlands once again, markedly disgusting stench and ever-present swarms of blood-sucking insects both testifying to that fact. Brown water and stretches of soggy land surrounded them as far as the eye could see.

"Nearly at the coordinates," Leo said.

"Can't imagine what will be there," Colin replied. "I like Brenda, but are we sure she's all there these days? There's nothing here but muck and bugs."

"Brenda wouldn't steer us wrong," Maira said. "She didn't know the whole situation, but whatever she sends us to will help."

She sounded like she was trying to convince herself as

much as anyone else. Colin shrugged. It wasn't like this side jaunt could make their situation any worse. It might delay the inevitable, but that was it. Sooner or later, they had to confront this band of rogues, and it wasn't a fight they seemed likely to win.

Colin was still struggling to process his emotions around that. On one level, he couldn't imagine leaving without at least trying to settle matters. On another, he desperately wanted his new cell to leave anyway. If one of them got killed in this insanity, he would never forgive himself. Just like he'd never forgiven himself for David's assumed death.

Of course, at the end of the day, the decision wasn't up to him. He wouldn't have left any of them behind, and they weren't going to abandon him. One way or another they were committed to this. Colin didn't know if he believed in destiny, but if it existed, he thought this must be what it felt like.

"Point of interest detected," noted ISAC.

"Huh," Colin said.

All of them looked around. There was still nothing but swamp in every direction. A few birds flew past. Something scaly splashed around in the nearby muck. A couple of hundred mosquitoes had brought their families for dinner. There was nothing Colin could see that would qualify as a point of interest.

"Are we sure we're at the right coordinates?" Maira asked uneasily.

Colin pulled the map up on his HUD. To judge by the movements of the others, they were doing the same. Sure enough, the blinking point was located right underneath them. Tilting his head, Colin stepped to the edge and peered around. There, to his surprise, was a rusting metal hatch. It was right next to the side of the fanboat.

"Oh," Colin said. "I, uh, I may have found it."

The other agents crowded over to the edge next to him to look.

"Is that actually it?" Maira asked.

ISAC highlighted it in orange for them. It was indeed the point of interest. If they wanted to know more, they would have to check it out. The only other option was to leave it behind and head for Houston. Colin shrugged.

"All right. I'll go down first. Yeong-Ja, you stay here. This one might not be best for somebody with a bad leg."

"Very well," Yeong-Ja said. "I'm on watch."

Colin took another look around at the endless stretches of swamp. "Yeah. You do that."

He clambered over the side and dropped to the ground. To his surprise, he landed with a dull clang rather than the squishy sinking he'd expected. There was metal plating around the visible hatch. He paced it out curiously. This thing was a fairly sizable vault.

Maira and Leo both landed nearby successively. Colin crouched, and the three of them together managed to turn the wheel on the hatch. It was surprisingly functional. The surface had definitely rusted, but in a strange way it didn't seem to go deeper than that. It was as if someone had designed it to do so, in order to help disguise it.

The hatch unlocked and swung open. The air that flowed past was utterly dry and stale. This place must have been protectively sealed for who knew how long. Colin got his flashlight out and shone it down into the dark. There were great iron cubes down there, lining the sides of the container. Each one had a glowing orange light on the front of it.

Colin climbed down into the vault proper. As he did, his watch chimed.

"SHD agent credentials authenticated," said ISAC. "Agent identified: Colin Harrison. File uploaded. Processing. Specialty equipment distributed."

One of the cubes hissed and opened. Colin examined it with some trepidation. It was a safe. Inside, to his surprise, lay a crossbow, a quiver of bolts, and a device he didn't recognize. He picked up the crossbow. It was ruggedly designed and patterned in camouflage. The device was a sphere, marked by black, silver, and green parts. Curious, Colin took all three items and emerged.

"Usage brief activated. Item: Explosive-Tipped Crossbow and Bolts. Crossbow is designed for all-environments usage. Each bolt is equipped with an explosive payload. When armed, the bolts will prime upon impact and detonate after a brief delay."

"Oh," Colin said. He blinked rapidly. "Thanks, ISAC. What about this doohickey?" He held up the orb.

"Usage brief activated. Item: Mender. When activated, the Mender will hover in the vicinity of the controlling agent. The Mender is a prototype device, capable of both distributing emergency armor repairs as well as first aid to injured combatants."

"Where has this been the whole time?" Colin asked in astonishment.

He turned to find Maira standing nearby. She held a weapon he didn't recognize in her arms. It was marked by six launch ports on the front of it. She had her head tilted curiously. Colin had to assume she was getting a brief on her new device much as he had. Behind her, Leo was already climbing out. He had, of all things, a minigun strapped to his back.

Colin scrambled up and out as well. Yeong-Ja was peering from above in the boat.

"What's going on down there?" she asked.

"Division Christmas, or something," Colin said. "I think I underestimated Brenda."

"Now hold on," Yeong-Ja said. "Am I being left out of this?"

Colin laughed. "Here, uh, wave your watch out over the opening."

Yeong-Ja leaned out as far as she dared and did as he'd asked.

"ISAC? Can you pick that up? Agent Cha can't access the vault directly due to an injury. Can you facilitate scanning her watch from here?" Colin asked.

Colin could hear the watch chime from up above. He looked down to see another of the safes was opening. He climbed back down into the vault to retrieve the items being dispensed for the wounded agent. One was a sniper rifle of intimidating proportions, the other a drone. Picking them up, Colin climbed back to the surface.

"Merry Divs-mas," he called.

Yeong-Ja reached down and retrieved the items from him. That freed him up to climb back into the boat himself. Once he was back on board, he found Yeong-Ja staring at the new rifle in her lap with wide eyes.

"I think I might be in love," she said.

Colin couldn't help but laugh at that. The other two

were soon back on board as well. He could see it in each of their eyes, the same thing he was feeling. It was a renewed determination. Stripped of every advantage they had in the course of the mission, they had felt increasingly hopeless. Maybe this unusual resupply would make the difference, or maybe it wouldn't. It felt like it put them back in the fight though. Now, at least, they had a chance.

"Is there anything more we can do to tip this in our favor?" asked Maira.

"You don't think the supplies will be enough?" asked Yeong-Ja.

Maira studied the advanced missile launcher she was carrying. "I think these are impressive weapons, but we're still not at our best. As far as we know, our enemies are fresh. I'd take any advantage we can get."

"I suppose if we have any aces in the hole, now is the time to play them," the sniper agreed.

"Well," Colin started. "There is one possibility."

He was reluctant to put the idea forward. So much of this mission had gone wrong that inviting further variables seemed like a mistake. The two women had a strong point, however. If there was anything they could do to strengthen their position, it was now or never.

"Well?" Maira prodded.

"We could ask the Molossi for help," Colin said.

The reaction from the rest of the agents was immediate. Maira flinched like he'd suggested setting themselves ablaze directly. Yeong-Ja frowned and scratched the back of her head. Even Leo's brow furrowed with concern. Colin forged ahead quickly.

"Look, I understand. Our contacts with them haven't exactly been smooth up until this point. But things have changed. We know what was behind that now. Colonel Georgio thinks they have his son hostage, but they don't."

"Having seen how they treat their allies, I'm not sure there's much difference," Yeong-Ja said softly.

"Even so, it changes things," Colin said. "If we tell him we're going to where David is right now, that if he helps us maybe we can take David alive..."

"And what if he refuses? What if he tries to stop us, even?" asked Maira.

"We won't tell him where we're actually going, not until he's agreed to help us," Colin said. "What can he do?"

There was an uneasy silence against the backdrop of the noisy swamp wildlife all around them. Colin could tell the rest of his cell were trying to answer or justify his question. In truth, he welcomed the effort. If they could think of a good reason to shoot this down, he'd be just as happy to forget about it. None of his conversations with Marcus Georgio had gone the way he'd hoped they would. But they had to assess every facet of the situation and the Molossi were something that could not be ignored.

"Worth a try." Leo shrugged.

Maira and Yeong-Ja both nodded in turn.

"All right," Colin said. "ISAC, will our radios reach Houston from here?"

"Affirmative," said the AI.

Colin took the handset off his shoulder and held it loosely. He took a deep breath and keyed the radio.

"This is Agent Colin Harrison of the Strategic Homeland

Division. I'd like to speak with Colonel Georgio of the Molossi."

He paused. The only answer on the radio was scratchy static. The other three agents looked on with anxious eyes. Colin avoided their gazes and swallowed hard. Would the colonel simply ignore them? Would he–

"Agent Harrison."

There was no mistaking the voice. It was Colonel Marcus Georgio himself. Colin felt his pulse speed up. Discovering that David had gone rogue seemed like it should have eased his survivor's guilt. Instead, Colin felt like it had only made it worse. David might not have ever been an angel, but something must have pushed him across that final threshold. What else would do that but being abandoned to die?

"I must say, it takes a certain courage to reach out this way," the colonel continued. "Shall I say thank you for not killing any of my men on your way out of the compound?"

"I don't kill unless I have to, colonel. You don't have to thank me for that," Colin said.

"How noble." There was a note of genuine regret in the colonel's voice. "I assume this is not a social call. What has driven you to make contact?"

"We've found David," Colin said.

Static again. It was quiet enough that Colin could hear a frog leap into the swamp water nearby. It made a splash and then swam off, blithely. He felt a moment's envy of the little creature. Surely nothing it had to do today could be this miserable.

"Do you have him?" the colonel asked.

That was it. No protestations, no pretending not to know

what Colin was talking about. It was almost funny how matter of fact the man was about the whole issue. In a way, Colin admired it. It required a certain type of keen mind to adapt so swiftly to changing circumstances, to accept when the jig was up.

"No," Colin said. "We know where he is, though. Colonel, that's not all. He's not a hostage as you've been told."

"Where is he?" asked the colonel.

Colin frowned. "Did you not hear what I said? David isn't a hostage. He's a rogue agent. He's been lying to you to control you."

A pause. "I heard you, Agent Harrison. What is it, exactly, that you imagine this changes?"

Colin didn't know how to answer. The other agents looked as astonished as he felt. Maira shook her head slowly with a deep frown.

"It changes everything," Colin managed finally. "How can you not care that your son is lying to you? That he's used your fear for him against you?"

"I do care, more than you can know," the colonel said heavily. "It simply does not change the outcome. I discarded my son for his sins once, agent, and had to feel the regret of that when I thought he'd died. I will not make the same mistake twice."

"You knew," Colin said, astounded.

"I suspected. Does it truly shock you, Agent Harrison? Had he really changed that much by the time you knew him?"

Colin considered this in silence. He'd spent over a year doing his best not to think about those desperate December days in New York. Being here, seeing Marcus, having another cell… all of that had changed things. The memories had been bubbling up over the past few days. It was growing harder to ignore the truth that he had built up a set of protective lies around that time.

He had beatified David in his mind. In a way, Colin had had to. To think callously of a man he hadn't been able to save – a fellow agent, too – would have felt like a betrayal. It would have dragged him even deeper into guilt's embrace. It had been one thing when he'd thought David was dead and gone. Now he was alive and causing harm… Colin had to face the truth.

"That is what I thought," Georgio said into the silence. "I fear he is a monster, Agent Harrison, but he is still my son."

Colin cleared his throat roughly. "So help us. Help us stop him. With your help we can take him alive. We can put this whole matter to rest."

"I wish…" Georgio trailed off briefly. He sounded deeply weary. "Alas, we do not live in a world of wishes."

"Shit," Maira whispered.

"It's not as if we're going to turn ourselves in to you," Colin said firmly. "Helping us is the only way you can affect how this plays out. Be our ally."

"I understand why you believe that – you have been cagey with the information you have given me. However, I have my own card left to play. Have you thought about your Node recently, Agent Harrison?"

"Oh, fucking hell," Maira said, her face aghast.

"I don't believe the rogues even knew you had it, as they have not commanded me to destroy it already. I left it for that reason. A small rebellion, you see. A tiny way of remaining my own man," the colonel said.

"Colonel, don't do anything rash–" Colin started quickly.

"David needs me, Agent Harrison, and I will not let you hurt him," Marcus Georgio said.

"Node signal lost," ISAC announced.

At once, all of their SHD tech died. ISAC's most advanced capabilities shut down. Their new weapons deactivated with hums and clicks. Safety interlocks, Colin supposed numbly. There to keep the Division's most advanced weapons from falling into the wrong hands.

"I am sorry, for what it is worth," Colonel Georgio said. "If you choose to run, I will not chase you. I can promise you that. You can still save yourselves. I hope you will. Colonel Georgio, out."

The four agents sat on the small boat and stared at one another. Colin's hand covered his mouth. He could feel the stubble all around it. He always made it a point to stay clean-shaven, but it had been impossible on this mission. Impossible. Just like any chance of their stopping the rogues now.

"Whatever advantage we had," Yeong-Ja said, looking down at her now defunct weapon, "it's gone now."

"I'm sorry, I..." Colin didn't know what to say. This was something he hadn't even thought of.

"We all agreed to it," Leo said firmly. "It's not on you alone."

"So we fall back," Yeong-Ja said desolately. "We retreat to Kansas or Tennessee. Maybe we can regroup..."

"That's one idea," Maira said.

She had been frowning ever since the Node was killed. Yet

Colin saw something in her eyes. A gleam. It would be a lie to say he knew her well, as they had only been together a short time, really. Yet something about it made a spark of hope burn in his chest again.

"I might just have another," she said.

"So this is all the gear we took off that dead rogue," Maira said.

Said gear was lying on the floor of the boat. They had Marsh's weapons, his harness, his pack, even his modified ISAC brick. It was this last item that Maira picked up and showed to the others. They looked confused. She couldn't blame them. This was her wheelhouse, not theirs. She tapped a finger on the brick. The little activation light still glowed bright red, in marked contrast to the dull orange of all their own gear.

"This bastard is still connected to a full-strength network," Maira continued.

"That doesn't seem like it helps us, Maira," Colin said dubiously.

"Their gear will work and ours won't," Yeong-Ja agreed. "That seems bad."

"Normally I would agree with you. If it was just the three of you here, I think you'd be shit out of luck. As it is, however, I'm here, and that means this could be the key to us being back in the fight."

Leo had been listening quietly. Maira noticed he was smiling now, just a bit.

"If you can't beat them ..." Leo said.

"Join them," Maira finished.

"You want us to go rogue?" Colin asked, confused and alarmed.

"No, not really," Maira said quickly. "But what I can do is modify our bricks the same way our dead rogue's has been adjusted. I can take us off ISAC and the SHD Network completely and plug us into their network instead."

"Wait," Colin said thoughtfully. "That's…"

"That's brilliant," Yeong-Ja said with genuine delight. "Our gear does not directly connect with the SHD Network."

"That's right," Maira confirmed smugly. "They interface through our watches. If we're on this other network, so are they. All of our weapons and toys? Back online. It's not that extra edge I was hoping for, but at least we'd be on our feet again."

"Back in the fight," Colin said.

Maira nodded emphatically.

"Will it work?" Leo asked.

"I won't know until I try," Maira admitted. "But their gear isn't a different hardware set. It's all built on the same principles as ours. In theory, it's sound."

"Well, I don't see how it could make things worse," Colin said.

Maira winced. "Oh, please don't say that. Now we're probably screwed."

"Try it," Yeong-Ja said eagerly.

The two men nodded. Maira took a deep breath.

"All right," Maira said. "Be quiet while I try to work a little magic."

Maira got out all the tools she would need. Some were actual tools, screwdrivers and the like. Her tablet was also present, along with all the cracking programs she carried around. She retrieved the ISAC brick from each Division agent. That part, at least, she understood. She'd spent plenty of time and energy examining the fundamentals of SHD tech during her time at the Kansas Core.

The question was, how had the rogues modified it? Maira had her guess as to who had done it, at least. The same person who had allowed Rowan to steal control of their devices before. This was the work of Theo Parnell. He was dead, of course. She was starting to feel like perhaps the man was her ghostly nemesis. She constantly found herself having to undo his technological mischief.

Maira was distantly aware that the tip of her tongue was sticking out of the corner of her mouth. Call her superstitious, but that always helped her concentrate. She didn't pay it any mind. This was particularly fiddly work. She put her friends and allies out of her mind as well. Letting herself be distracted by worry could lead to disaster for all of them. The best thing she could do for them was focus.

Once she thought she had grasped the changes the rogues had made to the brick, the trick was recreating those changes on each of theirs. She didn't have all the bits necessary for such work. Some of it she had to get creative with. She ended up cannibalizing some parts from the dead rogue's watch as well just to help see the job done.

It must have been an hour, maybe more, but it was finally ready. Maira blinked and rubbed her sleeve across her eyes. They felt dry and scratchy. She probably hadn't been blinking enough. That didn't matter. Colin probably had some eyedrops in that wonderbag of his. She looked up to realize all of them were staring at her.

"OK," Maira said, feeling in the limelight. "Let's hook them up and see what we've got."

"If this goes wrong, will the rogues be able to find us?" asked Colin.

Maira hesitated. "Maybe. If this goes wrong, we should probably call it and run as fast as we can for a lot of reasons."

Leo snorted. "Do it."

They each reattached the modified bricks to their gear. Each one still glowed that dull, listless orange. No connection. Maira took a deep breath and lifted her tablet. A single program remained to be run. She tapped the control on the screen.

"ISAC offline," the AI announced.

Even the limited functions they'd still had available shut down. The faded light on their gear died away completely. They sat in uncomfortable silence, with only the slosh of the muck around the boat and the calls of wildlife to keep them company.

Then, the lights came back on. They burned bright red like distant volcanoes. Their watches swiftly followed suit. Maira looked down at the shining crimson ring on her wrist. It was a strange thing, to see something she'd learned to hate and feel such a sense of triumph at the sight of it.

"ANNA activated," a new voice said.

It was a distaff counterpart to the bland masculinity of ISAC. There was something more to it, though, Maira thought. A little more attitude, perhaps. The sense that whatever program this thing was running, it wasn't as restricted. That, as long as they were connected, they were encouraged to break the rules, too.

"Greetings, rogues. Are we ready to cause some trouble?" ANNA asked.

Their gear came back online. HUDs rebooted in front of their eyes. The new weapons reactivated with the same series of clicks that had announced their deaths. A complete reversal, Maira thought with no small triumph. They were back in business. She looked around at the rest of the cell, each of them eyeing their restored weaponry, faces lit by red glows.

"I say it's time we visit Houston," Colin said.

"Yeah," Maira agreed. "Let's go sightseeing."

CHAPTER 16

To say the night had been a cold one was a powerful understatement. The gloves Colin wore did little to keep out the December chill. He would have given almost anything to swap the ones he had now for a nice pair of heavy-duty mittens. Unfortunately, those had a way of making it hard to hook his finger on the trigger of a gun. Mittens weren't suited to rescuing an agent in a city on the brink of anarchy.

David led the rescue mission. Colin and the others of their cell trailed a short distance behind him. Colin did his best to stay alert. The city had been bad enough when they first arrived. It was more dangerous with every passing day. It was hard to feel like the Division was succeeding. There was already talk of a need for reinforcements if there was going to be any hope of containing this crisis.

Jason walked beside Colin.

"I was thinking we should do something for Christmas," he said softly.

"Oh?" Colin asked.

"Yeah, you know, just something within the cell. A little gathering. Secret Santa maybe."

Colin chuckled. "Might be hard to buy gifts."

Jason's head snapped around like he'd been slapped. Colin blinked. He had only meant...

Jason's eyes were glassy, empty. An echo like thunder rolled over the street. The other agent toppled. He hit the ground bonelessly. No effort to save himself. He's dead, Colin thought in a daze. There was a messy hole punched into the side of his skull. Still, Colin dropped to one knee and tried to scoop the contents back inside. His hands shook.

"Fuck! Sniper!" screamed Serena.

She grabbed Colin by his collar and dragged him back into the side of a building. Assault rifles were chattering, too. David was still standing in the middle of the street, glaring down toward the end. A bullet pinged off the icy ground near him. With a snarl he whirled and followed after them.

"Where's the agent who put in the call?" yelled Serena over the roar of gunfire. She leaned out and fired back in short, controlled bursts.

"This wasn't supposed to go like this," growled David.

Colin blinked at him in confusion. It was like he was trying to think through a fog. Jason had been right next to him, alive. Then he was gone. That wasn't possible. He hadn't even had a chance to save the man. He looked down at his gloves. They were soaked with blood and covered in bits of bone and brain matter.

"Obviously not!" barked Serena at David. "Can you see the agent? ISAC!"

"Zero matches," ISAC said.

"What does that mean?" Serena said, bewildered. "Was the distress signal a fake?"

"Obviously," David said acidly. "This is an ambush."

"Doc, I need you to snap out of–" Serena started to say to Colin.

An RPG screamed in at high velocity. It hit the building above them and blasted the wall in. The overpressure hit them like God's fly-swatter. Colin was slammed to the sidewalk hard enough that he split his lips against the concrete. He came up with his ears ringing but his mind finally focused. He staggered to his feet and kicked the door of the storefront in.

"Get into cover!" Colin roared.

Serena staggered past him. David ducked past a second later. Colin followed them inside. It had been a clothes store before the Poison. Now the dark little shop was the site of an unexpected last stand. A second RPG impacted the building. It blew in the shop front windows in a rain of glass. Colin threw an arm across his face defensively. A shard still managed to nick his ear.

He swept the loose shards off his body and stepped to the empty window frame. Colin couldn't make out their assailants except for the occasional flash of a muzzle. He fired off a furious burst of return fire. It didn't do any good, but it briefly made him feel better.

"Doc!"

Colin's brief satisfaction evaporated. He turned to see Serena holding on to David. The man was clutching at his leg. A shard of glass a foot long stuck out from his thigh. Blood pulsed up around the shrapnel. Colin crossed the room in two strides.

"Cover us!" he called to Serena.

She darted past him. Colin heard her weapon open up behind him. He focused on putting pressure on David's wound with one hand. His other hand pulled his corpsman bag from his hip. His hands were still shaking. The bag fell from numb fingers and hit the ground, spilling some contents across the dirty store floor.

"Wasn't supposed to be me..." moaned David.

"Quiet, be quiet," Colin muttered.

"Colin!" Serena screamed.

Colin turned his head just in time to see a flame in the dark, headed their way. He reached out a hand toward her. The missile hit. Serena disintegrated in the blast. Blood and fragments of bone washed over him in a wave of grotesque heat. Colin was flung away from David. He skidded across the ground into a clothing display, knocking over a pair of mannequins. Painfully, he tried to drag himself back toward where David lay.

The roof began to fall.

It was night by the time Maira and her cell reached the city. In the end they had decided it was too risky to try to approach the Battleship *Texas* directly with the boat. The rogues were too likely to notice them. If they got spotted, who knew what tech the group had at their disposal. One Firefly would be plenty to send them to the bottom of the bay.

Instead, they left the fanboat at a nearby barge dock and proceeded the rest of the way on foot. Maira wondered if that was the last time she'd see the light little vessel. It had certainly served them well since they'd stolen it. If they didn't come back, she hoped someone else would find it and make good use of it.

It left them with about an hour's hike on foot. They walked most of the way in silence. It wasn't unpleasant. There was a companionable air over the group. Maira supposed that there was only so much they could go through together before they bonded by sheer necessity. In a way, that made this approach strangely more painful. They were heading to the ship together. Would all of them leave?

The last battle the four of them had faced as a group had been at Groves. To call it a disaster was likely being generous. Now they had to fight together once more. This time was going to be different, Maira told herself. It had to be. And if anyone was going to pay the price, let it be her.

Eventually the ship came into view out on the water. She was a massive shape of gray steel, more than five hundred feet long. A century ago, she had carried a thousand sailors to battle. She was connected to land by a single large ramp. Just as everything in the world was, the old ship suffered from a lack of maintenance. Rust had broken out across her hull like a bad rash. She rode lower in the water than seemed right. The quiet waves lapped against the hull, a constant sloshing background noise. Maira wondered if it could take too much longer before the *Texas* simply broke down and sank.

"Are we sure this is the place?" asked Colin quietly.

It was a fair question. From the outside there was nothing to indicate this was the center of all the madness they'd been through. The rogues were too smart to advertise their presence. All Maira could do was shrug helplessly.

"This is where the signal is coming from," she said.

"What if we just sank it?" asked Leo.

Maira blinked at him. "It's a priceless part of history."

The *Texas* was the last of the World War I dreadnoughts, and the only remaining capital ship to have served in both World Wars. She had once been a technological testbed, and then the first museum ship. The fact that the rogues were using it as their headquarters was an insult added to the injury of everything else they had done. It wasn't enough, apparently, to wreak mayhem across the region. They had to desecrate history, too.

"It's going to sink anyway," he replied.

"They'd get away," Colin said. "There's no way we could sink it fast enough to drown them or something. Think about it, would that work on us?"

"It would work on me at the moment," Yeong-Ja said thoughtfully.

Colin paused to consider. "Yeah, that's a fair point."

"Speaking of," Maira said. "You'd better set up in the parking lot across the way, Yeong-Ja."

The sniper frowned.

"I know," Maira said sympathetically. "But you're not up for a close quarters fight, and you're our fire support anyway."

"She's right," Leo agreed.

Yeong-Ja glanced between them then nodded reluctantly. "I will be there, and I will have my new drone airborne and keeping watch. Please don't make me come limping in after you."

"What's the plan for the rest of us?" Colin asked.

"We hunt them down," Maira said. It was increasingly hard to focus through the fatigue, but she said that with crystal clarity. They were all exhausted. It didn't matter. "We end this here tonight. We clear the entire ship."

"Sweep it room by room," Leo said.

"All right," Colin said. "But if David's here…"

"How do you want to handle it?" Maira asked gently.

"He's a rogue, and he's dangerous. I know that. If it's you or him, put him down." Colin took a deep breath. "But if you can spare his life…"

"We'll try," Maira said. "All right. Let's do this."

They set out toward the rusting hulk together.

Colin crossed the ramp first. He kept his new crossbow at the ready. It would have been nice to have time to practice with it, but it felt right in his hands. It was certainly a vast improvement over a handgun stolen from an incapacitated guard. The night was quiet. The ship lay in an undeveloped part of the city, marked mostly by cemeteries and soggy wetland.

"ANNA," Colin said quietly. "Are there any other rogue signals nearby?"

"Nope," the AI replied.

Colin frowned. It was possible the rogues were somewhere else right now. That would even work to their advantage. They could set a trap for their return. But it bothered him. It reminded him of the false signal back in… when David had…

"Scatter!" roared Colin.

They didn't question. Each of them sprinted in a different direction. They barely ran in time. Bursts of fire raked the deck in their wake. There were multiple shooters, Colin was sure of it. He ran as fast as he could for the other end of the ship. Luckily, the old ship was topped with a variety of structures and gun emplacements. He wove between them, putting cover between him and his foes.

Missed shots rang out behind him. Colin turned the corner

around the lowest tier of the great guns and skidded to a halt. Pounding boots rang on the deck behind him. Colin leaned out and loosed a crossbow bolt. He heard the thud of an impact followed by the detonation. Fire flashed against the night's darkness.

"You missed." The voice was cold as ice.

David. Colin cursed under his breath. He couldn't decide if he was glad he'd missed or not. He stayed low and reloaded the crossbow. David was a rogue, and the more that Colin confronted his memories the more he wondered how long that had been the case. Even so, did Colin have the will to use this new weapon? He imagined the bolt landing in the chest of the man he'd known, the man he'd tried to heal, and busting it open. Nausea rose at the image.

"My father said he'd disabled your gear. Another failure by the old man."

"He's doing his best to help you, David," Colin called. "I want to as well."

He needed to move. There was a raised part of the deck nearby. Colin climbed up on it and leapt toward the lowest gun barrels. He just managed to get his hands around one. Straining, he pulled himself up. He scrambled along the length of the barrel until he reached the roof of the gun housing.

"Help me how?" There was a genuine curiosity to David's question. "You both abandoned me when I needed you."

Colin stepped to the edge of the roof. He could see David below. His old comrade was prowling forward with an assault rifle held ready. Actually seeing him made Colin's chest ache. It was one thing to know all this. It was another to have to confront reality.

He could try to shoot now. At this angle the shot wasn't clear, but the bolts were explosive. Even a near miss might do the trick. He bared his teeth and put his finger on the trigger.

Colin frowned. The memories of that night were painfully vivid. Nothing was locked away anymore, however much he wished it could be.

He needed an answer.

"David," Colin called.

The rogue agent turned and looked up. He found himself peering down the length of Colin's crossbow. His only reaction was a small, cold smile.

"So, what now?" David asked.

"Now you tell me the truth," Colin said. He couldn't keep his voice from shaking, but he didn't care. His hand was steady. "Were you the one who sold us out that night in New York? Did you betray us?"

"Hm," David said. "Betray... no. I carried out the mission, doc. That city was dying, and none of you had the fortitude to see what had to be done to save it. So I found people who did."

"You were already rogue," Colin whispered.

David shrugged. "It's a label. Just a color on a watch. Look at yours. You're rogue, too. I bet you told yourself you're doing what must be done, right? I will admit, though, I didn't think you had it in you."

Colin took a deep breath. "Tell me straight. You sold us out. You got Jason and Serena killed."

"I did," David agreed readily. "What are you prepared to do about it?"

Colin's finger tightened on the trigger. David had survived

one brush with death. He had the chance to walk away when Serena and Jason had stayed on those cold streets. They deserved better. David was overdue an exit from this world. All Colin had to do was squeeze a little bit harder.

Colin let out an anguished breath. He couldn't. Not with the man just standing there. He wasn't a murderer.

David sighed. "You never did have it in you to do what had to be done, doc. As for me, I'm a killer."

David raised his assault rifle in a flash and opened fire.

Maira fled into the depths of the ship. They had lights in here, it turned out. They must have turned them off just in case. Now they were on and burning bright. It was like a maze of tight corridors all the same. She darted among them.

One of the rogues was after her. Maira was sure of it. Every time she paused, she could hear ringing footsteps. Someone was down here with her. They didn't sound big. Closer to her size, or perhaps even smaller. Unfortunately, that didn't mean they were any less dangerous.

"There's something interesting nearby," ANNA said.

Maira frowned. What did that mean?

"Can you locate it, ANNA? Take me there?" she whispered.

A red pathway guided her through the ship. Maira followed it as quickly as she could. The sound of pursuit had stopped now. Perhaps the rogue had given up. There wasn't much comfort in the thought; that would mean they'd moved their attention to one of her friends.

As if on cue, a minigun roared in the distance. Leo was fighting. Maira exhaled nervously and tried to move faster without making any more noise. She was down below the waterline, now. Below even the original one, not the new point to which the rusting ship had sunk. There was a clamminess to the air that made her wonder if the ship was already leaking somewhere. There was still no sign of her pursuer.

Maira stepped through a porthole into another chamber. This room had three exits, but the path ended. There were canisters in the chamber, a dozen of them. Each one was as tall as her waist. They had the look of sophisticated technology. She stepped closer to one and studied it curiously. Was it a container of some kind? A bomb, maybe?

"ANNA, what am I looking at?"

"Viral payloads. The Eclipse Virus, to be specific," ANNA replied amiably.

Maira froze. Her heart was suddenly pounding in her chest. She had heard of this, back during the hunt for Rowan O'Shea. The Green Poison had been bad enough, but Keener's band of rogues had isolated the virus and "improved" it. It was even more lethal now. It had wiped out at least one entire community.

"How much is here?" she asked shakily.

"Each payload contains sufficient viral particles to infect two times ten to the thirteenth power individuals under optimal circumstances. Dispersal methods will have a significant impact on actual effectiveness, of course."

Maira heard a clatter. She frowned and looked over her shoulder. There was no one behind her. She shrugged it off. The battle was doubtless raging throughout the ship, but this was important. There was enough virus here to devastate the population all over again, if not wipe it out completely. Maira couldn't imagine what the rogues wanted with it, but she didn't want to find out either. No one should have this power.

Was it as simple as blowing the cylinders up? Maira raised her new missile launcher then hesitated. This ship was not as sturdy as it had once been, and she was well below the water line. Firing her weapon in here might well punch a hole in the hull. That seemed like a bad idea, especially standing here when it happened. Targeting them directly seemed like it might contaminate the entire Trinity Bay, too. Was it worth it, to keep them from deciding where it was used?

Maira was very focused on what she was doing. When she heard the clatter again, it took a moment to sink in. Glanced behind her again. No one there.

The rogue stepped through a door to her right instead. Maira turned just in time to take a barrage of submachine gun fire directly to the torso.

Bullets hammered Colin in the chest. He fell backward with a wheeze, the air knocked out of him. The whole world blazed in white and red. He hit the roof he was standing on and lay there, gasping. The pain was extraordinary. A mule kicking him square in the ribs probably would have been gentler.

"Mender activated," ANNA said.

The little orb floated up from Colin's kit. He blinked at it, wheezing. It floated over next to him and gave him a shot right in the carotid. He yelped and swiped at it feebly, but it bobbed out of the way. Fire spread through his neck and down his body. Sweat broke out in its wake.

Colin knew this feeling. He'd just gotten a hearty dose of combat cocktail.

The pain fell away. His breathing eased. Colin looked down

at his chest. A trio of impact craters marked his armor. There was no blood. He moved and winced, but the pain was dull and distant now. Broken or bruised ribs, and his whole torso would be one massive hematoma, he was sure.

David was saying something in the distance.

The fire of the cocktail was burning hot in him now. He didn't waste time listening. Instead, Colin rolled to his feet and sprinted to the edge of the roof and leapt. David was just below still. Colin saw his eyes go wide, and then he plowed into the rogue agent feet first.

David went hurtling across the deck. Colin fell on his side. Stars burst in front of his eyes, but there was no pain. The cocktail saw to that. The rifle had fallen from David's hands. Colin didn't want it. He kicked it aside with a snarl and came to his feet. David was blinking and shaking his head, trying to rise. Colin gave him a solid kick in the side for his efforts.

David grunted and was sent rolling. Colin paced after him, fists clenched tight.

"You killed them, you son of a bitch! You tried to kill all of us, and left me to feel the guilt!"

David was getting back to his feet. He raised his face and Colin slammed his left fist home into his jaw. He followed it up with a right hook that smashed the rogue agent in the face and spattered blood onto the deck.

"I hated myself for you!" screamed Colin. "And what, you come back to torture your father as some sick game? To murder me? I'm tired of carrying the burden of the decision you made!"

Colin crouched over the other man and shouted. Part of him knew this was a bad idea. The rest of him didn't care.

Years of regret boiled over now into rage. He reached down to grab David by the vest and drag him to his feet.

David came up with something in his hand. Colin recognized the glint of brass knuckles a second before the world jumped three feet to the right. The sky spun above him like a top. His body's signals were all awry. There was pain, wasn't there? His head. He was bleeding. He spat blood. He had to get up.

David was standing over him.

"You were supposed to die two years ago, doc. It's all been borrowed time."

Colin got a leg under himself and tried to rise. David kicked him square in the chest. Colin fell back choking. He had to fight back. He had to do something. His limbs wouldn't respond. The cocktail could give you fire, but it didn't make you iron. The damage was still there. He couldn't breathe.

"If it's any comfort, I'll still finish the mission. I'm sorry you won't get to see it."

Maira fell.

"Oh, you're very hurt," ANNA told her.

She hit the deck with a cry. Her chest hurt like fire. Her armor must have taken most of the shots. They were low caliber rounds, they probably hadn't punched through. They...

Her hand found the place just below where her armor ended. It came up soaked in red.

"You need a doctor," ANNA said. "Should I call for help?"

"P-p-please," Maira sputtered.

"Begging?"

It was a woman's voice. She stepped from the shadow of

the doorway. She wasn't very big. Maira had been right. The thought almost made her laugh. A gurgling cough came out instead. There was copper in her mouth. It reminded her of holding wires there when she used to build computers at home.

"That's surprising. The Division doesn't tend to recruit begging types. I've heard of you, though. You're the new one, right? You're not a proper agent at all. Just some runt they pulled off the streets."

I have no idea who you are, Maira wanted to tell her. Complete nobody. Very apropos. The words wouldn't work either. She retched and spat red onto the deck.

"That's a nasty hit. Not a quick death, I'm afraid. You'll suffer."

The rogue agent stepped past her to check on the cylinders. She examined them carefully.

"Did you do anything stupid before I got to you? Wouldn't want to have the party favors go off early. Not when they're ready to ship out."

It clicked then. It was like a light came on in Maira's head. She could see it play out. The rogues had never wanted the fuel. They wanted the trade network itself. A pipeline that went to every settlement the Division was protecting. A perfect vector to spread a whole new plague. An end to any hope of stability.

They're going to kill everyone, Maira screamed at herself. Do something. Stop lying here and do something. The launcher had landed next to her when she fell. She picked it up with the hand that wasn't trying to hold in her guts.

The agent didn't pay her any mind. She, too, was very focused on the matter at hand. It was fate of the world shit, after all. Besides, the weapon didn't look like much of anything. It was too small to be a normal rocket launcher. Too bulky to be a pistol. To the uninitiated outsider, it had to look like nothing so much as a weird camera. A flare gun maybe.

Maira, however, had paid close attention to ISAC's briefing. With elaborate care she used her HUD to spread the missiles out across the room. If they didn't take care of the rogue agent, they'd still tear the walls down. She didn't target the cylinders directly. Don't blow them open. Just let them sink to the bottom.

The rogue finally glanced over and frowned. "What is that supposed to be?"

Maira grinned up at her with red teeth. "…quick… death…"

She squeezed the trigger.

David paused, brass knuckles raised for a finishing blow that would cave Colin's skull in. A cacophony of thunder echoed up from the depths of the ship. The whole craft canted a bit to the side. Tremors ran through the hull like an earthquake.

"What?" the rogue agent said in surprise.

The sudden slope of the dreadnought sent him stumbling. Colin knew his last chance when he saw it.

He hurled himself at David. It was not a graceful tackle. They both went down in a tangle of limbs. The little Mender hovered up next to him.

"Administer… sedative," Colin croaked.

David fought back. He hammered blows against Colin's sides, trying to break free. Every breath hurt Colin like fire. His ribs were well and truly broken now. It was going to be a long few weeks recuperating from this, if he didn't die first. He ignored the pain and just held on. The Mender darted in and with the same machine precision as before gave the rogue agent a quick jab in the neck.

"What ... the ..." croaked David.

His eyes rolled back into his head, and he collapsed.

Colin lay there next to him. The boat was definitely sinking now. Black waters bubbled and lashed all around them. Air must be escaping giant rents in the hull. He needed to get up, he told himself. He had to help the others. Any minute now. He would catch his breath and he would get right back into the action.

Somewhere in the distance a sniper shot rang out. A moment later Leo limped into view. He had obviously been in a fight. He was spattered with blood, and some of it was his. The taciturn agent had a hand clamped to his left arm. Red welled up between the fingers.

"Rogues?" Colin managed to ask through a throat filled with chalk.

"Two. Dead." A pause. "Yeong-Ja helped."

"That's good," Colin said. "Help ... Help me up."

Leo got him up in a fireman's carry. They both staggered toward the ramp.

"Maira, where are you?" Colin said into the radio. "Maira, check in."

"Vital signs have gone negative," ANNA announced. "A rogue agent has fallen."

CHAPTER 17

Colin sat beside the semitruck and waited. It was nice to just sit and not feel like he had to be on the run. Every breath hurt anyway. Movement just exacerbated things. Might as well enjoy the stillness while he could.

Leo paced nearby. "Sure about this?"

"Completely sure," Colin assured him.

"Why?" asked Leo.

Colin took a deep breath and immediately regretted it. "Because like Maira said about your brother... everyone deserves a chance to do better, for as long as we can afford to give them one."

"He's not gonna change. Some people don't," Leo growled.

"That's true." Colin glanced into the semi's bay. "He's not the one I'm pinning my hopes on, though. It's–"

"Stop making Colin give long-winded speeches," Yeong-Ja said from up above. "His talents do not lie there, and besides, it is causing him pain."

She was perched on top of the semitruck with her TAC-50 across her legs. She pointed off into the distance.

"They're coming."

"How many?" Leo asked.

"Just the one, as they promised." Yeong-Ja lifted the rifle. "I could still thin the numbers a little if you like."

"That would kind of defeat the point of this entire exercise," Colin noted drily.

"As you like," Yeong-Ja said with a shrug and dropped the rifle to her lap again.

The Humvee approached up the dusty road. The three of them watched silently as it pulled to a stop. A blonde woman sat behind the driver's wheel. The only other occupant climbed out the passenger side. It was Colonel Marcus Georgio. He stood beside his vehicle for a moment, as if about to change his mind. Then he squared his shoulders and approached them.

"I've done everything you asked," Marcus said as he neared them. He stopped and crossed his arms. "I released your driver and his semi. I came here, alone and unarmed."

"So you did," Colin said. "That's a good sign."

"What now?" Georgio asked.

"I heard the Reborn have offered a ceasefire and to come to the negotiation table," Colin said. "Their new leader is willing to discuss a staged phasing out of fossil fuels. He seems pretty reasonable."

Leo snorted.

"Yes. That's all true. What of it?" growled the colonel with thin patience.

"What will you do?"

"I haven't decided yet," Georgio said stiffly.

"I see," Colin said. "Well, he's all yours. Take him."

Colonel Georgio took a step toward the bay immediately then paused. "What, no demands? No threats? You're just giving him to me?"

"Yes," Colin said.

The colonel narrowed his eyes. "Why?"

"Because you've only seen the worst of the Division. And we've only seen the worst of you. And I want to believe that both of us can be better than that. Someone wise taught me that. So, it starts now. Your son is released into your custody. He's yours, no strings attached. I suggest you keep him contained. He needs a lot of help."

The colonel walked into the bay. He came out a moment later with David walking beside him. The rogue agent's hands were bound, and he was gagged, but he was otherwise unharmed. Georgio took him back to the Humvee hastily and urged him into the back seat. He stepped to the front and seemed about to climb in without saying anything more.

He paused.

"For whatever it's worth, I am sorry for what happened to the other agent. If nothing else, you could see the passion burn in her. I respect that."

Colin swallowed against a lump in his throat. He hadn't been able to save Maira. She had never emerged from the sinking battleship. It was another burden of guilt to carry. At least this time, it was for someone who deserved it.

"Thank you."

The colonel clambered inside the vehicle, and it pulled around and vanished back up the road. With a wince Colin slowly climbed back to his feet. His bandaged ribs ached abominably. It would be weeks more before he even started to feel better.

"What do we do now?" asked Yeong-Ja.

"Rest," Colin said. "There will be another crisis sooner than you know it."

"And then?" asked Leo.

"Then we do whatever we can to make things better. Because someone has to do it. Because the future is up to us."

EPILOGUE

Maira woke up with a gasp.

"Whoa, easy does it." A gentle hand on her shoulder kept her from trying to rise. "You are still in pretty bad shape. You're lucky to be alive."

Maira blinked against bright lights. The figure above her wore scrubs and a medical mask. She raised a trembling hand to try to touch her stomach.

"Nope, don't want to do that either. A lot of stitching there just to hold everything in place. Don't mess with that."

Maira tried to say something. Her mouth was so dry she couldn't. She licked her lips, but it barely helped.

"Would you like an ice chip?" the person asked.

Maira nodded desperately. The person placed the chip on her lips. It was cold and wet and possibly the most divine thing Maira had ever experienced. She let it soak down into her mouth. Afterward she felt like maybe she would be able to manage a few words.

"Where?"

She could hardly recognize her own voice. It sounded like the croak of some abysmal sea creature. The figure patted her shoulder comfortingly.

"You're in a hospital. Very good care, I assure you. We saved your life. Not many places left that could have done that."

There were blurry memories of what had happened. The bullets. The explosions. The dark waters rushing in to claim her. Then maybe a few more. Being pulled from the water? Lights? And pain. So much pain.

The rogues. They hadn't captured her, had they? Was she in their hands? Would they not have just killed her?

"Rogues?" she gurgled.

"Here? Oh, you think – no. Don't worry. Nothing of the sort. We don't tolerate those kinds of miscreants, I assure you."

Maira nodded. Her mind kept poking at her. There was something important. Faces. Smiles. Laughter. Tears. Friends.

"Cell?" she asked.

There was a long pause. At last the figure squeezed her shoulder. "I'm hesitant to tell you this now, but I don't want to lie to you. I'm afraid you were the only survivor."

Sorrow welled up in Maira, as thick and dark as oil itself. She closed her eyes tightly. Tears ran down her cheeks. She wanted to sob. All her weary body could manage was a whimper.

"I'm sorry. I know that must be difficult for you. For what it's worth, I'm glad you're here. We need you. There's important work to be done."

This was all too much to process. Maira could feel sleep rising. It was like a warm blanket wrapping around her. She needed it desperately. To heal and regain her strength. Still, there was one more question before she could properly rest.

"Safe… here?"

"Oh, absolutely, Miss Kanhai. Please relax and rest. Don't worry at all. You're in the hands of the Department of Homeland Security. This is the safest place in the world."